BEAR WITNESS TO POWER UNCHAINED

Yozo glanced to his right and took note of the downed saren. He wanted to help her, but the three figures twitched wildly, ready to jump in at him at the first sign of a break in concentration. He had no armor, unlike his comrade. The moment the little wretches latched onto him would quickly become disastrous.

The other three piled in, rushing the swordsman with such swiftness, even Yozo couldn't respond to the six clawed hands that thrust in, ripping at his clothes, shredding and binding up his sword arm, pushing him back against the wall where the other one-armed greyoldor sprung out from, joining the imminent feeding frenzy.

An azure bolt sliced into the side of one of the creatures that hung off of Yozo's shoulders, felling it to the ground. It shrieked and writhed as it clutched the still glowing hole in its side that fizzled with dark blue sparks.

The other three twisted pravens halted their ripping to look up, assessing what had happened to their ally.

Hamui's sneer was outlined and emphasized by the glow from his staff, hatred for the dark counterparts of his race clear as he lit the room with another bolt of blue, slicing the air between him and the group of darklings in a split second, melting the corner of one's head off, oozing glowing brains from its skull before dropping it next to Yozo.

<u>Lords of the Deep Hells Trilogy</u>

Book 3

Heart of the Maiden

This is a work of fiction. All the characters and events portrayed in this book are either products of the author's imagination or are used fictitiously.

Cover art by Andrey Vasilchenko

You can contact me at:

authorpaulyoder@gmail.com

Visit me online for launch dates and other news at:
authorpaulyoder.com (sign up for the newsletter)
instagram.com/author_paul_yoder
tiktok.com/@authorpaulyoder
<u>Paul Yoder on Goodreads</u>
<u>Paul Yoder on Amazon</u>

ASIN: B09BDG4MDN
ISBN: 9798512411964

Here's to all the unexpected twists and turns in life that weave a tapestry of character and story that makes us who we are.

Embrace this life, work to improve yourself, and enjoy each moment we're gifted.

LANDS OF WANDERLUST NOVELS BY

Paul Yoder

LORDS OF THE DEEP HELLS TRILOGY

Shadow of the Arisen
Lords of the Sands
Heart of the Maiden

KINGDOM OF CROWNS TRILOGY

The Rediron Warp
Firebrands
Seamwalker

LANDS
OF
WANDERLUST

Paul Yoder

Heart
of the
Maiden

Lords of the Deep Hells Trilogy

Book III

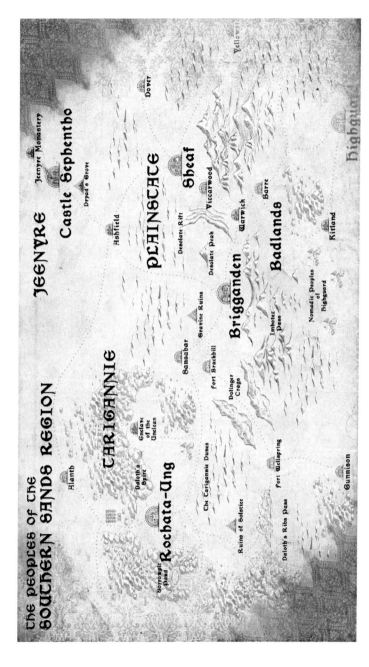

The Peoples of the
SOUTHERN SANDS REGION

JEENYRE

Jeenyre Monastery

Castle Sephentho

Dryad's Grove

Dover

Ashfield

PLAINSCATE

Sheaf

Desolate Rift

Viccarwood

Desolate Peak

Warwick

Barre

Gravine Ruins

Brigganden

Badlands

Sansabar

Kitland

Fort Brachhill

Dolinger Crags

Imbotec Pass

Nomadic People
of
Highguard

CARIGANNIE

Enclave
of the
Unclean

Hlanth

Daloth's Spire

Rochata-Ung

The Carigannie Dunes

Ruins of Solstice

Fort Welispring

Sorrowpit Pond

Daloth's Ribs Pass

Gunnison

Highguard

Yellow

PLANES OF ASH

The Blood Eye

HELL GATE

FALLEN TOWERS

SUITEN CANYON

CITY OF BLOOD AND ASH

ASHEN FIELDS

The BLOOD JUNGLE

RUINS OF MEN

SPIRE OF HOPE

HAVEN OF GREY ONES

ACID PLAINS

The POLYPS STRETCH

The SCORCHING SEA

The DEEP UNSEEN

Part One: Wayward Paths

1

THE SUN ROOM

The darkness lingered deep in the pathways of the old temple much longer than they naturally should have after being exposed to torchlight.

Denloth pointed to the recesses of the great hall, ordering the few torch-bearing arisen that accompanied them to light up the great chamber for him and his master to view.

Sand trickled down from the cracks in the ceiling, sprinkling through the torchlight, creating dull sparkles along the skeletons' paths to the edges of the long, dark chamber.

"Impressive," Sha'oul whispered, watching the torchbearers continue past pillar after pillar, showing just how grandiose the temple's stonework was.

"This is not some obscure cult's temple. This was a temple devoted to the great Dannon, God of the sun."

"Then what became of it? By the looks of it, this place has been abandoned for centuries," Denloth said, also speaking in hushed tones out of respect for the temple grounds they tread.

1

"Dannon's followers have receded, for the time," Sha'oul thoughtfully said, stepping off towards a side passage as he mused. "They will be back to worship him in time. Religions have seasons too. Some are thriving today that will dwindle centuries from now, and vice versa. Mortals are quick to forget."

"You seem to know much of this god," Denloth hesitantly voiced, wondering how many secrets his master knew regarding the temple they walked through now.

"I know much of many gods," Sha'oul retorted, humored by his companion's probing. "But more of Dannon than most, admittedly. He is one of the few gods that Telenth-Lanor still communes with. Dannon is one of the few gods that remains neutral to all other gods.

"Torchbearers," Sha'oul called, causing a clanking of bones as all six scurried to the spot they stood.

The archway along the section of wall they gazed upon was in ruins, most of the supporting stones crumbled beneath the weight of the collapsed ceiling high above.

"Do you feel anything within that chamber?" Sha'oul asked, his excitement for what lay beyond clear in his wicked grin, his yellow teeth showing orange in the torchlight.

Denloth reached out with his will, studying, tasting the aether beyond the cave-in. The presence of power within the old temple was undeniable, and sifting through it took a moment, but he did feel distinct threads of aether just beyond them, each emanating from a distinctly different source.

He breathed in and out slowly, coming back to his physical senses.

"There are...many auras just beyond. I sense Telenth, but I sense others as well."

Sha'oul's smile only widened, and he brought up a hand, a black ring immediately beginning to glow red as he tensed his fingers, moving them into a strange, ridged formation.

The sand that had filled most of the passageway began to sift up, sticking to the roof of the room, uncovering the path before them. Boulders began to roll off to the side, and the path was made clear as the sand solidified to the ceiling in a hardened glaze, showing them the partially collapsed room within.

They walked in, gazing upon the dozen or so black slate slabs that stood erect to either side of the room, quartz rods protruding from the floor on either side of the slate, and a beam of sunlight shining down from a fist-sized hole in the ceiling, extending up through an endless shaft, illuminating the room.

"What is this place?" Denloth questioned, following behind his master as they passed slate after slate until Sha'oul stood before one towards the middle of the room.

"It seems Telenth's rift gate is undamaged," Sha'oul said, sliding a hand along the textured slab, clenching his other hand so tight that his nails punctured his palms, blood welling up in his tight fist.

He shot forth his bloody hand, speckling the stone in red, tracing with his bloody finger a crescent moon and an eye beneath with a streak down the middle of it. This, Denloth knew to be the secret sign of the one they served. Few in Una knew it, and fewer still ever dared to invoke it.

"If this is a rift gate to Telenth, then to whom do the rest belong to? Surely not each to different gods. I have never heard of so many rift gates sharing the same region, let alone sharing the same room!" Denloth asked as his master finished his design, the significance of the chamber finally coming to him.

"Yes," the tall man laughed, seeing that his companion began to realize the power present in the room they had discovered. "The worshipers of Dannon were as ambitious as they were zealous. These rooms were called, *Sun Rooms*. Known by those not of the faith as rift junctions. A place where one might just as easily visit Aerath, the goddess of air, or Tekneon the god of the ages, as they might visit Fortia or Unerasct. I've only seen one other, and all rift gates there had been sundered. Though a few here seem damaged, that most remain functioning is a wonder."

"I have only seen two other rift gates," Denloth mumbled, approaching an adjacent stone slab, gliding his fingertips along the bumpy slate surface.

Sha'oul turned to consider his counterpart a moment before asking, "Have you never activated one?"

Pulling his attention from the slate, he said, "I have not," as he walked to the giant man's side, standing before Telenth's gate.

"Then today, you will have the honors of connecting our lord's realm to this one."

Though Sha'oul seemed sure of the offer, Denloth warned, "I have only studied the subject, and even that was just descriptions of the event with no mention to the detailed process of its function. I would need guidance."

Sha'oul looked back to the slate and quartz structure and smiled.

"Then guidance you shall have."

He lifted his massive, bloodstained hand, holding it outstretched towards the blood-inscribed slab, chanting in Felmortum, the harsh tones and syllables peaking with Sha'oul's twisted fingers. Denloth looked on, studying the words, the inscription his master had made, the hand movements....

Denloth's eyes widened as the slab began to move—or perhaps it was not so much as *moving*, but rather, an image was beginning to come into focus along its surface.

The quartz rods began to glow faintly, and the image along the slate quickly came into focus, the memory of his shared vision of the Plane of Ash he had beheld weeks ago coming back to him, seeing in more lucid clarity the grey waste, ash falling from an endless sky of gloom, a burning red orb in the distance faintly illuminating the hills and plains of soot.

There were creatures populating the desolate hellscape this time, and great and horrible did they appear to him, only seeing such abominations in tomes and fleeting images of like horrors amidst the Seam.

One such creature, close enough to them, turned and noticed them as they peeked through the dimensional rift into his endless life amidst the ash.

"Surely it sees us," Denloth ventured a guess, seeing that Sha'oul discontinued his chanting, standing back beside his companion now to watch as the creature loped in their general direction, sniffing the air.

"Perhaps...perhaps not," Sha'oul whispered, transfixed on the creature. "Though it is easy enough to view into the hells, from within, things are distorted at the start of a rift connection. It takes time for both dimensions to sync. I know, for I have been there—once."

"Then surely he can sense us?" Denloth continued to probe, seeing clearly that the creature meandered closer and closer to them, looking as though it were a dog that had gotten wind of raw meat.

The large man tilted his head slightly, considering the question. "Perhaps. *Sense* may be the wrong word for what that one is feeling just now. *Draw* may be a better descriptor. Always the draw to leave the realm of a Deep Hell is gnawing, ever at your thoughts. And you are punished for those thoughts, but persistent they remain, on and on through the ages...,"

Denloth considered his master's words as Sha'oul drifted off into thought, or through the old corridors of memory. And as he considered the words, the creature came to the rift's edge—close enough for him to now make out every detail of the beast—or man—he knew not which it was.

It stood a massive ten feet from the ground, its slumped posture indicating that it could stand even taller if it wanted to. Its face was that of a man, but by no means that of a normal man; it was one of nightmares, even for Denloth who had seen his share of horrors.

Its mouth was slack agape, rows of disheveled teeth arbitrarily lining his wide jaw, his wide-bridged nose burnt, holes along his skin, sizzling in the acidic ashfall.

His eyes were haunting. Sunken and so soot-smeared that they would have been lost in their depths, except for the soulless, blindingly white eyeshine.

A jagged rack of antlers grew from its skull, and its middle was worn away—spine and ribs on clear display. Its claw hands were bloodied, though the blood seemed dried and old.

It looked at Denloth then, and its haunting stare didn't waver now as it began to walk towards them, towards the edge of the portal, raising a clawed hand to the surface of the stone, and entered the Sun Room.

"Stand back," Sha'oul said, Denloth immediately complying with the order. "Let's give him some room to enter."

The bloody hand lingered in the temple air, testing what it had happened upon for a moment before dipping its antlers and head through the gate, squeezing its torso and limbs through the relatively small portal.

It stood, stretching out into the cool, dim Sun Room, looking to Denloth, then to Sha'oul, awaiting an answer for its presence.

Sha'oul spoke to it in Felmortum, and though Denloth wasn't well practiced with the language, he had been studying it long enough now to understand his master's words.

"All to blood, and blood to ash. The Great Ashen One has need of you here in Una. I serve him here, and you serve me now. Disobey any command, and you will be sent back straightway, and the Ashen One will not be pleased."

The creature tilted its head, looking around at its surroundings for a moment before returning to gaze upon Sha'oul, nodding its head in understanding.

"Good," he crooned, ordering, "await us in the great hall."

The beast looked in the direction the man pointed him, and began to lope to the sandblasted threshold, stooping under, exiting to join the skeletons that awaited at the archway.

"A wendigo. Not the most intelligent, or loyal creatures found in the Plane of Ash, but devilishly powerful, and somewhat cunning when it knows there's blood involved," Sha'oul spoke in a soft voice, only loud enough for Denloth to hear.

"Not the most loyal, you say?" Denloth asked, side-eyeing the lumbering beast out beyond the archway.

"No," Sha'oul admitted, "but with simplicity of mind comes simple and powerful fears, and above all, they fear our god. It will obey the Ashen One's chosen. Even if it does test me, I have dealt with countless wendigos through the ages. I will force it to submit before me if it comes to it."

As Denloth stood, considering the creature that now leaned down to shine its beady eyes in upon them, Sha'oul clapped, breaking the eerie moment, standing before the rift gate once more, indicating for Denloth to step up to the slab.

The only sound in the room was from the slightly glowing quartz rods sticking out of the ground, both the rods next to the slab, and one of the neighboring rods beside another rift gate, humming a low, vibrating tone.

"It will be safe to activate the rift again so soon?" Denloth asked, watching the energy in the rods continue to buzz at a consistent frequency.

"Two minor demons will not stress a rift like this. All of those rods," he answered, indicating the sixteen undamaged rods that still stood next to their respective rift gates, "will help dissipate any excess aether as the rift remains active."

"And what if no rods were present to absorb aether?" Denloth quizzically asked.

"Then we would absorb it, or our souls would try, and would fail. The aether ejected from the tears between realms is a chaotic energy. None that I know of know how to utilize it, though, rift makers have found how to neutralize it, hence the augmented rift crystals that hum before us. It will take hours, if not days for it to complete the process of defusing the stored aether, so when one uses a rift gate, the need must be great," Sha'oul answered.

"Alright," Denloth said, stepping up to the rift, inspecting the symbols Sha'oul had drawn with his blood. "Where do I begin?"

Sha'oul began to slowly step behind the black slate, looking upon it, considering the mechanics of the device before answering, "You...summon the Seam—easily as I understand it—do you not?"

Denloth nodded, agreeing with his master's assessment.

"Then you should have no issue calling forth a rift. Focus is the key. You had mentioned that in your early years you were a priest of Hassome—he is a master of focus. Surely your upbringing will aid you in this task.

"Simply think upon the one you summon, the land, the smell, all associations you have with that place. You do not need to have set foot in that realm, though this does help, but simply knowing some details of the place you call to helps the rift to puncture. After that initial connection is made, maintaining a rift is simple."

"What of the blood and the symbology? Do I need to perform the same ritual?" Denloth quizzed.

"Not...necessarily. Once an offering has been made through a rift gate, the connection remains until the gate is destroyed; but this," he said pointing to the blood drawings, "helps my focus, strengthens my call to the Planes of Ash. If you can activate a rift without the token, then it is not necessary. I simply enjoy offering supplication to our lord."

Denloth considered his words, clearing his mind as he began to draw up all information he had researched on the Planes of Ash, having fresh insight on its landscape only moments ago to aid his concentration.

Sha'oul had barely made his way around to his understudy when the rift lit up, the gateway to the Planes of Ash engulfing the stone's surface, the rods' glow and hum doubling in an instant.

Though Denloth's eyes were closed, deep in concentration, Sha'oul watched as the herds of wendigos, mogroths, egladava, and all other manner of fetid creatures roaming the ash fields all looked in unison at the rift's window. There was something not right, he knew.

"Denloth," he whispered, but his student was smiling now, feeling his way easily through the rift's aethereal mechanics, his robes beginning to flutter as if a light breeze played about him, though there was no airflow within the temple deep where they stood.

Rods close by began to glow, and the two slates next to Telenth's rift began to open, slowly at first, but once their faint images graced the slate surface, it lit, fully open; one showing what Sha'oul knew to be the Planes of Rot, the dominion of Jezelethizal, and another of the Hellflow, Zullenseer's domain, both one of seven lords of the Deep Hells.

"Denloth," Sha'oul called, beginning to worry as he saw the horrid hellspawn in all three realms now looking directly at them, all with a look of starving beasts viewing prey.

The rift behind them blinked awake, a realm a swirl in blue aether-like ribbons and banners came into view, a place which he suspected belonged to the god Hassome, Sha'oul noticing that Denloth was not only activating the Deep Hells rifts, but the High Thrones as well.

Three more activated in a blink, and all rods pitched into a scream-like noise, all now glowing a blazing white. A gaseous light ripped from Denloth's closed eyes, the energy shaking the man slightly as he hovered in concentration.

"Denloth! End it now!" Sha'oul yelled over the howling rods, seeing that each of the portals were quickly overtaking the stones they were bound by.

All at once, the stones returned to their solid state, the rifts cutting off abruptly, though the rods were still rattling at their tips.

Denloth collapsed, and to avoid the horrendous cacophony within the room, and from absorbing any stray rift aether, Sha'oul quickly gathered up the robed man and fled to the Sun Room, its blinding light shining out into the great hall as though a sun had just been activated within its small confines.

The wendigo had fled all the way to the entrance of the great hall's archway, and Sha'oul didn't blame it as he gathered the thoughtless skeletons and retreated from the inner depths of the temple, hoping that Denloth had not done irreversible damage to not just their lord's rift, but to their standing in Telenth's eyes for intruding in domains where they did not belong.

2

THE CALL OF BLOOD

The sun bore down on his exposed skin, flaying him wickedly, his hands and face blistering and sizzling open as he trudged ever closer to a clump of vegetation in the sparse desert.

He was past the pain by now. His former master's voice had come back strong, and once in his mind space, refused to leave, forcing him south—always south.

He could not refuse the urge to comply. He could barely focus on a single thought, or take in information of where he was at, what he was doing, or what he saw before him. All perception was tainted by his master's visions, and all of his mind was flayed open, exposed and raw before Telenth's proddings.

Every attempt to think hurt more than anything he had experienced in his previous life before Telenth's influence—and it felt like another lifetime ago that he had been the one others called Nomad, and even more so when he had been known as Hiro.

He could do nothing but comply with the endless stream of

commands fed to him directly into the creases of his mind.

"South. Go south."

He collapsed under a thick sage bush, the small patch of shade along the dirt cooling his skin slightly, shielding his broken and pocked skin from the scorching sun.

He had expected punishment and resistance from his master for the disobedient diversion, but instead, the voices calmed, allowing him precious moments in the dirt of reprieve from the killing sun, allowing the day to grow long as he fell into a fitful slumber.

He awoke, not to the barren desert that he had hazily remembered, but to a place that seemed more real to him recently than any other faded memory of a place.

His first breath was one filled with ash, particles as fine as dust assaulting his raw lungs, causing him to cough and gag as he worked at opening his eyes in the stinging, acidic environment.

Blinking through the tears, his throat and lungs numb now after long bouts of coughing, he got up on a knee, looking out through squinted eyes to see that he was on a vista of a slick sponge-like mound overlooking a vast expanse of ash, vein-like vines weaving across the endless plane through it, plumes of spores spouting out small mouths in patches of horrid fauna scattered through the terrain.

He remembered this place, from what was left of his memory. It was a hell he had languished in for eternities past. The smell, the taste, the pain....

"What do you want with me?" he croaked out, tormented beyond his ability to maintain his composure.

He was exhausted, and not just physically so. What fatigued him more than the ache of muscle, his sustenance deprived belly, and weakness of blood, was a weariness of mind. His thoughts had been robbed from him, for how long, he didn't know anymore. All memory seemed in a distant place, and all pathways which constructed his ability to think independently, seemed broken up, or perhaps better put, redirected. His thoughts were no longer his to think, and the only clear memory he now had was swathed in blood red, pain, and ash.

11

"Sha'oul," a million voices hissed, the sharp word slicing into his mind like endless needles slowly sinking into his exposed brain.

His ears were ringing, his vision ripping apart, and every inch of his skin felt like the mantra of *Sha'oul* was nipping at him, persistently gnawing deeper and deeper into his flesh.

"Find him," the voices whispered. "Follow the call of blood."

Each word assaulted him, driving him insane. Each syllable sending itching barbs of pain into his mind, only to rip it out afterwards.

"I will go! I will find—" he shouted in desperation—sobbing. He drew a ragged breath, vomiting out the name of the one he was tasked to find, "–Sha'oul!"

There was no answer from the omnipresent voice, no note of approval for his compliance, only ash. Ash that continued to eat away at him inside and out.

He collapsed into the knee-high ash drift.

Eyes watched him from afar. Tris had kept her distance from the crazed man. Though Naldurn had ordered her to trail Nomad, she had also seen the bright red mark across her face where the man had slapped her, and Tris knew that if the man was quick or cunning enough to catch Naldurn off guard, then he was more than likely to give her a terrible time if she got sloppy.

The man was resting, fitfully, but he had remained still on the ground for close to an hour—mumbling unintelligibly in his broken slumber.

He was on the ground one moment, and the next, he was standing.

The movement startled Tris, not just because it was sudden, but that it was impossibly abrupt. It was as though she herself was the one dreaming now, watching the man stand at an odd angle, his posture crooked as he slowly adjusted his head, looking over the dunes and towards the crags at their borders that lay miles out.

He bolted, running with a new purpose, sprinting so fast in the sandy terrain that after a few minutes of trying to keep up with him, Tris slowed and then stopped, looking out at the man atop a dune peak, marking the direction he was headed.

"Dolinger Crags it is then," she huffed, watching for a while longer before checking the low hanging sun, determining the time it'd take her to make her way back to the highway.

She'd be setting up camp on the edge of the dunes tonight. But on the morrow, she'd make her way back to her Shadow Company. Naldurn wouldn't be pleased to learn of Nomad getting away from her, but they now had a good heading of the direction the man was headed.

She hoped her report would be enough to please Naldurn. It would have to be, because she was not going to hunt that man alone in a desolate canyon.

3
REGROUP POST VICTORY

It was far past dark when Metus trotted back through the bloody gates, corpses piled high on either side. He was completely spent from the day's madness.

Hathos spotted his sultan's entrance and alerted Bannon immediately, still working with the rest of his troops to count their dead, tend to their injured, as well as oversee the prisoners of war they had captured.

Bannon rushed up to the sultan's dolinger, helping to guide it by its reins to a more secluded yard, considering it best to talk with the sultan in private, not sure how his leader was managing that night after the fissures in composure he had witnessed earlier.

Helping him down from his mount, Bannon asked in a soft voice, "How do you fare, Sultan?"

Metus stared off, taking a long moment to gather his words, the shock of the brutal war still catching up to him.

"Gather the leadership. I need to speak with them. Just…give me a few minutes to consider an agenda."

"As you wish, my sultan," Bannon answered, bowing before trotting off to find Hathos, Undine, Tau, and Naldurn.

The troops were busy, and amidst the bustle of all the tasks that needed doing, it took Bannon some time to find each company leader, delegating what urgent tasks that still needed to be done to their lieutenants.

Gathering them in the backyard of a small, adobe house, Bannon went and retrieved Metus, the two entering the small yard together, Metus ordering everyone to be at ease, each taking a seat along the low wall or taking one of the few rickety back-porch chairs that lined the house.

Metus looked up from the unlit firepit, eyeing each officer there before starting.

"Though we won the battle, it is but a technicality. We have lost many soldiers, and if there was anything I could have done differently these past few days to have avoided these many deaths, I beg your forgiveness for not having the foresight to have done it."

The officers shifted uncomfortably, not wanting to interrupt Metus' apology, but each knowing that he was not to blame for the death of their troops.

"What are our casualties? Where do we stand?" he continued.

Hathos took the question.

"We're still searching for missing bodies, but most companies have a preliminary headcount. These numbers may change into the night as we possibly find wanderers, and...if the injured take a turn for the worse.

"Undine, with Blood Company, reports eight dead, twelve injured, with five of those gravely injured. Tau, with Shield Company, reports sixteen dead, seven injured, with four of those gravely injured. And Naldurn, standing in for Kissa for Shadow Company, reports six dead, and three injured."

Metus pinched the bridge of his nose, tiredness or remorse clouding his features as the numbers sunk in before replying, "That's thirty dead as of now, is it not?"

"That is correct, Sultan," answered Bannon.

"Twenty-two injured?" Metus guessed.

"Yes," Bannon once again confirmed.

"Then that only leaves us with forty-five, not including us here, Kissa, Tris, and Eilan, all three of which are away on other tasks," Metus concluded, mumbling, "That's just over half of the Hyperium, either dead or injured."

The rest remained silent until Metus questioned, "Other reports—what is each company occupied with currently?"

Hathos and Bannon looked to each of the three company centurions.

Undine answered first.

"The Blood Company is handling the prisoners. There are sixty-two Rochatan soldiers in all that surrendered. There are not many injured. We're trained to deliver sure blows. Those that are gravely wounded, we're bringing to their people to take care of as we don't have any medics or supplies to spare."

"Let us know if you need any help from any other companies with handling those prisoners. They're not armed, but they still outnumber all of us combined, let alone your company," Bannon offered, Undine nodding his understanding.

Tau spoke up next.

"Shield Company has had the most casualties. We're doing what we can in searching for survivors. It's a large battlefield. We moved what bodies we could from the gateway. It was filled with corpses. We'll need it clear when we ride out, and moving bodies is a task best done sooner than later.

"We're also retrieving what dolingers we can while outside the walls. Many were slaughtered, most probably ran off. There's a corral in town we're penning them in. There's a good two dozen in there now. We're finding horses too. Not sure yet how many the troops have snagged. I was helping organize that when I got called here. We'll need mounts if we plan on making it out of this region in a timely manner."

"Good thinking, Tau," Metus agreed, everyone then looking to Naldurn.

"We searched for Darious' hiding spot. We've located him and told him to have his people stay underground until notified. I figure the sight might be a bit much for them to take. We'll need to move them before the sun hits these bodies though. The smell will be hard for the townsfolk to handle, I'm sure.

"We also have word that Henarus is awake. His priest had something to do with that. He did what he could for the prophet and is now with others in my company, tending to the wounded. Our medics are stretched thin, though, and so are our supplies, half of which are on some missing dolinger apparently."

"Very well," Metus nodded. "You've all performed your duties tonight with honor. Bannon, Hathos, make sure to provide what direction and support you can to each of our companies."

Bannon was quick to answer.

"It will be done, Sultan."

"Now as for what's next," Metus began. "I have made a promise to Darious and his people. I mean to keep that promise. We will have the people here gather what they can carry, find as many horses as we can gather, and escort them back to the Plainstate. We will settle them in Barre and have our physicians do what they can for their leprosy."

This will take logistics and orchestration. For that reason I'm going to lead them back myself, and I will take with me any Hyperium that are too bad off to continue. We will be dividing our company on the morrow."

Bannon's eyes furrowed considering Metus' plan.

"It's not that I don't understand the need to see to our wounded, or to see that Darious' people are well handled, but frankly, where does that leave those who are not returning?"

"Perhaps I approached this poorly. Let me explain myself," Metus sighed, looking to each of his leaders that stood by him faithfully. "I forced myself upon this company, against your and Leith's advisement. I selfishly headed up this operation, even though there are far more experienced and capable minds to head a mission as important as this. I see now, my inability to command in the field may have cost lives. If this mission is to ever have a chance at succeeding, I need to remove myself from the lead, and perform the duties I perform best, which are back in Sheaf, providing aid and support as you and the others do what you do best."

Bannon considered Metus' line of reasoning, neither he nor the other officers having a response to Metus' argument.

"I can lead the injured back, and handle the refugees, but we still have an arisen problem on our hands, and Reza and all the others are still in grave danger. If they are found, and word of this battle finds its way back to the judges, it is doubtful they will be granted anything other than a swift execution. They will need to be extracted from Rochata-Ung, and together you will need to see what can be done about the arisen army.

"It is clear that we will have no help from Tarigannie, Brigganden, or any other nation. You are to assess if a targeted attack is even an option at this point, then return or send for reinforcements. I can have our army at the border, ready for your word. We'll just have to hope that Rochata-Ung does not interfere with *us* trying to defend their lands for them," Metus said, harshness entering his voice at his last thought.

"I see," Bannon said, chin in hand, considering his leader's intentions. "Mind if I ask you some particulars?" Bannon probed, not sure how ready Metus was to level and reason with them on the details.

"Please," he responded, Bannon seeing clearly that Metus wanted nothing but honest advice from his council.

"So you will be taking all gravely injured Hyperium? So you will have no other able-bodied help within our company to assist you in taking care of the injured? Excluding Darious' people of course. You would not want to risk infection to our troops. Can you see to a host of refugees and some twenty-odd wounded soldiers on your own?"

Metus was silent for a moment, sorting through the described image in his head before asking, "Who do you suggest come with me? I will not take more than a few from what able-bodied Hyperium we have left. They will need all the numbers they can."

"I will come back with you," Bannon answered easily.

"You're needed here with the rest of the Hyperium," Metus reasoned.

"Am I? Or am I needed back at Sheaf? Not to downplay Leith's versatility, or Amlici's readiness to command the Plainstate's army, but with the reinforcements operation you mentioned putting in place, as well as continuing to station enough troops along our borders, cities, and towns, there will be need of senior leadership at home in the days to come. I cannot rightly let you go unguarded back through that mess, Brigganden. And besides all that, I've been stepping on Hathos' toes this whole time. He's more than capable in running an operation like this. Once Reza, Gale, Jasper, and the others are reunited, they'll be set to perform the second half of this mission."

Metus smiled for the first time that long night. The way Bannon had put it made it seem as though they still had hope in setting things right. He was more than welcomed to the thought of having his company on the hard road ahead.

"Now then, you want to deploy the rest of the Hyperium back to Rochata to extract Reza, Gale, and Eilan who were with you before your exit; Kissa, Jasper, and Arie who we sent back in for the first three; and Cavok and Terra who were supposed to pick up those two enchanters. Am I forgetting anyone?"

"Tris," Naldurn added. "I had sent her to track Nomad for a ways, then to return and report. She's resourceful—she'll likely find the Hyperium before long, even if she has to backtrack our trail.

"Right," Bannon approved, continuing his thought. "Once all have been gathered, the Hyperium, led by Hathos and Reza, are to head south where we suspect the arisen army to be. Perhaps by then they will have recovered Tris, which would be able to point them in the direction Nomad was headed. That'd lead them straight to the arisen lord."

"That's right," Metus agreed. "At which point, upon finding the arisen army, Hathos and the Hyperium, and Reza and company, will survey the arisen forces and determine if there's any possible line of attack, specifically, any reasonable path to kill the arisen lord. If there is not, or the forces of Rochata-Ung once again come to harass, return to our borders north of Brigganden. We can offer reinforcements from there, or, if that avenue is found to be hopeless, we can regather ourselves in our own lands and formulate our next strategy from there."

"I have a suggestion," Hathos said in a quiet, but commanding tone. Metus and Bannon looked to the Hyperium Primus of all three companies and waited for him to explain.

"To extract Reza and the others will require some cunning. We just decimated one of their cavalry units. They will be hostile to our presence. We have sixty-two prisoners. We can bring them back in a show of goodwill. They will be focused on this exchange. In the meantime, Naldurn and a few of her Shadows will have gained access to the city, locate our people, and see them out of the city walls, south to the Tarigannie Dunes where we will rendezvous."

"Once Rochata have their people back, they may send a force after you again," Bannon offered, considering the next step in the plan.

Hathos considered the snag. "Let's hope Tris has information on Nomad, and let's hope Nomad guides us quickly to the arisen's forces. If Rochata comes face to face with the arisen army, they may be forced to believe all our warnings."

"There's a lot of hope in that plan," Bannon gruffed.

Hathos let the statement settle in for a moment before admitting, "With the size of our force we have left to work with, and the task laid before us, hope will have to be an element we're comfortable working with."

There was a somber moment of quiet, each in the leadership circle contemplating the plan thus far, trying hard to ward off, or get used to, the increasing smell of death that lingered amidst the town before Metus took a deep breath in and exclaimed, "Indeed. Which is why, Hathos, if at any point during the mission you feel your chances at completing your mission becomes too risky, abort and head back to the Plainstate."

"That sounds like a plan," Bannon said, adding, "Hathos, you'll probably want to head out by morning time. With the Hyperium on the move, Rochata's focus will be on you and not on us. We'll be much more vulnerable traveling with the sick and wounded. Being run down by another deployment would be certain doom for our company. Gather what able-bodies you can tonight, organize your troops, take what supplies you'll need for the road, and get the prisoners ready to head out. We'll be doing the same sometime tomorrow after letting the refugees pack what they can for the journey."

Metus gazed off, the group weary from not just the battle, but from all that remained ahead of them. His eyes were fixed on a dead Rochatan soldier, slit through the stomach, his entrails already a gathering place for the desert flies.

Snapping out of his daze, he announced, "I'll visit with Henarus and see how he fares. With luck, he'll be good enough to continue on with the Hyperium. The more gods we have at our aid in this war, the better.

"We have a great deal of work to do this night. Let's waste no more time here. See to your men and women. Let's be ready to leave this place at sunrise. Gather our dead and see to a funeral pyre. I hate to leave the Rochatan dead unburied, but there's simply too many of them, and I don't trust the prisoners to roam the fields for cleanup. The dead will have to remain to molder as a warning to Rochata-Ung."

Metus paused, his breathing quickening slightly. "And I hope that if they do receive that warning, they pay special attention to Set's body...," he said, Bannon's concern for his sultan's mind state returning, "...and to know that any crooked judge that crosses me and my people, will receive no mercy by my hand.

4

THE BLOOMING LOTUS

"There's the college gates," Reza said, being careful to keep her voice low as she motioned for Gale and Eilan to see from the shadows of the backstreet they were hiding in.

It had been a few blocks since they had seen signs of the city guards looking for them, Eilan weaving them quickly and skillfully down and through a network of low-traffic streets to get them to their destination without much trouble from the pursuing guards.

Eilan casually looked down the main street leading to the gates, checking to see if there were soldiers around, then tucked back into the shadow of the overhanging building they were lined up against.

"I see no guards the way we came. We may have outdistanced them. If we're committed to entering that campus, we'd better make our move now," she said to Reza, who ultimately was the one her and Gale knew the decision rested upon.

"It's the only lead we have to find Cavok and Terra. Nowhere else to go," she said, walking calmly out of the side street with

Eilan and Gale close behind, the three walking up to the long gates that stretched many acres to both sides, gating in the beautiful cherry tree covered campus grounds.

A young man stood on the other side of the gate, watching the three as they approached, asking, "What brings you to the Blooming Lotus today?" in an unconcerned voice.

"We wish to see Zaren Zebulon. It's urgent," Reza answered shortly, getting the feeling of guard's eyes upon their backs the longer they stood out in the open.

The young man perked up, remembering the last time a stranger had asked for the old enchanter.

Stumbling slightly with his words, the boy answered, "I don't know if he's still here. I heard he was preparing to leave this morning. I could check for you—"

"Please. Let us go with you to find him. My message is urgent—every moment counts," Reza begged, knowing that if they were spotted by the guards there, things would get incredibly more complicated.

The youth looked to the other two beside Reza, then went to unlock the gate, letting them in off the street.

"Thank you," Reza sighed, waiting as the young man locked the gate behind them, leading them quickly down the campus' main path to the large archways.

They were just coming up the steps when Reza heard a familiar voice call out, "Come on, old man. I wouldn't have agreed to have you along if I had known you were bringing all that rubbish," Cavok said, walking out of the shadows of the building's hall to find Reza standing there, stunned at her good fortune in catching the man before they had left campus and into the city.

"Cavok! Thank the gods!" Reza called out, giving the large man a quick embrace as he turned from shouting at the old enchanter lagging behind to consider Reza, Gale, and Eilan.

"What are you three doing here?" he asked, not seeing the other company he had left them with the previous day.

"We ran into trouble. Had to split up," Reza explained as the three others slowly caught up to Cavok.

Terra embraced Reza, wearing a welcoming smile as she went to stand next to Cavok, whom she often shadowed the past few days, his sturdy structure seeming to provide her with needed security.

An all too familiar praven bounded up to greet Reza, an old enchanter all in robes hobbling up just behind, looking somewhat pleased to once again see the saren knight.

"Reza Malay," Jadu, the little praven uselessly announced to everyone, adding after a moment, "Hey, did those lesions ever completely clear up from that poison you contracted last year or do they still vex you? That type of skin condition often comes in waves, you know—"

"Jadu! This is not the time for antics! Tarigannie is in danger, the arisen lord is on his way, and Sultan Metus was separated from us while being chased by guards!"

"So—the talks with the judges ended poorly?" Cavok asked, not sounding the least surprised.

"Yes, Cavok—they ended poorly," she hissed, exasperation beginning to creep in.

"So, I'm guessing we're moving to plan B?" he said as he crossed his arms, easily looking over Reza's head to survey the city beyond the gates.

She took a steadying breath and said as calmly as she was able, "Unless Metus secretly conveyed a plan B only to you, then no. We don't have a plan B. We just need to get the hell out of this death-trap of a city—" she lowered her rising voice to a whisper and continued, "—before the guards find us and string us up for defending ourselves and killing half-a-dozen murderous thugs in the streets."

Cavok looked to Terra, side-eyeing her for falsely judging him so harshly the other day with the guard he had put to sleep in the alley.

"And you think I'm rough with guards? You ain't seen Reza angry and cornered," Cavok patronizingly whispered.

The gate youth stood there bug-eyed, knowing at that point it was too late to slip away. For the second time in the last day, he had somehow managed to become an uncomfortable fly on the wall as Master Zebulon's guests divulged terribly incriminating information that Denny had rather not have heard in the first place.

In the silence, most in the group became aware of the extra pair of ears, and Cavok gruffed to Zaren, "You going to do something about this kid, or am I?"

Zaren furrowed his brows, locking eyes with Cavok. "There's no need," looking to the youth, explaining, "Denny has been witness to much more...*deviant* transactions and information, which has granted him a number of private enchanting lessons from renowned *yours truly*—hasn't it, Denny?" he coerced.

Denny shrugged, nodding his head convincingly as everyone looked to him.

"Not a word, Denny, or I'll find you in the dead of the night and use you like a rat in an experiment, playing with your reactions like a cat with a mouse...."

The boy swallowed, remaining deathly still, unblinking.

"See. Denny's not a problem," the old man casually said.

"Hells, I was just going to put the kid to sleep for a few hours," Cavok said, eyebrows raised at the ruthlessness of the old man.

"Enough," Gale cut in harshly. "As Reza said, we don't have time for this. We need to find a way out of this city, and currently, the gates are on heightened alert looking for us. What are our options?"

"Need a way out of the city, eh? I might know of one—well, I know of a few, but one in specific that's close by," Cavok offered, all eyes back on him once more.

"Zaren and Jadu probably know of it. There's a gate northwest of this college. It's used for travel between here and Alanth. Many orchard workers come and go through it daily. It's a smaller gate, but if push comes to shove, we'll be dealing with much less resistance from gate guards there than the main one to the south."

"Perhaps the guards up at that gate haven't even gotten word of us yet," Eilan suggested.

"Well, if they haven't yet, they soon will. If we're going to make a move on that gate, we had better get moving on it," Gale added, asking Cavok, Zaren, and the others, "Are you lot ready to move out?"

"Denny, go fetch us some student enchanter's robes," Zaren sighed, sliding a hand down his face, mumbling, "I haven't even set foot outside of this damned college on this ludicrous job and already we're in trouble with the law. Why did I agree to get mixed up with you lot again?"

5

OF SCHOOL ROBES AND WILDFLOWERS

"Keep the hood on, Jadu," Reza hissed at the little praven who was fidgeting with the oversized robes he had been tossed.

"Why? They're not looking for me, it's you they're after," he replied back in the busy street they were in, getting a not-so-light smack on the back of the head from Eilan, trying to silence the loud praven before he gave them away with his idle talk.

"Ow!" Jadu yelped, rubbing his noggin, looking up to the two vexful women, throwing his hood on before he could be assaulted further.

"The gate's ahead. Looks like it's a bit busy," Cavok said, leaning down to announce to Reza.

"It's apparently harvest day or some fall festival. Let's hope this congestion doesn't hold us up too long," she softly replied from under her red-velvet hood.

Zaren, leading the *class* of first-year student enchanters, all robed in the same drab, flame-retardant, red hooded robes, hobbled up to the short line leading out of the city gates, everyone waiting for the incoming company of orchard workers to slowly move their fresh haul of apricots, pomegranates, and melons along down the main street, headed to the market proper.

"Can I buy one? Those look lovely!" Jadu called out to a cart as it moved along down the lane.

One of the workers took note of the child-sized man swimming in robes, chuckled at the comical scene, seeing Cavok's large frame beside him, tossing him a ripe apricot for the smile.

A guard on the other side of the lane took note of the small act of kindness, a smirk playing on his lips as he went about his duties with a little more warmness in his heart.

Reza glared hard at the little man that was bringing far too much attention to their group, but with Cavok's hand humorously ruffling the praven's hood and hair, she let out a sigh and attempted to put him out of her thoughts, knowing how riled he was going to make her if she didn't let it be. Then it would be *her* who would be the one drawing attention to the group. She envisioned an image of her strangling the little man in the streets, which gave her a slight moment of joy.

"Headed?" the gate guard tersely asked Zaren as they finally inched their way to the small raised gated archway as the last of the orchard crew made their way through the one-cart sized pass.

"Field trip for some Blooming Lotus first years," Zaren grumpily replied, not out of character in the least as he ill-temperedly rocked in place, leaning on his staff.

Seeing the way clear, having answered the guard already, Zaren started to hobble through the gate, but the guard held a hand in front of him, holding him up as Zaren gave a stink-face at the man in armor.

"One moment, they've been waiting a while to get through," the guard explained as a few groups of travelers made their way through the archway, some with donkey's hauling their belongings, some with carts, and some bringing live animals for the market.

"Field trip, eh? Sounds fun. Whacha got planned for 'em

today?" the guard asked, attempting to engage in a bit of small talk with the grumpy old enchanter.

"Floral picking. Damned students don't know a nightshade from a canterbell," Zaren grumbled, frustrated at having to actually play into the role of a college professor, even though that technically was one of his many titles.

"Fun," the guard sighed, his interest in the group instantly deflating.

The last of the outsiders made their way through the gate, and Reza, keeping a nervous eye on the whole scene, stiffened as she saw three familiar figures saunter through the gates in their direction.

Arie, Jasper, and Kissa casually made their way through the gate, Arie looking up as Reza blurted out, "Good day for traveling?"

The three stopped, noticing the group that they had been sent back to the city to rescue.

"It is a *very* good day to travel," Arie replied, a smile easily coming to her as she silently thanked the gods that luck had decided to grace them at least once that day.

"Where are you lot headed?" Kissa asked, playing along with the anonymity ploy, guards still flanking both sides of them.

"Flower picking!" Zaren barked out, quite done with stalling at the gate, playing games.

"We passed some vivid wildflowers just a ways back, not native to the region. Might be worth a look...if you'd be willing to pay us as your guide there. A small finder's fee, nothing much," Arie soothingly said, selling the offer so convincingly, that even one of the guards perked up, listening in on the talk of colorful exotic flowers.

"How gracious of you. How does a silver strip sound?" Reza asked, Zaren taking the hint that Reza was engaged in some ploy she no doubt wanted him to play along with.

"That's a fair price. It's not far off the trail," Arie agreed.

Reza smiled back, "Then please, lead the way."

The guard listening in on the conversation smiled dumbly as he breathed in a lung of fresh, fall air, his faith in humanity restored as the birds chirped in the nearby acacia tree, lending to the peaceful exchange.

The large group started out of the gates, making their way under the portcullis just as they heard the sound of horse hooves ride up, officers announcing to the guards on duty descriptions of on-the-run dignitaries from the Plainstate to keep an eye out for, ordering to double the guards on duty at the gate.

"What about that lot that just left?" Reza heard the mounted city guard ask as they made their way slowly past the new batch of travelers waiting to get into the city.

"Just a class from the enchanter's college. No strange foreigners there. Well, no foreigners there; can't rightly say about the strange part," the lead guard answered unconcernedly.

"Am I glad we found you when we did," Arie breathed next to Reza.

"Believe me, me too," she said, letting out the breath she had been holding since they passed through the gate.

6
THE SOFT LIGHT OF AN OLD MEMORY

The day had been long, and without mounts, they had been forced to hike to Daloth's Spire from the northern gate, making their way off trail along the foothills as hidden from view as possible.

It was well past sundown when they finally decided to take a break, Zaren refusing to move another step that day, halting their progress prematurely.

Cavok, Jadu, and Zaren were the first to doze off, and after Gale, Eilan, and Jasper briefly caught each other up on the day's events, they too took the forced stop as opportunity to rest, leaving Reza speaking with Terra, Arie, and Kissa in hushed tones in their fireless campsite.

"So Metus went east with the Hyperium, and five-hundred Tarigannie horsemen were riding after them last you saw them?" Reza restated, wanting more clarity on the brief update Jasper had given earlier that day on the hike.

"And they were catching up fast. Their horses were fresh. Our dolingers have been on the road for nearly a week now," Arie confirmed.

"That's why Jasper didn't want to stop tonight. Metus could be in great need of us," Kissa added, more than a little annoyed by Zaren's mulishness.

Well, some are not used to the road," she said, thinking of how old Zaren actually was, and how surprised she was that he even made it as far as he had that day on his own two legs, as well as Jadu, considering how short his legs were.

"Speaking of which, Terra, you should rest while we have time to do so. No need for you to be up," she said, looking to the young girl who did seem well and tired, but also excited to be in the presence of the three strong women.

"I will in a bit, if you don't mind me being here for a while longer," she said, attempting to sound as mature as the presence she kept, though each still looked at her as though she were a child staying up past her bedtime.

"As long as you don't lag behind like that Zaren fellow over there...," Kissa mumbled, and Reza decided to leave it at that, getting back to the topic at hand.

"So tomorrow, we find their trail—won't be hard to find with so many riders—then we follow. Are we sticking together as a group, or sending anyone up ahead?" Reza asked.

"Though the old man's pace will be an annoying setback, I do not want to split up again. We've done that too many times already, and thankfully, have been lucky enough to rejoin without too many issues, but now that we're together, let's keep it that way," Kissa answered as she looked to the stars, charting them to determine if they were still headed in the general direction she thought they had been.

"Agreed," Arie said, smiling. "When I first saw you at the gates, you were so stiff, I thought I was going to need to catch you if you fainted out of shock."

"I didn't make a show of it," Reza shot back, a bit embarrassed, remembering how cool Arie had played her role, never being the one for theatrics herself.

"You did look quite startled. It was a bit of a show," Kissa added, her tone slightly more playful than her usual hard edge.

Arie and Terra chuckled, seeing how Reza had so easily been made to blush.

Reza turned to Terra, who quickly stopped giggling.

"Perhaps it *is* time for you to turn in," she said harshly, meaning it as a joke, but the sarcastic nuance flew past the young girl.

"If you say so," Terra breathed, abashed that she had so quickly managed to end her time with the adult women.

"Reza—" Arie scolded as Terra got up to join Cavok's side, having slept next to the hulking man for the past few days on the road.

"Terra, wait," she said, trailing after the girl, catching up to her halfway to Cavok.

"You're right, it is late, and today was exhausting. I'd hate to be a burden tomorrow. I was trailing behind a bit today…," she whispered, refusing to look into Reza's eyes.

"You were fine today," Reza said, resting an uneasy hand on the girl's shoulder, trying to think of how to dig herself out of the awkward hole she had placed herself in.

"Oh," she exclaimed, fidgeting with something at her collar, Terra turning to look at what Reza was pulling off from around her neck.

"I meant to give this to you, well, for a while now. I just didn't know when or how…," Reza gently said, handing the amulet she had recovered from Bede's body the previous year.

The talisman had the symbol of her faith clearly inscribed along its worn surface. She knew who it had belonged to. She had seen it many times in her childhood, had let it been used as a trinket to keep her toddler hands busy while her grandmother and mother had talked….

"Bede…," Terra whispered, tears welling up easily as she played with the warm metal in her hands once more.

"I would have given you it sooner, but—" Reza fumbled for words, "—I'm bad with this kind of thing—" she muttered, but was cut short as Terra buried her head in Reza's chest, hugging her in the dark, Reza patting her on the back to help ease the girl's emotions.

Noticing some dim light glowing, Reza gently pried herself from her embrace, whispering, "It glows—"

"Oh. Yeah, it is," Terra said, slightly sobbing, but the oddity helping her to regain her composure.

"Just like it did...for Bede," she said, remembering the significance of the small detail.

Reza slowly looked from the warm light and up to the girl's face, whose eyes, still moist, seemed weighed down with exhaustion.

"If I don't get you to bed soon, you're going to fall asleep while standing right in front of me," Reza said, putting an arm around the girl, walking her over to Cavok's side, seeing that she got into her warm enchanter's robes before bedding down next to the slumped-over tattooed man. She knew Terra would be kept warm and safe next to Cavok. She had slept to his back many times over the years. She knew that the man did not move once asleep.

As she was about to turn back to rejoin Kissa and Arie to further discuss the plans of the following day, her eyes lingered on the enchanted girl, lightly brushing the small, warm, glowing pendant, closing her eyes to fall into sleep.

7
SICK AND DYING

"Are they ready?" Metus asked Darious as the burly man walked up beside the sultan and his war general as they finalized the number of horses they had left in the corral.

"They are more than ready to leave this place," Darious said, even the hardened man resorting to covering his nose and mouth with a rag momentarily as another wave of putrification drifted their way from the slaughter a few blocks down.

"Then let's get these horses hitched to some wagons and get the injured and disabled loaded. Tell your people to bring what they can carry. We'll only be using cart space for necessities for the journey," Bannon ordered as he waved for one of the injured Blood soldiers left behind to help round up their company.

They had seventeen soldiers heading back with them, all bad off enough to only serve as a hindrance to the rest of the Hyperium that had headed out earlier that morning back on the road with the prisoners of war.

Bannon was quick to round up his people; a total of fifty-eight men, women, children, and elderly. Most could move without aid, though a few were bedridden, needing to fill up space on some of the various carts and wagons they had in store.

The Shield Company had gathered quite a number of horses early in the night before dawn, thirty-two in total. The rest of the dolingers and horses found were used by the fifty or so Hyperium troops that had departed that morning.

They had burned their dead troops in a communal pyre before daybreak, and with it, all troops had been accounted for, confirming that indeed thirty Hyperium soldiers had been slain in battle the previous night.

Metus knew it was going to be a long day, but no part of it would be longer than the time they had to spend in the rotting town, signs of death on clear display on all sides of them.

<hr/>

The backcountry trail to Sansabar was smooth enough a trek, up until they reached the canyon. The paths were narrow, and the caravan had to travel single file to squeeze through the rocky pass.

The long off-road day trek was beginning to wear on everyone as not everyone had seats on the carts or on horseback. Metus and Bannon led the group alongside Darious, who knew the occasionally used back trail from the enclave to Sansabar.

"Call for a stop!" a voice yelled from a ways back in the canyon, getting the three's attention at the front of the line, which they promptly did.

"Stay with the lead," Metus called to Bannon, motioning for Darious to come with him to investigate what the trouble was.

A cry of pain came from the narrow part of the canyon, and around a horse-pulled wagon stood a group of unclean onlookers that made room for Darious and Metus as they arrived.

A man patted the horse that pulled the wagon, trying to calm the beast, another refugee remaining pinned, wedged between the narrow canyon walls and the cart, the wheels crushing the man slowly as the anxious horse nickered and bucked its head, pulling the cart an inch further into the wedged man's crushed frame.

"Get these people to move on. They're spooking the horse. And if this horse decides to bolt, we're all getting run down," Metus quietly said to Darious, the man slowly moving to whisper to everyone to make their way out of the canyon.

"Do you think you can work on backing that horse up once its calmed?" Metus asked the man attempting to handle the animal, who was doing much better once the crowd in the front had all moved on down the canyon.

"What do you think I've been trying to do?" the man snipped back, reining at the horse to scoot it back till its haunches were touching the wagon.

"All of you in the back, you've got to pull the wagon. The horse shouldn't be fighting you now," Metus called, moving next to the horse to attempt to push the cart back, hoping that those behind heard him and were going to start helping him.

The wagon creaked and the man let out a painful cry as the cart started to budge. Metus felt the others pulling now, and with a loud snap of the man's ribs, the cart lurched back a few feet, dropping the man to the ground who had fainted from the pain and shock of half his chest caving in.

"Grab him. Get him out of the way," Metus called to those who were pulling the wagon, and after the man was drug back a ways, he motioned for the man leading the horse to move it forward, slowly, to get it out of the canyon before it could cause any more issue.

Metus shrunk into a side pocket of the canyon, letting the wagon pass, then rushed back to the man who had a circle of unclean standing around him.

"Let me see," he said, asking for space as he knelt down to inspect the man's vitals.

Blood started to seep from his mouth, slowly at first. He coughed, spraying blood in the air, Metus shielding his face just in time. The man's head lurched to the side, passing away before Metus could think of what to do or how to help.

"We lost one of our men just now. Looks like he lost too much blood through the night," Bannon morosely said as Metus made his way back to the front of the line, adding, worry present in his voice, "What happened? There's blood on you."

"One of Darious' people—died. Wedged between a wagon and the canyon—caved his chest in," Metus wearily offered, wiping what blood off he could as Darious ordered for the caravan to begin moving once more.

The caravan somberly started moving again, slower this time, and with less chatter.

The night came on, and in the distance, they could see the lights of Sansabar speckle the horizon. They would not make it to town that night, and in fact, they did not plan to lead the caravan through there at all, other than to send Bannon on a supplies run with what little gold Darious had to offer for trade.

They were still in Tarigannie, and they needed to cross the border sooner than later. Having the whole Enclave of the Unclean there would not only put Sansabar on edge, but news would travel fast to the capital, and they did not need Rochata-Ung officials knowing where they were or had been.

Setting up camp, the enclave and the Hyperium hitched up lean-tos separately from each other, the fear the Hyperium had to contracting leprosy being a legitimate concern shared by the troops and Bannon.

Sultan Metus finished up his rations well past after dark, having been more than busy helping tend to other immobile soldiers as they bedded down for the night.

Gods he wanted nothing more than to hide from all the misery and despair—to leave the moaning and cries that came on once the sun had gone down. He knew he couldn't, but the thought persisted, like a gnat that kept returning to buzz in your ear.

Taking a few swigs of water, he got up from the side of a wagon he was perched at and went looking for his general.

"Looking for something, Sultan?" a soldier on makeshift crutches asked, seeing Metus poking his head around the wagons.

"General Bannon," Metus stated.

"Ah, yeah," the soldier said, immediately more downcast than he had been, "General Bannon's with the medic. Jose and Lennon, they both ain't doing so good. They're over there,"

The soldier pointed Metus to the right cart, and he peeked in to see one of the Shield Company medics drizzle a brown glass vile of myrrh along the gruesome, deep gash the Blood soldier had along his thigh and abdomen.

Tears streamed from the soldier's eyes, or beads of sweat, Metus couldn't tell which, and the man writhed as the medic worked at cleaning and suturing the part of the open wound that had not already been sewn.

Bannon kept a wet cloth over the man next to the other two, soothingly talking to him words Metus could not understand as the man shook violently, sweating his clothes and bandages through.

Metus moved to Bannon's side of the cart, inspecting the soldier closer. He had been stabbed somewhere around the armpit on the left side. His bandages were deep red, and his skin was pale. The shivers came and went at random. Listening to Bannon's speech up close, he realized it was a chant, religious perhaps, but not in a language that he knew of.

"The boy's deep in fever," Bannon whispered to Metus, not taking his eyes off the shaking pale man.

"Is it contagious?" Metus asked, not sure if he should be worried about the announcement.

"No. This is the warrior's fever. One sustained from battle wounds. Infection, when it gets deep in the blood, will begin to rattle a man apart."

Metus looked to the poor soul who didn't even seem conscious and asked, "Will he live?"

"If he beats the fever…perhaps," Bannon reverently said. "We will know tonight."

"Others may need you Sultan. We are taking care of these two for now. Go, tend to your men," Bannon said, eyes still on the soldier as he started up his strange chant.

Metus took one final look at the two gravely wounded men, and then walked away.

Looking to the camp, he could see eyes on him. His men and women. The ones he had brought on this mission. The ones that had followed his orders. The ones who had paid the consequences for his orders and actions with their own bodies.

He wanted to go and hide, if only for an hour, to escape all the lingering, sleepless pain and death. To clear his head.

He went to the closest soldier who looked longingly for some form of comfort, a bloodied bandage over her right eye, blinded from battle. She was part of Shadow Company. Perfect sight was one of their qualifiers in that company, he knew. She would have to be dismissed after all this was over, if she survived the trip back to Sheaf.

He wanted to hide away that night.

8
ALLIES AND ENEMIES

"Jadu, get Zaren up, we're losing daylight," Reza said, her voice cracking in irritation, not happy with either the praven's disinterest in rousing his master, or the old man's ability to oversleep.

"He sleeps well past sunrise most days. He's not going to like being woken up so early," Jadu argued, looking at the sleeping old man bundled up in his robes with more than a little hesitation.

"We do not have time for beauty sleep, Jadu!" Reza scolded, adding, "He's your teacher, you wake him. We're moving out *now*."

"You're not the one that's going to have to do extra mantra concentration exercises," Jadu grumbled under his breath as he went to nudge Zaren slightly harder, calling for him to wake up.

"That old enchanter better be up in the next minute or *I'll* deal with him," Kissa harshly whispered to Reza in passing, the rest of the company idly waiting, ready to begin the day's trek.

Eilan came silently down the boulders they were camping next to, her haste denoting urgency.

"Dolingers and horses coming this way. Quite a few. Lots of soldiers on foot as well. Could be the Hyperium," she reported, Reza and Kissa turning from glaring at the sleeping old man to consider the scout's news.

"How far out are they?" Kissa asked.

"Still miles out. Time enough for us to move to intercept if that's what you're thinking," Eilan answered, both looking to Reza to help them make the decision.

"If it could be the Hyperium, then we have to try to make contact. Let's at least get moving to do so. Kissa, Eilan, Gale, Jasper," Reza called, the two elite guards coming to join the planning circle once hearing their names called. "You four, scout it out. Make contact if it is the Hyperium. Let them know we're here. I fear we'd be too slow to catch them with *some* presently in our group."

"Try and keep up," Eilan smirked at Gale and Jasper as her and Kissa took off sprinting down the sand mound they had camped atop of, slashing cuts in the sand dunes with their feet as they slid down to the hard desert floor.

Even with their armor, Gale and Jasper sprinted off, just as quick, and Reza watched as the group of four bolted off to intercept the unidentified force, which still was not within her view.

By the time Zaren was up, and not in a pleasant mood about it either, Reza and the others could easily see the large force moving out in the plains before them.

Though there were more than a hundred in the band, only fifty or so were mounted, the other half were marching on foot, though their clip was swift.

"Arie, mind telling us what you see?" Reza asked the haltia as she perched atop a small boulder, squinting, looking intently as the four small figures she knew to be Kissa and the others moved to intercept the lead of the mounted forces.

"Kissa has made herself known to their leader," she quietly said distractedly. "They've called for a halt now."

Zaren and Jadu hobbled up to join the group perched at the

dune's edge beside Terra and Cavok, Cavok taking the praven up on his shoulder as he used to do for Jadu to get a better look with the aid of a bit more elevation.

"They are sending riders this way now, six of them. That's the Hyperium all right. They're coming to pick us up," Arie announced, smiles easily coming to most in the group, grateful to see that the Hyperium had somehow weathered the terrible pursuit of Rochata-Ung's horsemen.

"They're sending riders?" Zaren asked, his voice more crackly than usual. "Thank the gods. One more day of walking and I would have had to have delved into my transportation spells. Didn't know I was signing up with such a rudimentary group."

"You can summon a mount?" Reza incredulously asked, glaring the old enchanter down once more.

"I didn't say a mount," he bickered, looking up to give the statement some further thought. "Though I suppose I have a summoning spell somewhere in my book."

"Why didn't you use it yesterday?"

"My dear Reza, one does not simply perform magic willy-nilly. What happens when you truly need a spell? Conservation is the key to preservation—"

"Enough," Reza said, cutting off what felt like the start of a longwinded speech. "Don't tell Kissa you could have done that all along. She'd kill you."

"Why are only half of the Hyperium mounted?" Cavok asked, his deep voice cutting through the bickering.

No one ventured an answer directly, but Arie softly spoke, "We'll soon find out," as the approaching six Shadow Company riders rode up to the dunes in a sprint, the dolingers heaving from the exertion.

"Get on," the lead rider, Naldurn, ordered, Reza jumping on with her as the others partnered up, the six mounts starting back to the main body of the Hyperium, arriving within minutes at somewhat a slower pace with the extra weight than they had arrived.

Naldurn rode up aside Hathos at the head of the company, the others filling in around as close as they could while the company started their march forward again on course for Rochata-Ung.

"Our numbers were reduced last night, as you can see," Hathos calmly spoke to Reza as they trotted along, answering the question that had been gnawing at her from the time she had come to realize the marching troops were Rochatans and not their own.

"By half? Is Metus...," she asked, not wanting to know the answer to the unsaid question if he had truly been slain.

"No. The sultan, along with Bannon and seventeen injured are headed back to the Plainstate along with the enclave refugees. We suffered losses, but not as many as you see vacant in their ranks here."

"Then what's the plan? With half the Hyperium and without Metus and Bannon, why are we returning to Rochata? They have a force large enough to easily slaughter us if they wish. And judging by what it looks like you did to their horsemen, my assumption is, they *will* wish," Reza questioned.

"I'm expecting them to. Hopefully they will come at us with their full force," Hathos quietly said, Reza having to strain to hear the soft-spoken man.

He did not meet eyes with her, but could feel her confusion at the seemingly suicidal path the group was on. He spoke to her, attempting to unravel the schemes he held.

"Your extraction went better than planned. This bodes well with us. It seems the gods have cast us a considering glance."

Looking up to the rising sun, eyeing the distant speck that marked the sprawl of buildings and walls that made up Rochata-Ung in the distance beyond the miles of rising heatwaves warping their vision, he turned his piercing gaze and continued.

"We fought and killed hundreds of their soldiers at the Enclave of the Unclean. This is an act of war. Though they started it, they will want to finish it. They will retaliate.

"We deliver the prisoners of war back to them in a gesture of good will. It will not halt their pursuit, but it will slow them down. They wouldn't simply leave exhausted and wounded troops to fend for themselves out here in the burning desert.

"If we can find the arisen army, bring the Rochata forces to them for them to see the threat themselves, our quarrel might pale in comparison to the looming threat that the arisen lord poses. They may find that we are, as we announced from the start of all this, their allies, not their enemies. Let's hope at least. If they continue their attack on us at that point, then they truly are idiots."

"Reza," Naldurn uncomfortably scolded, adjusting in her saddle, Reza having subconsciously been squeezing her tighter and tighter around the waist as Hathos had been explaining his plan.

"Sorry," Reza offered, placing her hands along Naldurn's hips instead, taking a few breaths as she attempted to wrap her head around the new direction their mission had taken along vastly more dangerous paths.

"Where's Nomad?" she asked after a moment, looking around the troops for signs of him.

"He...escaped us," Naldurn answered. "I tried to stop him, so did Henarus, but he was too wild for us to contend with."

Reza reflected on the news for a moment before Naldurn continued. "I sent Tris, one of our Shadows, to track him. We hope to link back up with her soon. That's our only lead other than when he left, he was headed south."

"And Henarus? Is he alright?" Reza asked.

"Yes. The prophet is battered, but lives. He is in our company with his priest," Hathos answered.

"Hathos, I see a force ahead," Eilan cautiously called out, her partner moving their mount closer to the Hyperium Primus.

"I see it too," Arie confirmed, the two haltia's eyesight penetrating a great distance beyond that of their human counterparts.

"The army is large," Eilan warned. "More than five hundred."

Hathos considered the information in silence for a moment before offering conjectures. "Perhaps a regiment of backup? Either to support Set and his cavalry, or to call his company home. One of such reckless command is sure to not go without the occasional censure and recall."

"A half force is not what we were hoping for," Undine voiced to Hathos' side. "The smaller the unit, the faster they will be to run upon us."

The morning light shone brightly off their leader's breastplate, and the only consolation to Undine's grim words from Hathos was his unflagging march towards their enemy that once again outnumbered them many times over.

9
BAITING THE STRIKE

The dark halls were only lit by a faint glow along the ritual braziers that let off a ghostly wisp of a flame, whatever magic still giving them life, seeming on the verge of flickering out at any moment.

Denloth halted under a tall archway behind Sha'oul who stood, turning his head to look off into the dark beyond.

"The eyes of a god are upon us," the tall man said after a moment of pause.

Denloth reached to sense the aether currents, feeling the strands and presences of all the influences nearby. He could feel most strongly his master's aura, overwhelming and vivid in its pulsation. He could also feel the strangeness of the new creature Sha'oul had brought into their plane of existence, as well as the faint stirrings of the army of arisen beyond the temple walls. Behind them was the pounding of energy pulsations from the Sun Room, but beyond that, he was not sensing anything else.

As if he knew that his companion struggled to sense the presence he spoke of, he offered, "Up along the cliffs, overlooking this canyon. Do you feel her? A...saren. A strong one. One close to her goddess."

Denloth immediately refocused his attention, searching far out past the canyon, trying to feel for the one his master spoke of.

"I cannot detect her," he finally admitted, frustrated at the strain which had begun to give him a headache.

Sha'oul smiled, considering his student's failure. In this area, tasting the presence of another's essence, he was well matured, more perhaps than any he knew. Knowing the location of his enemies, and allies, had served him many times over the years, costing those that would have ruined him their victory.

After the display in the Sun Room, he had begun to worry slightly of Denloth's reach and potential. The display had been impressive to say the least—worrying at most. If the student had the potential to outgrow the master—what need was there for a master then? He recalled what he had done to *his* master centuries ago.

"You have no former dealings with Sareth, have you?" he asked at length, probing Denloth's gaps of experience.

"No, not intimately," Denloth confessed. "I have studied her in tomes, but rare is it that I have even seen a saren."

"We will soon rectify that. I'll make sure you have the chance to get *very* intimate with one of her chosen," Sha'oul grinned, savoring his thoughts of the schemes already hatching to snare the holy one overlooking them in their dark temple corridors.

Sha'oul picked up his pace now, Denloth curiously in tow, seeing that his master had an immediate purpose about his heading.

They walked into the torchlight at the end of the corridor where the torch-bearing skeletons waited, along with their new dark friend, the wendigo.

Sha'oul transitioned to the foul language that Denloth lightly knew, listening carefully as his master talked to the beast.

"Child of ash, what is your name?" the tall man demanded, standing shorter and smaller than that of the large beast, but imposing a much larger presence than the other in all other ways.

"Lunt," the creature croaked at length, eyeing his new master cautiously, already fearful as to what power it was giving away as

48

it gave up its name, the one the Lord of Ash knew it by.

"I have need, and you shall serve. Fail to perform thy duties, and I shall rip you from this existence and deliver you to Telenth-Lanor myself to pay for your shortcomings. This is his war, not mine, not ours. If you fail me, you fail him, and he will render all to ash who hinder his designs."

Lunt's dead eyes strayed away from Sha'oul as he spoke, the fear of their god burning a hole in his soul as he was addressed. Even Denloth could feel something supernatural about Sha'oul's delivery, as if he were using some sort of coercive magicks to drill the point home.

"I shall serve faithfully," Lunt agreed in its cutting dark language, cowering as his tall frame bent over, a fat stream of rank urine streaming out from its genitals, physically submitting before its master.

"See that you do," Sha'oul said, going on to issue his command. "Your task is simple. Command the arisen troops northwards, out of the canyon, then along the road south between the crags and take the fort at the trail's end. The numbers there are a trifle, you will take it without much resistance."

He stepped forward, placing a palm on the beast's cowed forehead between its antlers. Denloth felt a transfer of sorts, or an endowment of authority, pass to the creature, it standing up after receiving its new mantle, walking off out of the hall with the skeletons in tow, a new sense of purpose fresh in its gait.

"You send away our army? Are we not going with him?" Denloth whispered, not certain of his master's heading.

"The one that sits up above along the canyon walls would not come down otherwise. Surely she has been there for some time surveying. She will notice I am not in the presence of my army. Perhaps she will think this is the opportunity she has been waiting for. A chance to strike at me when I am alone and vulnerable."

"And you *would* be, save for me. Why open your defenses like this? I still fail to see," Denloth pressed, not liking how cocky his master was appearing just then, knowing that in terms of his own tenaciousness, he had lived thus far by playing the long game, being cautious, calculating, and waiting for the opportunities to come to him, not chasing too far ahead of his reach.

"Will we be alone? How many Oathbound still beckon to your call?" Sha'oul casually asked.

"Three," Denloth answered.

"Two less than you had before we left the mountains," Sha'oul tossed out, reflecting upon the deduction in troops. "They still remain loyal to you?"

"They do," Denloth confirmed.

"I did not relinquish command of my greyoldors. Seven of them I also have at my command. The power I sense along the cliffs, though potent, is not numerous. A small force at best. Our ten abreast us will be more than sufficient to deal with this annoyance. Once she is taken care of, we will have one less god to worry about to oppose our march on Tarigannie. I do not want a threat floating over our heads as we make our move. For now the moment of weakness is planned of our own doing, but if not dealt with, later that weakness could be legitimate. That is not the time to have a god eyeing us," Sha'oul finished, walking out of the hall, his tattered cloak rippling in a smooth line as it followed his movements.

"Then we must prepare for battle with this woman," Denloth said, consigning himself to the direction his master had taken them, following him out of the hall, headed towards their reserve guards.

"No, Denloth," Sha'oul grimly said, his face stern as they turned to the corrugated chatoyant sandstone-lined room that was littered with seven hair-like pods hanging from the roof, gleaming eyes of seething hatred staring out at the two as they entered.

"We must prepare for war with a *god*."

10

A DIRE GAMBIT

The night they had arrived at the overlook, overshadowing the temple a hundred yards below, they had hopes of a swift assault; but the arisen army had moved very little, and with such a force guarding the entrance to the temple, they had seen no opportunity to gain entrance to the lair.

Days had gone by, and the camp of saren was beginning to want for rations and fresh water, as with Fin's encampment.

Most of the saren were performing tasks: hunting, looking for natural cisterns to water the horses, or keeping watch on the arisen army. Only a few were still at camp with Lanereth, Fin, and the others.

Wyld and Yozo languidly were gathered in their lean-tos, conserving their energy while they waited for the order they had all been waiting for from the start.

Malagar and Fin sat along a shabby tree line of cedar trees that provided the only natural shade along the desert plains canyon shelf. Lanereth beside them went over yet another plan she was considering for infiltrating the temple far below at the canyon's floor.

"A trip around the canyon may take a day, two at most. Maybe there's a topside entrance to that temple that we can't see from over here," she suggested, Fin shaking his head, not liking the plan.

"If there's not, then we'd be stuck with another day's journey to come back around. There's no route down into the canyon from the east side of the crags. I've looked. It's a sheer cliff face. At least with this side there's a route down in. If the arisen made a move while over there, we would miss our shot at getting to that temple in time," he said while drawing a rough sketch of the canyon in the sand.

"I agree with Fin. Patience is the answer. They will not stay put in there forever. They can accomplish nothing in the bottom of that pit, and Denloth is clever enough to know that. They will make a move soon," Malagar spoke, sitting back in the heat of the sun, the scant shade the cedar tree was providing barely covering his head.

Lanereth considered the two's input, not enjoying the prospect of sitting around for who knows how many more days burning away under the Tarigannie sun, squandering their rations, waiting for their enemy to make a move.

"We have enough food and drink left to last us two more days. On horseback, it's half a day along this road to Fort Wellspring; almost a full day back north to Sansabar. We can wait only till then, then we must resupply and hope we don't miss anything," she said, more than a little beaten down at the long distance they had traveled from the Jeenyre mountains, only then to have to set camp under such harsh conditions.

Everyone looked up as one of the saren knights ran back into the camp from the canyon lookout post. Wyld and Yozo peeked out of their lean-tos to listen in on the report.

"Something large, all covered in shrouds, came out of the temple. All the arisen are following it. The army is mobilizing," she hurriedly rushed out, catching her breath from the sprint.

Lanereth stood up, looking to Fin and Malagar as they went to join the remaining saren still at the lookout a few hundred meters out. She ordered the knight to go and find the others and have them report back to camp before she ran off after the two men.

They were already perched alongside Revna who lay flat along the lip of the canyon wall, watching the hundreds of moving figures shuffle unnaturally towards the large, shrouded creature that loomed at the head of the forces, antlers smoking in the sunlight.

"It came out a few minutes ago. Just started moving the troops when Liv came and got you," the priestess whispered, all the while keeping her eyes locked on the activity below.

"That...is not the presence I felt the other day. That's not the arisen lord," Lanereth said, the others taking note of the High Priestess' concern.

"Yeah, as far as I know, Sha'oul doesn't have antlers," Fin agreed, asking, "But why does the army follow that *thing* then?"

None had an answer. Instead, they all watched a minute longer before the antlered figure began loping off north along the shaded side of the canyon, taking the arisen horde along with it.

"It'll take that number of arisen a while to move out, but move out it seems they are doing. Though, I see no arisen lord among their ranks," Lanereth said, backing up to begin heading back to camp to see about gathering the rest of her knights.

"Nor Denloth that I could see," Fin added, following her as Malagar stayed at Revna's side.

Most of the sarens had not wandered far for their tasks with the exception of Hassa, who had gone looking for water with Hamui on horseback earlier that day.

"All are here but Hassa and the praven," Sarah reported as Lanereth jogged back into camp with Fin at her side.

Lanereth considered the announcement for a moment, eyeing all six knights and Tove, her priestess.

"We may need to move without them. We may not get another shot at an opportunity like this, and the window may close quicker than we have time to scour the countryside searching for them," she said, looking to Fin to confirm he concurred with her reasoning.

Fin looked uneasy about the prospects of facing Denloth or the arisen king without Hamui. He had witness terrible magicks from both, and though he knew the priestess had some chance at combatting the dark sorcerers, he had not actually witnessed saren magic before for himself.

"I don't like going in there two people short either—Hassa is my best fighter—but the opening has presented itself," she pressed, all now gathered around the two as they discussed whether or not they were going to mount the assault they had all been waiting on for days now.

"That's another thing. Why order his army to head out without him? It could easily be a setup," Fin said, hesitating to dampen the energy he was feeling mounting in everyone. He knew getting pumped before a battle helped, but it could also cause people to make dumb decisions.

"Trap or no, the majority of the arisen lord's forces has just moved out. This is as good a chance as I see our small force will get to catch him alone to deal with him. If we can take him down, all his force will be untethered from his command. This is our chance, Fin. Would Reza do differently? Would she hesitate when the target is clear, unprotected before you?"

Fin was taken aback at the mention of Reza. She was younger than him, but he respected Reza's ability to execute military operations immensely. Her fiery spirit knew no fear when charging into war, but...would she agree with Lanereth on this one? He couldn't say.

"Something doesn't seem right about this whole setup," was all Fin could reply, but Lanereth waited, needing a confirmation of if he and his crew were in or out of the strike.

At length, he reluctantly answered, "Yozo, Wyld, you two ready for this?"

Yozo nodded slightly, resting a hand on his sword, ever at his side, and Wyld puffed up her chest, stretching out her arms, flexing for battle being enough of an answer for him.

"Then, we fight at your side," Fin grimly said, turning back to Lanereth, adding, "May Sareth and any other merciful gods watch over us this day."

"Sareth is the only goddess we'll need," Lanereth stiffly said, calling for all her sarens to gather their war gear and get ready for the assault, Fin doing the same.

The army had all but moved around the bend by the time the crew was assembled and ready for the operation. The lingering memory of the number of abominations that had just been there still haunted the vision of all along the cliff's ledge as they stared down into its gaping expanse.

The trail down was rough, and it took them a good half hour to scramble and descend to the bottom of the canyon from the many tiered ledges on the side of the canyon they had been perched atop of.

Kicking a severed arm off to the side, Fin scanned the silent canyon, looking to his crew, seeing that Malagar and Wyld were both equally ready to resolve their score with Denloth.

Yozo, however, seemed neither overconfident, nor skittish. Fin had come to appreciate the man's stoicism in the face of battle. It reminded him of Nomad, in a way. He knew he would not have to worry about him in a tuff, and that was always a relief when fighting with someone at your side.

"Say your final prayers," Lanereth ominously said to her small platoon. "It may be our last chance before battle."

The group made their way across the canyon floor to the steps of the temple, all gazing upon its impressive façade. It was ancient, and either man or time and weather had defaced much of its design, but there still remained imbedded opal and obsidian stones, laid in a pattern showing the sun and moon along many cycles, arching over the entrance.

The archway stood twenty feet above them, ten foot wide, and one by one, the sarens crossed the threshold between light and shadow, disappearing into the long-forgotten halls of a distant god.

Fin was the last one in, giving a hopeful look to the cliff walls from where they had come, half expecting to see the burly saren knight with the humorously small praven along her shoulder, making their way down the canyon to join them—but like the canyon floor, the rim remained quiet and empty.

"Sareth," Fin whispered, looking to the sky one last time

before following the rest into the darkness, "you'd better goddamn be there for us."

11

PLUNGED INTO DARKNESS

The dim hallways were stale, no traffic breathing air in or out of the glowing hallways for decades, perhaps centuries. Lanereth walked confidently through archways, flanked by her two priestesses who held symbolic staves with the sign of their goddess.

Behind them were seven swords and shields, the saren knights marching as quietly as they could, attempting to compensate for the heavy armor they all wore.

Fin, Wyld, Yozo, and Malagar were close behind, guarding the rear, eyeing the many black corridors that split off from the main path they had taken.

Lanereth called for a halt, holding up her hand as she tilted her head to listen to a noise deep in the temple.

"What is that buzzing?" she asked, all in the company straining to listen to the high-pitched hum further ahead in some distant room of the temple.

None had an answer, and she produced a hefty, marbled cylinder from her robes. Whispering words, lips pressed against it, the cylinder began to lengthen, forming into a solid pole, a clear, perfectly smooth crystal at the top.

She touched the end of the staff to the ground, and a dull shockwave of sound echoed out in all directions.

Everyone was still, only able to guess as to what their leader was doing.

The sound came back, rippling in from some of the side corridors. She had her eyes closed, deep in concentration.

More shockwave sound ripples came to her from ahead, though these were distorted.

"Whatever it is, it's in some way affecting the aether currents, and it's up ahead, through that archway in a room off to the left."

"A noise, a disturbance in the currents. If they have set a trap for us, that room on the left would be my first guess as to where they're going to spring it on us," Fin whispered, walking up to Lanereth as the group stood there, waiting for the order to proceed forward.

"Fin, we don't have the remainder of the day to get lost in this place searching for our quarry. It's too massive. What, do you advise we take that tunnel?" she asked, pointing to a side corridor beside them. "Or that passage, or that one?"

Fin looked off into the dark hallways, realizing she was right, at least about searching pointless avenues that showed little to merit investigation.

"If they're here, they're up there, and that's where we need to go, trap, or no trap," she ended, stepping forward into the gloom, her sarens following behind as they passed Fin by.

Shaking off the gut feeling of trouble, he picked up the pace, falling in beside Malagar and Yozo as the group continued down the dim hall, passing through the threshold at the end of the line of archways, the room beyond opening up into a great chamber, tall, thick pillars holding up the great hall's ceiling that towered fifty feet above.

Deep into the chamber, they could see very little, but to the left of the room shone a bright light that illuminated just enough for them to see how far the chamber spanned.

None spoke, all in awe of the structure's grandeur, and of its ominous stillness.

The high-pitched hum was easily located now that they were within the chamber, and just as Lanereth had said, the noise was calling out from a room off to the left along with a bright light that shone from the doorway.

The group slowly made their way along the wall, inspecting the emulsified sand glaze that was smeared along the structure's roof. The whirring came from within the room which drowned out all other sound.

Lanereth looked to all thirteen comrades that stood at the ready, each willing to brave the darkest threat the Southern Sands had seen in many years head on.

Fin, Malagar, and Wyld stepped up, nodding that they were ready to enter at her command, Yozo holding back with the other knights.

"He's in there. I can sense him," Lanereth whispered, the slightest tremble in her voice, and Fin couldn't tell if it was one of fear or excitement.

He slipped his hand in his vest, drawing something out of it, though, what it was, Lanereth could not decipher.

"May Sareth be with you this day, High Priestess," Malagar whispered to her side, breaking her attention away from the oddity Fin held.

"May she be with us all," she affirmed, and with that, she entered the room, Fin and the others close behind.

They walked through the plastered entrance to see a dozen black slate slabs, standing out of the ground with two shining quartz rods, rubble, and destroyed structures to the left of the room.

She stopped and so did everyone else that now looked at what Lanereth had set her eyes to. At the end of the long room stood two figures. She knew who the tall one was; she could feel the taint emanating from his presence. He had the touch of a devil upon him. She immediately knew that this was the arisen lord that they sought.

They made no move, and as the cascading light of the crystals continued to shine, enveloping everything in the room in a blinding light, the buzz continuing to drown out anything they could want to say, she stepped forward, and all followed her advance.

Every step was heavier than the one before, and those at her back could feel that in that room, fates and futures would be made, or cut short, everything they had trained for their whole life, leading up to the peak of this moment.

She passed four screeching crystals, coming to a slab bright with blood along its black surface. She stared, transfixed by the imagery for a moment before a slithering voice cut through the wall of noise, penetrating their minds.

None understood the harsh language, but Fin and Malagar had heard it before, and as Wyld's posture hunched, as though ready to pounce, Malagar grabbed for her wrist worried that Denloth was attempting to, once again, hypnotize the kaith through some dark means.

She lashed out, throwing Malagar's grip from her just as the bloodied slate opened into a rift, the Planes of Ash appearing before them.

The harsh voice called again, and Wyld tackled Lanereth from behind, knocking her off-balance, tumbling towards the rift as the mind-controlled kaith drove her into the hellish realm.

Malagar made one last attempt to snatch at the two, but they were thrown into the ashen realm, and without a second look back, he lunged in to attempt to retrieve them, but as soon as he entered, the rift stone shattered, blowing apart beside Fin and two of the other saren, the slate shrapnel cutting them badly and throwing them to the ground.

Fin's ears were ringing from the blast, an even shriller pitch than before. He opened his eyes wide, blinking, trying to regain use of his faculties quickly before Denloth and his master could take advantage of the vulnerable state he was in.

One of the saren knights further from the blast rushed up to him, helping him up, dragging him back away from the exploded rift that Malagar, Wyld, and Lanereth had disappeared into.

Fin looked around and saw a priestess and knight, that had also been close to the blast, were equally staggered and were being drug back to the entrance of the room in an attempt to regroup, the two figures at the end of the room leisurely moving up to their location.

Fin stammered, trying to shout a retreat, but his words came out garbled. He did not know the extent of the two saren priestesses' abilities, but he knew with their leader, their High Priestess gone, two of his troops gone, and having started down two comrades to begin with, the odds had gone from dire to nonexistent with winning the fight.

The figures approached their front line and the curtain of light that clouded the room began to ripple and wave in space, right before a dark knight ripped into existence between the group. Fin beheld the golden wings shooting up out of the knight's formfitting helm, a beady red glow emanating from within, the light penetrating its inner shadows, showing a blood-slicked skull housed within the black steel.

"Oathbound," Fin uttered, just as two more dark-plated knights ripped into being next to the first.

He looked around to the door behind them, looking for their escape, but Yozo and the two saren knights that still stood on the other side of the doorway had their backs to him, and looking past them, he saw why.

Little figures lurked in the dark just beyond the light. He would have looked past them but for the many pairs of moving glimmers in the dark, bobbing and twitching in agitation, waiting for those at the door to leave the light for them to pounce.

They were flanked and without their leader.

12

STRIKING THE MATCH

"We will attempt an audience with them. Tau, Undine, come with me. All others, stay here and await our return," Hathos ordered, the three promptly riding off towards the hundreds of horsemen riding towards them.

They rode at a leisurely pace, not wanting to press their horses' and dolingers' health, knowing full well that a good deal of galloping was in their future.

The sun marked the riders, their polished armor gleaming in its light, and from the opposing force, five riders broke ranks to meet them.

The eight men slowed, pulling up as their horses nickered, pulling at their reins, seeming desperate to continue the charge as they showed their large teeth and eye whites.

The two groups sized each other up, each waiting for the other to begin talks amidst hoof stomps in the dry desert dirt highway.

Hathos broke the agitated silence with his calm, collected voice, announcing, "Our company was hunted down and attacked yesterday by a High Judge named Set. His forces came upon us unprovoked, and we did defend ourselves, killing many in his command. We bring back the remaining prisoners in an attempt at finding some measure of peace between our two states."

The lead horseman listened patiently while reigning his horse in, holding Hathos' eyes intently the whole time. In a stern voice, he warned, "You will return our men to us at once. We will escort you to Rochata-Ung for further talks."

"Talks? You mean sentencing. We have no interest in being accused of war crimes by a corrupt court of which we are not guilty to. Accept your prisoners and be done with us," Hathos spat, not in the mood to mince words, rearing up his horse in a frightful display, as he turned and galloped off with Undine and Tau following close behind, leaving the officials in their dust.

With both sides returning to their attachments, the opposing forces waited in the hot desert heat as their leaders rejoined, barking out orders as they rode up.

"Leave the prisoners, we ride south through the dunes," Hathos shouted to his crew, dolinger and horse riders leaving their posts around the Tarigannie survivors they had been closely watching.

Seeing that they were being freed, the remaining Rochatans cheered, rushing down the highway toward the large cavalry unit far down the road.

Hathos watched the freed men run for a moment longer, looking back to his men and women, offering a silent prayer that luck would be on their side that day, waving an arm for all to follow his lead, starting them off with a light gallop towards the endless dunes south of them.

By the time they had made it to the first of many sand ridges, Hathos turned to see if they were being followed, waving Undine and the troops onward as he ordered his horse to a halt along the first dune's peak.

The prisoners had been collected, and they had lingered in the same spot for a while before eventually turning back, heading down the road to Rochata-Ung.

Hathos released a held breath. If they had pressed an attack there and then, he was not sure their tired forces could fend them off or outrun them for long. They needed time. They needed some distance—at least temporarily.

He did not doubt Rochatan officials would respond poorly to the news the prisoners would give them of their massive defeat. There would be retaliation; and now, they had a direction, a heading to hunt for them. South—where the arisen army lay—or so he hoped.

"So much hope. So many ways this could end in disaster," he murmured under his breath as he turned to catch up with his company that had now well passed him.

Rarely did he operate on such an elaborate risky network of gambits, but he had been given little choice. Though as loyal as he was to Sultan Metus, and as well-meaning the sultan had been in taking up with the company on the mission, he had put his leaders in difficult situations and had asked the world of them. If he was to dig them out of the hole they had been led into, he knew a few miracles would be necessary, which was the leading reason for his insistence on bringing the prophet with them. Even with his head injury, he knew the power the man held in swaying the tides of fortune and fate.

He caught up quickly with his centurions, drawing them close for orders.

"They return to Rochata today, but they will be on our trail tomorrow, after their men are safely returned and details of the massacre are made known to their High Judges. We'll use that time to move deep into the dunes. They are infamous for their harshness and difficulty in traversing them. It should slow their pursuit even more. We will camp this night and give the men and mounts rest. They all need it."

Kissa, Undine, and Tau nodded their heads in approval, glad to be following their leader's clear vision directly once more.

"Move out, see to your companies," he ordered, catching Kissa before she rode back to her Shadows.

"See that you keep a few Shadows on watch. I want to know well before anyone crosses our path or is on our trail. And Kissa— good to have you back with us."

She nodded sternly, adding, "I'll see to it done. Six of my finest will scout for us in all directions."

The two trotted off, Kissa to her post and Hathos to Henarus to check up on the injured man which was doubled up with his priest on a larger steed.

The man's injury did concern him, but that night, he would see what could be done to relieve him of his brain fog from the blow he had taken to the head.

The saren had been able to heal the woman and child. Perhaps he could utilize her or the abilities of her other strange companions. Metus did value them as a high priority, though he wondered if his sultan *overvalued* the mismatched band of misfits.

He suspected he would be able to find out for himself in the days ahead. He would need all the help he could get with the monumental task before him.

13

BEAR WITNESS TO POWER UNCHAINED

Fin peered around the archway, seeing at least half a dozen gleaming eyes in the shadows waiting for them to exit the light of the room they were in. Looking back in front of them, he saw the sarens giving ground as the three ominous dark knights slowly advanced forward with Denloth and Sha'oul close behind.

There was no way around it, he knew. They were going to have to press one way or the other or risk being attacked from both sides. With the tides of the battle turned so badly for the worst even before blows had been thrown, he made the call.

"Revna! Fall back!" he called, and though she was only fifteen feet further in, the ringing of the crystals drowned the order out, and instead of running, he saw her staff lighting up as she chanted, a pearlescent shockwave blasting the Oathbound in front of her and her sisters.

A magenta hue flickered from two of the Oathbound as they

were thrust to the ground, the one on the far right disappearing just before it was hit, reappearing behind the saren's defensive line, shoving a rondel dagger in a saren knight's side before she was able to react, the point jerkily splitting the chainmail and gambeson she wore, causing her to clutch her side and draw away in pain.

The other two Oathbound recovered quickly, two saren knights taking the recovery time to charge them. The other priestess shouted blessings upon the two knights, imbuing their swords with radiant light just as they struck out at the two dark ones, which brought their shotel's up just in time to bind up the attack.

The black metal the shotels were made of began to turn a dark red, rattling, cracks beginning to form where blade met blade.

One shattered, the bright longsword slamming through the curved sword, slicing through parts of the Oathbound's armor like wax, searing the abomination housed within the iron tomb of armor.

A bright light flashed, ejecting the embedded sword back, the saren halting the momentum just before she was cut by her own blade, standing at the ready once more as the damaged knight discarded his broken sword, drawing two stubby sickle daggers, coming at her again.

Still rattling, the other Oathbound pivoted its curved blade around the saren's longsword, digging the tip into the woman's neck, driving her back, swinging wildly in defense, managing to shatter the blade that likely just landed a fatal wound upon her.

Two daggers flew over her shoulder as she turned to fall back, both points hitting their marks, sinking into the Oathbound's helm slits, toppling the dark knight to the ground, dropping its broken sword as it fell.

Fin caught the mortally wounded saren, quickly realizing that if she did not staunch the blood spurting from her neck, that she would be dead within moments.

Another saren stepped up and took her fallen sister's post, squaring off with the dark knight that was getting to its feet, drawing a pair of twin sickle daggers.

Revna was there suddenly, laying hands upon the throat-stabbed saren, performing a healing, Fin could see, as her hands began to radiate with light, Fin removing his hand from her neck to find the tear closed, a bright red scar rapidly forming.

Another flash of magenta sparked to his left, and he could see the Oathbound that had Seam-jumped into their ranks being battered by two saren knights, bashing along its armor and stabbing through slits as it attempted to ward off the assault.

A purple bolt of crackling electricity tore through the room over everyone's heads, striking the sandblasted archway, bringing down large chunks of sandstone in the doorway, dust covering their exit, shutting out a saren knight and Yozo who were still out in the hallway keeping the shadows in the dark at bay.

"Shit," Fin coughed, the sand pelting hard against his cloak, pushing him back to Revna's side as the two frontline saren knights did their best to fend off the Oathbound's assault.

<hr/>

An angry purple light struck the roof of the doorway, felling sections of roof, filling in most of the archway, the dust from the explosion drowning out the blinding light that had been keeping the shadows in the dark at bay.

Yozo's blade came out, cutting a line in the dust as a small praven figure lunged in at him, its erratic bouncing and hopping throwing off Yozo's strike slightly, lopping off digits when he had been going for the creature's whole arm.

The creature's teeth gleamed as it snapped at Yozo's face but was forced to lunge back against the rubble that was still coming down as Yozo's sword sliced at it once more.

The falling rubble smacked the greyoldor against the crumbling stonework which partially buried the creature, giving Yozo time to face the other three figures that were hopping in at him.

Runa, the saren knight that stood guard alongside Yozo, rushed the nearest set of eyes, swinging her shield widely, attempting to catch the childlike figure in the head with the shield, but it skipped jerkily away, the other two shadows lunging in as the opening in the saren's defenses was presented to them.

Bringing her shield back in tight against her body, the creatures clamored over and around the wall of metal franticly, clutching and ripping at the corners of her armor, seeking the soft flesh that lay beneath.

Runa let out a scream of frustration, bashing one of the greyoldors in the head with the pummel of her sword, sending it to the ground, the other one managing to crawl around to her back, gnawing at the chainmail coif as the third creature lunged beneath her shield, binding up her legs, toppling her to the ground, all three corrupted pravens scrambling franticly to mount her, tearing at her armor once more.

Yozo glanced to his right and took note of the downed saren. He wanted to help her, but the three figures twitched wildly, ready to jump in at him at the first sign of a break in concentration. He had no armor, unlike his comrade. The moment the little wretches latched onto him would quickly become disastrous.

The greyoldor in the doorway wriggled free from the imprisoning rubble, reaching for Yozo's silken robes, but this time, not being able to leap away, Yozo made a short-arched slash, lopping off the outstretched hand, causing the creature to recoil back into the smokescreen of the sandy downpour along the doorway.

The other three piled in, rushing the swordsman with such swiftness, even Yozo couldn't respond to the six clawed hands that thrust in, ripping at his clothes, shredding and binding up his sword arm, pushing him back against the wall where the other one-armed greyoldor sprung out from, joining the imminent feeding frenzy.

An azure bolt sliced into the side of one of the creatures that hung off of Yozo's shoulders, felling it to the ground. It shrieked and writhed as it clutched the still glowing hole in its side that fizzled with dark blue sparks.

The other three twisted pravens halted their ripping to look up, assessing what had happened to their ally.

Hamui's sneer was outlined and emphasized by the glow from his staff, hatred for the dark counterparts of his race clear as he lit the room with another bolt of blue, slicing the air between him and the group of darklings in a split second, melting the corner of one's head off, oozing glowing brains from its skull before dropping it next to Yozo.

A few charging footsteps of one in heavy armor preceded a shield point as it thrust one of the greyoldor's straddling Runa in the stomach, driving it into the stone floor, the dull shield pressing through the small creature's middle until it punctured, grinding through skin and organs as Hassa skid the thing along the floor with her shield, tossing it off to the side as she slashed at the other two surrounding her shieldmaiden.

The remaining greyoldors disengaged, reassessing the new threats.

Runa got to her feet, smashing in the head of the one that languidly writhed on the ground with its entrails exposed.

Yozo took the reprieve to reposition himself, sprinting to Hamui's position, lining up next to him to face the three that had roughed him up, which now eyed the group calculatingly.

Hassa swung her mace at the scurrying greyoldor that was latched onto the back of Runa. It leapt off at the last second, Hassa having to pull the swing short to avoid from slamming her comrade.

The other praven continued to bind Runa's legs, tripping her up just when she had gotten her footing back, ripping into the woman's groin with its teeth, clawing her midsection as it made its way underneath her layered armor.

Hassa tried to help her sister, but the other greyoldor snuck back in, tugging at her cloak, pulling her off-balance as it poked for vulnerabilities, jumping off to the side as she made a blind swing at it once more.

Yozo and Hamui could see they needed to finish the three remaining greyoldors quick, hearing the trouble the two sarens were having with the two that proved to be too quick for the armored warriors, but the three that lurked closer and closer to them were not yet committed to the attack, twitching irritably, blood dripping from the side of one and from the severed arm of another.

Yozo lunged in, knowing he could wait no longer for their charge, focusing on the furthest one on the right who had a faintly glowing hole in its side.

It was sluggish from the wound, which Yozo suspected would be the case, and as he slashed in, it struggled to tumble off to the side, no footing to dodge the follow up thrust to its throat as Yozo deftly stabbed through its neck, removing his blade to swipe away the middle greyoldor's lunge towards him, forcing the thing to skip to the side, just as Hamui thrust his hand forward, grabbing it by the wrist, electricity popping along its body, crackling angrily as the thing went rigid. Hamui surged another wave of energy through the creature, its eyes exploding from its skull with the blast, easily indicating its life had snuffed.

Hassa swung angrily, missing again and again. The hopping greyoldor bounded easily about her, distracting her, then attacking when she tried to go to Runa's aid.

Runa was on the ground again, the greyoldor that harassed her continuing to rip the armor from her, slashing and gnawing at her exposed parts. She backed up against the rubble doorway, clutching at her shield to protect her vitals as the creature tore at her limbs, bleeding her out slowly.

Giving up on the nuisance that plagued her, Hassa dropped her shield and mace and rushed the distracted little greyoldor that was gnawing at Runa, snatching him up by his leg and neck, and brought him down on her knee.

The snap of the greyoldor's spine resounded through the cacophonous chamber as the other greyoldor latched onto her neck, gouging into her throat as she finished dealing with the other lifeless greyoldor, tossing it off to the side.

Runa struggled to get up, watching horrified as the greyoldor crunched deeper into the tall saren's neck, buried beneath her coif, blood gushing out into the wretched thing's mouth and face.

Hassa fell to her knees, collapsing before a mangled Runa, who lifted her sword, bringing it down in vengeance upon the oblivious greyoldor who was too involved in reveling in the fountain of blood it had struck to notice the blade slice into its back, again and again, until it collapsed onto the large saren it was feasting upon.

Runa heaved a few times, collapsing against the wall, taking in her final breaths, looking to Hamui and Yozo who were squaring off against the final greyoldor, slumping lifeless as Yozo once again drew his blade, arcing a slice at the armless greyoldor.

The greyoldor dodged, then dodged again as Yozo followed up the swing, tumbling, when Hamui shot a blue bolt at his fallen counterpart, blasting off one of its feet. As the greyoldor went to leap away, the fresh stump stole its spring, and Yozo slashed cleanly through its midsection, sheathing his sword as the small body crumpled in two sloppy heaps on the dark, stone floor.

The knights fought on, and the sarens were holding up against the Oathbound, but with each new reanimation of the wicked plated bloody skeletons came more of a toll on the sarens' strength, wounds beginning to mount.

Dark energy tentacles burst forth from Sha'oul's hand, each greatly darkening the space around its licking tendril, reaching out to Tove, the other priestess, latching around her limbs, beginning to drag her to him.

Slashing an Oathbound down, shoving the other one out of the way, a frontline saren rushed the giant of a man, swinging at his outstretched hand.

The sword slammed into his hand but was deflected harmlessly off as a network of purple tendrils flared into a barrier around the point of impact.

The saren swung once more, chopping in at the arisen lord's head, but the web of tendrils appeared, almost like a second skin, deflecting the attack with a hiss.

Sha'oul backhanded the saren before him, sending her tumbling back amidst the Oathbound which took the opportunity to thrust several times in at the saren, their blades beginning to come back bloodied as her shieldmate ran in to shove them off of her.

Tove screamed, and her shouts, even a few strides away, were audible over the crystal's buzzing. Her cries of pain and anguish got Fin and Revna to their feet.

"Revna, I need to get to Sha'oul or we're all dead! Can you do something about that hex?" Fin shouted, eyeing the giant of a

72

man, seeing now that a simple stab likely would do nothing to the hexweave protected avatar.

She nodded, understanding what Fin was asking of her. "I'll do what I can," she shouted back, though, she was not certain she could break any barriers the dark warlord wore. She would try her damnedest, nonetheless.

Sha'oul clenched his fist, and the dark tendrils squeezed Tove, silencing her, two fat tendrils arching up, shoving into her open mouth, undulating and expanding, sapping the color from her as they piled their way down her throat, rendering her into a lifeless husk within moments.

The moment was so violent that it stunned all watching as their priestess was reduced to a husk before their eyes. The Oathbound continued the press unphased, however, and the group's shock was taken advantage of, two of the Oathbound Seam-jumping at two of the closest sarens, leaving streaks of brilliant phosphorescence in their wake, shoving the stunned sarens in the sides and back, felling Alva and finishing off Liv, who had already been waning from the multiple stab wounds she was suffering from.

"I'll hold them," one of the knights, Jezebel, shouted back to Revna and Fin who knew they were planning an attack against the arisen lord. She swung out at the Oathbound knocking a helmet from its slick, bloody skull, everyone in the group now seeing the horrific face of the foes they fought.

"Now Fin!" Revna shouted, holding aloft her staff, as another saren fell to a mortal blow off to their side, the tides of the battle quickly turning. She shouted prayers to her goddess as she began to light the room around Sha'oul beyond the blinding light that blanketed everyone already.

Fin bolted around the engaged Oathbound, the two wounded knights doing their job in keeping the reanimating skeletons busy as he rushed directly at Sha'oul. He leaped through the air just as Revna's prayer crescendoed, white flame jolting down on the tall man's dark armor of undulating tendrils, the flames jabbing in through the net-like barbs, hooking and ripping the hexweave shell apart.

Fin landed on the man's broad chest, latching onto his thick armor, holding him eye level as he lifted his hand, about to strike.

Sha'oul snatched the man by the arm just before the strike, laughing at the nerve the man had to come at him unarmed.

"You think to strike me down with your fist, little man? You had better come at me with more than that," Sha'oul spat, throwing Fin behind him, Fin rolling fifteen feet down the line of rifts before coming to a stop.

"If a brawl is what you desire, then I shall entertain you," he said, lifting the tendrilled net around his body aloft as the flames continued to rip holes in its weave, thrusting a hand at Revna, sending the corrupted net of hexweave upon her, wrapping her up, sending her to the floor, the tendrils seeking ways to enter her body as it wrapped around her mouth, gagging her from praying to her god for further aid.

"Denloth, see to the others," the arisen lord said, turning to Fin, who was just now getting back to his feet after the tumble.

Denloth stepped up to take his master's position, facing the only saren knight that was not occupied with an Oathbound. He smiled, knowing the small failing party of knights would soon be put down—knowing that the saren he eyed knew the truth of her fate as well.

She squared up, regardless of the odds at that point, not giving the wicked man further satisfaction that he was seeking in her despair.

Switching her sword to her shield hand, she unlatched a throwing axe, raising it to throw it at the warlock just as Denloth raised his hands up, a spectral purple glow shooting forth from his countenance, images of skulls and anguished faces flying out, penetrating through the saren knight, freezing her for a moment as Denloth began chanting incantations, preparing for his next attack as Jen worked her muscles free of the hex-like starch that stiffened her limbs.

Fin stood up, stance off-centered, showing Sha'oul only one side of his frame. He had learned a bit of brawling from Matt over the years, and he was no schlub when it came to fisticuffs, and seeing that Sha'oul had literally thrown off his hexweave barrier that would have stopped most physical attacks, he smirked, looking forward to driving his fists into the tyrant's face.

Sha'oul unclipped his gauntlets, dropping them to the floor, revealing blackened, cracked hands, the taint of the arisen ingrained throughout his flesh beneath his armor.

He walked towards Fin, beckoning Fin to make a swing at him.

The blinding lights from the crystals all about them had, by that point, permanently damaged his vision, Fin guessed, and the ringing was about to split his head in two, but he held his stance firm, debating on if he should take the bait or wait for the huge man to make the first move. He knew that with what he had planned, he only had one shot at getting the upper hand.

"On with it," Sha'oul gruffed, striking deceptively swift, slapping Fin, sending him tumbling another ten feet towards the back of the room.

Fin got back up, but Sha'oul was upon him, snatching him up by the cloak, holding him aloft for a moment before Fin swiveled out of his cloak, pulling out a dagger along his chest bandolier, plunging it towards the giant's chest, Sha'oul blocking the dagger with his own forearm just before Fin could complete the blow.

Sha'oul gripped Fin's arm, snapping it in half with one hand, grabbing the man by the neck, bringing him face to face. He opened his maw, exposing jagged black and yellow teeth, his rank breath overwhelming Fin as he brought him in, intending to begin feasting on him.

Fin swung with his free hand, and Sha'oul allowed him to, laughing at the weak, last display the man exhibited.

His laughter ceased abruptly, a sharp pang indicating something amiss. Fin brought back his arm, his hand clenched firmly on the cloaked dagger Sultan Metus had given him, jabbing its blade back into the crease of the shoulder and neck.

As Sha'oul felt a blade dig deep into his chest, he reflexively flung Fin off to the side, slamming him into one of the crystal nodes, then continued to tumble another twenty feet further. The crystal snapped, slamming into the floor, exploding, setting off the crystal next to it.

The pillar next to Sha'oul burst, blasting him down, attempting to hold himself up with his good arm as the room erupted in chaos, flickering lights and explosions running amuck along the Sun Room's various quartz pillars.

Denloth ducked upon the initial explosion, and Jen, seeing his distraction, lunged in at him, sword point leading, but his obsidian ring flashed magenta, and he fell back into a fold in reality, the image he left warping into a dissolution of a shadow of himself before fading into the blinding light of the room, leaving her there, thrusting into the rippling space in front of her.

Two of the Oathbound that had been slowly dissecting the flagging saren knights, Seam-jumped into the void, streaks of opalescent scars tearing into the sandstone where they had been standing.

The last Oathbound started to follow his comrade's trail into the Seam but was tackled by the knight it faced, Sarah kicking the stumbling arisen's helmet off, following up with a deep stab into its chest cavity. The Oathbound exploded into a storm of armor and bone shrapnel at the fatal blow, sending her flying back to the entrance of the room, dazed and bruised.

Amidst all the commotion and explosions, Sarah attempted to sit up, having to dodge to the side just as a red wave of aether slammed into the rubble that had collapsed in the doorway, blasting it clear, Sha'oul's large figure in a dead run, his right arm slumped as he rushed for the door.

He raised his good hand, releasing the binding hexweave that had been slowly strangling Revna, draining the life from her on the floor. The tendrils weaved around him as he smacked aside the two knights that tried to hold him back, rushing through the door only to be met with a blade slashing at his neck, the tendrils barely holding the killing edge from his flesh.

Hamui shot a crimson beam towards him from behind, blasting a hole in his hexweave barrier, searing his ear off, grazing his head as he grabbed Yozo's sword blade, only to have another blade jab into his thigh, digging in through the unprotected area.

He yelled in frustration, cursing in a dark tongue, waxed tapestries along his armor melting and burning off as his body lit on fire, forcing Yozo back, but another beam shot in at him, this time shattering the rest of what protection the tendrils had to offer, the weave completely unraveling now.

His chanting continued, and more scrolls burned up along his armor, wax melting into every groove of metal, and a ball of flame lurched forward, engulfing Hamui, tumbling him along with it until it rammed into a pillar, cracking it at its base, exploding violently.

A longsword dug into his back, Sarah suffering through the licking flames to score a hit, but Sha'oul was empowered now, and all he looked upon were doomed.

His flaming eyes met hers, and from them shot a flicker of light, flitting quickly into her face, blowing her brains out from the back of her head a blink later.

He looked at Yozo, his stare emotionless. Yozo stood firm, but the flaming devil seemed beyond him then, the element of surprise spent, and he watched as the flaming man turned and loped off out of the room down the corridors.

Out of the room rushed Jezebel dragging Fin with her as Alva lunged out of the screaming room with Revna over her shoulders just as more quartz explosions sounded off, sending shrapnel flying into the two still in the doorway, blowing them down.

Yozo rushed to their aid, pulling them further out of the doorway, peering back into the room quickly to see if there were any other knights alive needing to be extracted.

Yozo let out a steadying sigh. With the amount of carnage that last blast had done within the room, he didn't think it necessary to even risk going in to check, three of the quartz nodes still intact and whirling violently.

"Come. Help me get the others out of this place," Yozo said to Jezebel that was rousing from the blast, the only other reliably conscious member remaining in their group.

As he shouldered the two sarens, Jezebel kneeling down to scoop up Fin, all three unconscious, Yozo looked over to the cracked, burnt pillar and saw a charred body.

Burnt bone stuck through skin along his charred face, everything hallowed out by the extreme heat of the ball of fire that had slammed into him.

"Rest in peace, Hamui," Yozo uttered as the two left the room, leaving behind the temple halls which had now become a tomb.

Part Two: Planes of Ash

14

ENDLESS ASH

"Wyld, come back!" Malagar shouted, immediately entering a coughing fit as the caustic air entered his tender lungs.

"Wyld—" he coughed out, collapsing to his knees in the hardened ash slopes they had been deposited on, the canyons of dingy mustard-colored sediment towering behind them as Malagar and Lanereth attempted to simply continue to breathe in the hellish environment.

The kaith's Seam scars flickered in the distance as she bolted into the canyon pathways leading up the mountain.

A short crack sounded above them followed by an echoing thump, a flash of light splitting through the heavy acrid cloud cover, some sort of lightning announcing the acid rain that came moments after.

Lanereth cried out, the polluted rain sizzling into her skin and hair, Malagar forsaking Wyld to her own fate as he struggled to get back to Lanereth, the two of them making their way into an alcove against the corrugated basalt cliff walls.

The downpour rushed through in sheets, the torrent of noise that came and went with the deluge disorienting the two beyond the sting that slowly ate away at their clothes, skin, and hair.

They looked on as the storm began to lessen, the main downpour passing on through the sickly fields below them, working through coughing fits, attempting to acclimate to the harsh air.

"Where are we?" Malagar chuffed out, looking out over the hellscape before them at the waist-high polyp field of frilled fungus that seemed to stretch on forever.

"Planes of Ash—" Lanereth hoarsely whispered, barely getting out the words before doubling over, hacking violently once more.

"We must move," Malagar managed out, grabbing Lanereth's wrist, gently tugging her along as they made their way up the canyon path they had been deposited at.

Stumbling along the ridged incline, another sheet of acidic rain rushed over them, drenching them once again, eating holes through their surface-level clothes, causing them to grunt and moan out in pain as they squinted out through red, burning eyes, tripping along through the canyon.

Lanereth wobbled along, holding to her staff for support, the sizzle of acid along her skin causing weakening tremors to run through her frame. Malagar rushed up ahead, looking for cover.

The corridor eventually opened up into a wide canyon room, blocked by a rock shelf, rust-colored slime lightly coating the walls and floor.

"The air," Malagar said through catches of breath, "seems better here."

Looking around in the canyon room they had stumbled upon, he could see dark holes along the room's floor. Bones and half portions of some sort of creature laid cluttered all about, half morphed into the surrounding ash and basalt surface of the walls and floor, as if the formation was a living thing itself, slowly absorbing any that had had the displeasure to die upon its surface.

The canyon did continue upwards, but only after a tall shelf that loomed before them, parts of corpses hanging from its edge as if strung up like an effigy to ward off all who visited.

The slot canyon they had made their way into did have some overhead coverage from the rain. If another downpour happened upon them, the overhead shelves promised at least partial coverage and dryness. He knew how flash floods could rip through canyons like the one they were in now and hoped that the ominous holes along the floor were present further up to provide drainage. If a wall of acid water were to rip through the canyon, he knew that would be the end for them, but it was a threat they could do little to nothing about at the moment, so he set the worry aside for the time being.

Lanereth's coughing fits had died down, but she was still not in a position to speak, wheezing through waves of pain deep in her throat, chest, and along every inch of her skin, holding desperately to her white staff.

Malagar fared better, the leather he wore protecting his vitals from the direct exposure to the rainfall they had suffered through. He was shorn, as well, and as he looked to Lanereth's long plaited hair, each strand soaked with acid, he realized she was being eaten alive with each passing moment.

He hastily began to disrobe, taking off his jerkin and other protective gear, seeing the robed saren shivering in a mesh of disintegrating cloth, her hair falling out in clumps as she lightly pulled a handful of it out as she itched at her scalp.

"Lanereth, we need to get you out of your robes. They're falling apart anyways," Malagar hoarsely said, stripping down to his still dry linen undergarments.

She shivered in response, hunched over, holding herself.

Malagar kneeled down, tentatively pulling on Lanereth's rags, her top disintegrating before he could even work at pulling it over her.

Tearing the rest of her garments off in swaths, he slopped the deteriorating silk cotton patches from her body, taking a strip of dry hemp from his light gambeson to pat her dry with.

Each touch of the rough material on her melted skin sent painful shivers through her, and as Malagar was beginning to make progress with wicking off the yellow film of acid from her skin, she made an effort to stand for him to continue the painful process on her lower half.

Standing erect split her skin in places, and she held back cries of pain as she forced the movement.

Malagar brushed his brow to keep sweat mingled with acid from getting in his eyes. Bringing his hand down, he saw that he had scraped off a layer of skin with the subconscious movement.

He did a quick pat down of his own head and areas that his armor had not protected him from, skin sloughing off all along his scalp and sections of his arms and legs.

He had gotten off much lighter than the saren, he could see. Standing before him naked, only a simple necklace remaining on her upper half and her staff that she clung to at her side, he could easily tell the damage to her extremities and head were severe, though, thankfully, much of her torso only received minimal burns, having shed the drenched clothes just as the dampness had soaked through.

"We need to clothe you," Malagar said, seeing that she was eyeing the armor. He guessed she hesitated for the same reason he did—the both of them knowing that covering her open skin with hemp and leather was going to be an excruciating process. He knew moving around in it with her skin so raw was going to be a living hell for her.

"Let me—" she started, clearing her scratched up throat before continuing, "—attempt to reach out to Sareth, first."

He readily nodded, hoping for her sake that her goddess would be able to help them in some way.

She raised her staff high, stretching out her body, opening new cracks in her skin as she prayed, shouting out into the canyon that loomed over them. Her voice seemed muffled somehow, like the walls were absorbing her prayers, or that something in the air snagged her voice as it rose.

Though her words were beautiful, angelic even, he could hear the pain etched in between each breath, and the vision of her naked melted body reaching to the yellow ashen sky, calling out in desperation to her deity, surrounded by walls of ash, slime, and bone, caused him to give in momentarily to despair, knowing that there would be no heavenly answer there in their hellish canyon.

15
A FIGURE ALONG THE CLIFFS

Flames along his outline fluttered out as Sha'oul stumbled out of the temple's entrance, the sun already well over the canyon's edge, the air outside cooling rapidly as a gust made its way through the crags.

Black blood seeped through the seams of is disheveled armor, pooling on the cracked sandstone tile beneath him as he looked up to the long climb up the canyon wall he had before him.

He ripped off a plate of armor, dropping it to the ground, shedding weight that would only slow him down and overexert him at that point.

He burned one last spell from the surface of his pauldron before tossing it, a white-hot flame appearing at his fingertips. He brought the flame to the corner of his neck, searing closed the stab wound, the one the man with the hidden blade had inflicted upon him.

He would see to that one's death personally.

After cauterizing the rest of his deeper wounds, he released the flame, leaning upon the archway, catching his breath for a moment before slugging across the canyon floor.

The sun was low on the horizon by the time he made it over the canyon's edge. The wind blew stinging sand high into the atmosphere, tinging the sky an ashen yellow just before dusk.

He looked down to the ancient temple one last time, distantly concerned for how his enemy fared, knowing that he had cut it close in the Sun Room. He had been caught by surprise more than once, and he had played the battle too casually. He would not underestimate those that had been hounding him for so long a second time.

And what of Denloth, he mused. His warlock had abandoned his post at the very moment he had needed him most. A simple blood penance would not be enough to forgive him of such a dereliction.

He started forward. He knew his army would have only made it to the exit of the great canyon's entrance on the north side by the time the moon was high, and now, with no aid, he knew he was truly vulnerable. He needed to rejoin his ranks as soon as possible.

The light sandstorm made it difficult to make out much of what was ahead of him, and though it would make finding his way through the barren waste bothersome, he also knew it would help to obscure him if indeed those who he had just dealt with did gather the nerve to immediately resume their hunt.

He halted in his tracks, more than a bit stunned to see a figure standing in front of him, the desert wind dying down a bit to reveal the complete mess of a man, sunbaked and disheveled almost beyond recognition to any that might have known him.

Though dressed as one native to the region, his features belonged to one foreign—one he had been shown many times in recent months in visions. The one that had been stricken with a hex by his late warlock, which bound the man to him, both body and soul.

"All to blood...," the man croaked out, his throat dry as the desert he walked upon, "...and blood to ash. The Great Ashen One has need of me. I serve him, and so, I serve you now. What is your command?"

Sha'oul's surprise melted to wicked pleasure. He had been waiting for this one to come home to him for some time now. For once that day, the fates had smiled upon him.

"Come," Sha'oul said, his voice deep and smooth in contrast to his new companion, "follow me."

Nomad gladly did. For the first time in days, the burning in his mind began to subside.

16

THE BLOOD EYE

"Watch...over me," Sha'oul wheezed out, taking a knee as he struggled to lay himself on the ground, the night's travel having sapped him of what strength he had left from the fight the day before.

Nomad, in his comatose state, did not respond, but stood idly watching the horizon, struggling with urges that fluctuated between complete obedience to the man, and drawing his sword and murdering him in his sleep. He remained frozen, not able to make any progress with his compulsions in either direction.

Sha'oul remained oblivious to his servant's internal struggle as he fell into a deep slumber, his consciousness going into a long, silent blackness devoid of thought, his body aggressively at work knitting itself back together, his deep wounds mending at a quickened pace.

The night wore on, and Nomad had drawn his sword many times, looming crazily over Sha'oul as he slept, shaking his head of murderous thoughts through the haze of exhaustion he had been riding, having had no sleep, food, or drink for many days, the only thing keeping him sustained at that point being his fealty to his new lord, the Ashen One, which hounded him in the waking moments, and more so in his slumber.

The dead of sleep was broken instantly, and Sha'oul shot up, his nostrils filling with soot as he rose out of a field of ash, grunting through the sting of a landscape he had long-stretching memories of—very few of which being fond ones.

He snorted out ash and composed himself, looking up to see an angry red slit in the sky high above him, a shadow titan, blurred by the distortions within the altered realm looking down upon him.

He could see no eyes, or even features of the blurred being, but he knew its attention was upon him, and he knew who had called him to the realm, at least in spirit through the dreamworld—Telenth-Lanor, the Lord of Ash himself.

He kneeled, his face resting inches above the ash bank he was in, waiting for his lord to commune with him. The wait was long, and he trembled, knowing full well of his recent failures. He knew the fate that awaited those that failed with their respective callings.

The ground shook, and millions of voices called down from the rift in the sky, speaking as one.

"Like the ash you wade in, so is your fate."

"No!" Sha'oul cried out, the large man cowering in the presence of the faceless god as he stared silently down upon him.

"I was betrayed! Denloth is not faithful to our cause!"

"He is not faithful to *you*. You alone are responsible for his failure," the ominous conflux of voices said, their words worming in through his ears.

"Allow me a final chance to prove I am worthy! My army is at the ready, we shall still take Rochata-Ung, and from there, all of the Southern Sands. Allow me this!" he pleaded, desperate to steer the threatening imminent retribution away from him by his merciless god.

"Silence," boomed from the rippling warp in the sky, the psychic wave blasting down on him so harshly, Sha'oul sagged as his body tried to decide if it was going to fight to continue to sustain him.

"You offer excuses. You have failed. If you were to attack the pitiful desert city in your current state with your army of dead, you would see defeat. It matters not to me. You think our plans hinge on your mission? Your ego and ignorance know no bounds. You are but ash and blood, fuel for the quickening of our designs."

Sha'oul remained silent, as ordered, waiting in agony through the rumblings of the heavens above as his god deliberated over him.

"You may yet serve one final purpose. Though you lost my favor and your reward this day, you may still serve me that I might lessen your punishment."

Sha'oul bowed low in the ash, laying himself prostrate before the deity, weeping in open relief and sorrow.

"You will take your army and camp before the ruins of Solstice to the west. Here you will find an arch. Call forth to me from there, performing all the rites necessary to see here the opening of the mouth of hell. Old and broken may the ruins be, but with the sacrifice of blood may this once great gate open wide to the heavens and hells once more. Few in Una still know the old magic, but I will guide you. I will be with you this one last time.

"Fail me upon this task, and all is lost for you. The Deep Unseen will be thy place of eternal torture, until all is rendered to blood, and then to ash. And only after every soul, thought, and even god has been reduced to ash shall the Unseen be released from their hidden grave beneath the scorching sea to behold the endless grey, released from their tortured existence to be the last ones to render to ash in despair and relief to know that now, all things have ended."

Sha'oul's mind had been drilled into during the speech, so much so that he had lost his sanity for a time, driveling nonsensically. Telenth ravaged his brain; millions of psychotic voices licking his mind raw with their barbed tongues, eating at his innards as he beheld a portion of the awful glory of his god.

He was lost in consciousness, wandering the discordant halls of painful uncertainty for an unknown amount of time.

He lay curled up in the fetal position, scratching at his skull, ripping the flesh from his scalp in an attempt to rid himself of the mind worms that riddled the insides of his head.

A hand roughly shook him, and in an instant, he heard his name, someone calling to him.

"Sha'oul!" Denloth shouted, recoiling slightly as the large man's eyes shot open from his terrible nightmare, the fear still raw in his unusually distressed expression.

He sat up cautiously, looking around at his surroundings. The nomad was there, hand on sword hilt, standing at ready to slash Denloth down at the first sign of hostility towards his master. The desert sun had begun to rise, the youthful pink of the morning still casting its precious hue to every dune and rise in sight. Denloth kneeled beside him with one of his Oathbound standing at his side between him and the nomad, the two ready to go to blows at any moment.

"You practically scratched your scalp off," Denloth announced, still not sure what the strange behavior from his master meant, treading lightly as his master seemed in a terrible way from when he last left him.

"You traitor," Sha'oul spat, trying to stand, but falling on all fours as his brain attempted to properly reconnect itself to his body.

"The Sun Room was exploding. Surely you didn't mean for me to remain there and die in the explosion?" Denloth asked, fearing to offer the large man a hand up as he clearly was attempting to stand in order to do him harm.

"I expect my servants to stand firmly by my side in battle!" he hoarsely barked, infuriated with it all, his carefully laid plans, years—centuries even—in the making, falling pathetically apart so quickly over the course of one day—one fight.

He admitted, he had been careless with the little man with his invisible dagger, but if Denloth had not bolted at the first sign of the turning of the tides of battle, they would have completely wiped the trite resistance band out that day, and he would not have been so badly injured. Injured enough to fall into deep sleep—the one place Telenth could hound him freely. The one place Telenth had the most power in all of Una.

"You do not know what you cost me back there," he said,

clenching his fists so tight that his sharp fingernails gouged deep red lines in his palms.

He released the tension in his hands and fell back to the desert floor, looking into the sky as the morning light began to burn his skin.

"You have no idea...," he said, calmed now, the bout of rage passing as he accepted the fact that what had happened, was done, and killing Denloth at that point would simply lose him another ally in the one mission left to him that lay ahead.

Telenth would not accept a failure on his part. Though he had already fallen from his lord's graces, there was more, much more, he could lose if he did not fulfill this final command flawlessly. Denloth could be useful to him still, and he needed to put aside his petty grudge he had with the man now and move forward with a clear head. He could reflect upon Denloth's torturous death after all this was over—but not now.

"Sha'oul. I tried to return immediately, but the broken rifts warped the Seam. It took me a good deal of time, and much risk, to find a path back to this region. I lost an Oathbound in the attempt. I did not mean to leave you there alone," he whispered, kneeling beside his resting master, sincerity clear in his voice.

"Do not leave me again," Sha'oul spoke. "Too much is on the line. I need my allies resolute—loyal."

"Yes, my lord," Denloth readily committed.

"The Ashen One himself came to me in a vision. He has new orders for us," Sha'oul said, sitting up, his strength and coordination returning to him after a time.

"We have an important task ahead of us, and our minds must be clear. There will be no room for error," he said, trailing off momentarily, lost in thought, tasting the fresh memory of ash in his lungs.

"I require a great number of lives. We will produce a slaughter that will fill the sands for miles around with blood. We will open a rift larger than either of us has ever seen, and Telenth will guide my hand in its making," he announced as he stood up facing Denloth, meeting his eyes intensely, full of purpose.

His back was turned to Nomad, the thrall being a forgotten detail. Nomad's eyes were locked upon the man, his face placid, but his eyes screaming of murder as his glare had not once left Sha'oul the whole night through.

17
THE HOARISH NIGHTMARE

Lanereth's prayers went unanswered, and though she waited for a long while in pain, reaching up to the clouded sky, only the soft crack of distant thunder returned.

She whispered into the crystal tip of her staff, Malagar assuming that she was making an attempt at a spell, but nothing came of it, and she recalled the staff to its travel size, reducing into a small, marbled cylinder.

"Sareth does not hear me. My spells are useless here," she drearily announced to Malagar who had already suspected as much.

She shivered, reaching out to Malagar, and he took her hand, thinking that she needed support, but as soon as she made contact with him, he realized that she was performing a healing on him instead, his open sores and raw skin patching over before she released him.

"I thought your spells were no good here?" Malagar asked, amazed at the small miracle of health she had bestowed upon him.

"A saren's ability to perform a healing is not dependent upon Sareth. She gave us this blessing from birth. It is the one light from her that can never be revoked, even in the depths of hell," she tiredly explained as she began to work a healing on herself, recycling her skin's health with that of her blood.

For a less experienced saren, the maneuver to heal oneself was a reckless and dangerous one, but she was one of the most practiced at the art in all the region. She worked with precision focus to take just enough from the blood and her vitals to mend some of the worst parts of her boiled skin.

The healing took time, and the toxins that polluted her blood now sickened her, causing her to tremble to the core, but at the least her skin was not flayed, and that was an exchange she gladly took.

She took the hemp and leather jerkin and gingerly put it on, Malagar helping to cinch the sides to fit snugly to her torso as she deposited her compacted staff in a leather side pouch.

His suede obi belt had held up well against the rain and he secured it around her, ripping off the edges of the hemp underneath that had begun to soak in the corrosive moisture.

He started to loosen the lacing of his gauntlets, but she placed a hand on his, stopping him.

"This is more than enough. You need protection too," she said, already concerned that the two articles of armor he had given her now put his core at great risk, leaving him bare chested, no protection offered if even a light drizzle of rain happened to catch them off guard again.

"As you wish," he said, strapping the gauntlets back on, lacing them up.

"The Planes of Ash, you said?" Malagar asked, looking up into the mustard-colored sky high above the canyon walls.

"I—believe so. What other planes of hell would the avatar of Telenth have access to? Besides," she added, pausing a moment to catch her breath, a wave of exhaustion hitting her, "from my studies—this fits his realm to the T."

"Is there a way back, or are we simply doomed here, destined to live out our days in this hell with no escape?" Malagar asked, a tinge of frustration edging in at their predicament.

Lanereth clutched her pendant, looking off in thought for a moment before admitting, "I know of no likely escape."

"The air and rain itself are enough to kill us before nightfall. How are we to survive in a place not meant for mortals? There must be a way out, back to Una!" Malagar said, pacing along the canyon's walls.

"You're right," Lanereth hazily said, considering his statement further. "The air *was* killing us."

Malagar stopped pacing, looking to Lanereth, confused at her odd restatement.

"It's not now, though. The air is much more breathable here, don't you think?" she asked, looking to him for an answer.

He took a deep breath in, a little too deep, the spice of the air triggering him to cough a bit until he could recompose himself and answer, "Maybe slightly more breathable. Still, barbs seem to be in the air."

"Yes, though still not pleasant, the deeper we got into this canyon, the easier it was to breathe now that I think of it. Why is that do you think? Is it the elevation?" she asked.

Malagar thought for a moment and shrugged, inspecting the bones morphed into the wall he was next to.

"For all we know, it could be this weird rock formation," he said, scraping his finger along it, "or this pink slime."

He pulled his hand quickly back, wringing it out as he hissed through a wave of pain.

"What happened?" Lanereth asked, confused as she had not seen anything that would have caused such a reaction.

"That pink stuff," he said, rubbing his finger off on a dry piece of fabric along the scraps he had patted them down with. "Don't touch it—it stings."

"Here, let me see," Lanereth said, approaching the man as he picked up his idle pacing once more.

"It's nothing," he said, shrugging off her concern, looking up to the ledge that led up the canyon further.

"Give me your hand," she said, more forcefully, having seen

how clearly the sludge had stung him.

He relented, Lanereth grabbing him by the wrist, turning his palm up.

"Your skin, it's eating away," Lanereth whispered, a calming white glow coming to her hand as she rested it over his, the wound healing up quickly.

"Well...now we know the sludge is even worse than the rain. Better be careful to avoid it," Lanereth said in a matronly warning voice, almost scolding Malagar for his carelessness.

"Aye, that we should," he responded, grateful to the woman who had healed him twice now, quietly taking note of how the process drained her.

A muted crack warped the sky above, and they both looked to the rolling clouds overhead, both moving to get under the shelf in the canyon room they were in, doing their best to avoid the rusty slime that coated the walls.

Though the rains came quick, ripping through their spot in the canyon within moments after they huddled under the shelf, the downpour did not last as long as the first, and after a few booms of thunder, the cloud drifted past, the remaining drops of rain running into streams along the lowest point on the canyon floor, draining into the holes scattered throughout the canyon.

"At least we have air to breathe and shelter overhead," Lanereth uttered, the last drops of acid pooling together, draining down the canyon as they watched the weather pass them by, thankfully dry this time.

"But to what end?" Malagar sighed out, looking up further into the canyon past the wall of bones before them.

"I have a bit of water and morsels, enough for a snack, in that leather pouch in that jerkin," he said, nodding to the armor she now wore. "What of us after that?"

She clutched her amulet but had no response to the bleak question. The air stung, though not as badly as in the foothills, but the fresh rain vapors had stripped their eyes and throat of moisture.

Rain came down in the distant areas of the canyon, but just around the bend came a clacking sound, as if stones were pecking off the floor.

"Do you hear that?" Lanereth whispered after a moment, drawing Malagar close.

The two listened, and the sound returned, though this time, Malagar was able to identify the noise.

"Hooves," he whispered in her ear, eyeing the corridor, trying to guess how close the cloven animal was to rounding the bend.

A loud snort sounded, and the two could tell that it came from a creature with a large lung capacity.

"We need to go," Malagar mouthed, pulling Lanereth by the wrist, leading her to a section of the shelf that blocked their path that wasn't covered in slime.

Holding his hands together, he gave her a boost as she scrambled to latch onto the ledge, slowly pulling herself up as the creature's hoof steps sounded clear as it rounded the bend.

A large head with a damaged set of antlers, ten feet off the ground, peeked around the corner. Malagar looked back to catch a glimpse of the beast, its wicked slash of a mouth open, showing rows of horrid teeth, its empty reflective eyes shining brightly as it narrowed in on the two.

Malagar leapt high up the wall, getting a hold on the ledge as Lanereth reached down to grab his free hand, pulling him up and over as the creature came charging from around the corner, its hooved feet clacking loud off the basalt floor as it rushed to the two.

Malagar tumbled on top of Lanereth as he came up and over the lip, and the two watched as the human-like torso of the beast reached out with its long arms, grabbing up over the ledge, snatching at the pair.

Rolling backwards, Malagar barely dodged the giant hand as it scraped past him, but Lanereth was not as nimble, getting snatched as she went to crawl away.

Its boney fingers clenched around her. Lanereth cried out as its grip tightened, crushing her as she was dragged to the thing's open maw.

The creature reflexively jerked back in pain, releasing its grip, flailing its arm and squealing out an ugly cry as Lanereth was dropped on her back. Malagar rushed to her, taking advantage of the sudden flash of luck, dragging her back up the canyon as the beast tended to its smoking hand, plummeting to the canyon floor as one of its legs fell into a hole behind it.

Finally getting her footing, Lanereth shrugged off Malagar's helping hand, and the two sprinted higher up into the canyon, the walls shortening the higher they went.

The monster did not follow them, and after a long stretch of time of scrambling up the canyon slot with no more signs of rain or creatures to harass them, they came to the first, what looked like, hand-made structure they had seen in the distant world.

Taking a moment to catch their breaths and inspect the archway at the end of the canyon up ahead, they leaned against the ashen wall, keeping concealed as they whispered to each other.

"That looks constructed," Malagar said, eyeing the brick-like pattern along the sides of the canyon's exit, a long bone wedged into place, spanning the gap along the top of the walls.

"By what, is the question," Lanereth whispered, trying to get a good look of what lay beyond the archway, the clouds of yellow fog making it hard to see anything beyond.

"Doubtful it was made by one of those giants back there. That archway is only five feet high or so. Not that it couldn't climb over it, but if it were the one to construct such a structure, it'd be placing that bone arch quite a bit higher for ease of access, I'd guess," Malagar mused, looking to Lanereth who subconsciously clutched her goddess' amulet as she worried over the meaning of the structure before them.

"I saw the beast flinch when it grabbed you, almost like you had burned it. That trinket have anything to do with it?" Malagar asked, bringing Lanereth's attention from the archway to the amulet she rubbed in her hand.

"This is no trinket," she harshly corrected. "It's a relic, blessed by Sareth herself. All High Priestesses are endowed with one. It is our channel directly to Sareth. It is rarely used, only in times of great need."

"I would say this is a time of great need," Malagar remarked.

"I would agree. That's why I tried calling out to her earlier through it, but…," she hesitated, considering the possibilities, "I'm not sure she has access to even my call here in one of the Deep

Hells. If that's the case, I've been stripped of power, for she *is* my power."

"Well, you still have your healing," Malagar optimistically reminded her, his tone one of thanks, the sting of the burns he had received almost completely gone by now.

"Yes. That I do," she considered quietly, reflecting on it all before getting back on their initial subject. "Apparently, the touch of Sareth upon my amulet still has a strong effect upon the denizens of this damnable realm; enough of an effect to harm them if touched."

"Let's hope we don't get close enough to any other creatures here to have to rely upon it," Malagar said, looking back to the archway, still seeing no change to the drifting fogbank.

The two looked to the strange archway again, gleaning nothing more from it as they remained in their thoughts. At length, Lanereth broke the silence.

"We can't stay here, there's no shelter from the rain if it comes again."

"Maybe Wyld's up there somewhere," Malagar answered hopefully, peering off into the eerily silent mist up ahead.

Lanereth started ahead, Malagar following, the two passing under the brick and boned archway, stepping out into the light fog beyond, the sting of acidity already nipping at their flesh.

18

GRACE ALONG THE STILL DUNES

The night sky was clear, the air cool and crisp. The Kale moon shown down, casting a green hue along the normally pink and orange desert sands.

They had ridden hard that day, and all companies had been exhausted, ready for the order to halt as the night set firmly in.

No tents stood along the stretch of sand they had made camp at. No fire or communal sitting area erected. They bedded down and slept in their full gear, save their breastplates and helms. Within moments they could be ready to move and flee or fight.

Kissa called in the six scouts she had had patrolling during the day, sending a fresh set out to watch through half of the night.

Hathos found Henarus and his priest and asked how the prophet was faring. As they communed, he checked the middle-aged man's responses to help him gauge how he was handling the concussion he had sustained from Nomad.

"The travel today...was rough," the mature man confessed, patting his priest on the shoulder, smiling as he admitted, "Without Josiah, I likely would have fallen off my horse a few times."

"Your balance is off?" Hathos inquired.

Henarus nodded. "It is hard to concentrate, which is quite foreign for me. Hassome is the god of focus, after all. That is his domain, so clarity...," he said, trailing off, struggling to get through his statement.

"Rest," Hathos comforted, standing up, looking around camp.

"I will find Reza. The sarens are known for their healings. Perhaps even that strange enchanter might have a cure for you, but first I would seek the saren," he said, leaving the two to search for Reza's attachment.

Seeing Gale, Hathos beckoned him forth, asking where he might find his charge.

"Reza's with Arie over on the ridge," Gale answered, pointing him to the couple standing atop the peak of the largest sand dune that hid their camp.

Hathos quietly made his way up the sandy rise, catching only the tail end of the women's conversation as they went silent, turning to consider their visitor.

"Ah, Hathos. Good to see you," Reza greeted, looking back to the view they had been intently studying.

"What is it you watch up here?" he asked, seeing that Arie's interest was held by something on the horizon as well.

"We traveled far this day," she announced, pointing to the end of the dunes miles to the east of them.

"The Dolinger Crags are within sight far to the east," she said, pausing for Hathos to inspect for himself.

He squinted, trying to see through the pale green waves of sand that seemed to stretch on forever.

"I see no crags," he muttered after a moment, giving up on the search.

"I can't see it either, but Arie's half haltia. Sight is a gift to her kind. She says the crags lie ten or so miles eastward," Reza replied, pointing south of them, sweeping over the horizon from south to west.

"She also sees other landmarks. By her description, I believe I know what they are. I lived in this region for a number of years, so I've been down to south Tarigannie. I think I can make out where we are in the dunes, and that is a good ten miles from the southern edge of the Tarigannie Dunes. Fort Wellspring is to our south. Also Daloth's Ribs and the old pagan ruins lie to the west of us. The highway runs along all of those landmarks, and if Rochata-Ung does decide to make chase, if they do not simply follow us into the dunes, they may ride the roads around to head us off at the pass."

Hathos looked to the horizon of sand, seeing none of the announced landmarks, but considering the information and the available options.

"The real question remains, where is the arisen army?" he whispered, deep in thought.

"Knowing *that* would make things much easier," Arie admitted, adding, "I see no signs of movement out there currently though, only the lights of Fort Wellspring, and even that is barely within my view."

Hathos breathed in deep, collecting his thoughts, looking back to Reza. "Speaking of gifts we've been given, Reza, Henarus is not yet recovered from the blow your friend dealt him. I fear we may soon need his aid, and he will not have the clarity of mind to give it. Might you see what can be done in terms of a healing? We are in desperate need of a miracle."

Reza turned to the shorn head man, slightly uneasy at the request, never quite fully in good terms with her innate talent, even though in past months she had learned a great deal more about the flow and ways of the skill.

"Show me to him," she answered at length, following him back down the dunes and through the encampment.

Henarus clutched his head, clearly in discomfort, suffering through a migraine. His priest held an open canteen out for him, and he began sipping from it lightly as he winced through an episode.

"Henarus, would you mind a blessing?" Reza asked in a soft voice, the man opening his eyes, looking up to see her and Hathos kneeling next to him.

"Reza," he moaned, steadying himself as a wave of dizziness came upon him. "Yes, dear. That would be a godsend."

The prophet looked his age, more tired than Reza had ever seen the proud man. It hurt her to behold him in such a state. His presence was ever so firm and sharp, not much unlike her mentor, Lanereth.

She looked down upon Isis' ring, concentrating on it, reaching into the gift the dryads had endowed it with, drawing it up to feel its energy.

Though Leaf's warning of saving its energy for the fight against Sha'oul fluttered about her thoughts, she was convinced they would understand. Henarus was a powerful force for good and could bring much to their fight with the Lord of Ash.

She reached out, resting a hand upon the prophet's crown, seeping into his soul, searching for what ailed him. The ring soothed her, mediating her navigation, flowing life into the fog that clung to his mind, dispersing the darkness as she shown light into the pathways of his thoughts and memory.

She released, standing as she looked to the man who opened his eyes, smiling at the return of his cognition.

"Reza, what did I say about believing in yourself," Henarus beamed, standing to embrace his healer. "You have nothing to fear but your own self-doubt in who you are and what you are capable of, blessed child of Sareth."

She hugged him back, glad to have been able to help relieve his pains; gladder still to seem to be finally getting a firmer handle of her skill of healing.

19
FAVELA OF THE GREY ONES

The fog thickened, and Malagar clutched Lanereth's hand as the two began to cough through the caustic air, their skin beginning to pinch and sting from the tiny droplets of acid that hung in the air.

Lanereth tried to contest Malagar's desperate push into the mist, but every attempt to plea for them to stop and return to the canyon was interrupted with bouts of coughing and hacking as he yanked her along.

The thick cloud began to lighten quickly, and Malagar slowed their pace as they stumbled out into a clearing, slumping over when they got far enough away from the gas to clear their lungs and compose their breathing once more.

"Look," Malagar choked out between breaths, pointing to strange structures along the cliff face to their left; platforms, constructed of bone, cemented together with an ashen paste, creating frames in which many large cocoon-like structures hung.

The structures stretched on for miles, though they saw no activity or any inhabitants amidst the network of nests.

"What in the hells is that?" Malagar gruffed, fixated on the massive sprawl that stretched on endlessly.

Lanereth calmed her breath, shaking her head as she answered, "I have no idea, but with such a large network of nests, or whatever those cocoon things are, where are the creatures that built them?"

"Perhaps this hive has been abandoned?" Malagar speculated, looking back at the fog bank that they had run through, seeing that it had moved off a ways out behind them.

"What's that?" Lanereth asked, pointing to a large basin and funneling system on the outskirts of the settlement.

Malagar rubbed his red, irritated eyes, trying to get a better look at the structure Lanereth pointed to.

"Could be a water catch," he said, his interest in the find piqued.

The two stood, taking in their new surroundings for a moment, the view of the city in front of them the only landscape of any note, the fogbank still covering most everything else within their vision.

"What could possibly find this rain drinkable?" Lanereth scoffed before Malagar started off towards the funneling basin.

Following behind him, dread of getting closer to the network of web-like nests looming over them, they slowly approached the pool of clear water, kneeling under the protective hood that overshadowed it.

"Interesting," Malagar whispered, looking down into the depths of the pool, seeing chunks of black and white objects lining the floor of the pool a few feet down.

"Think this is drinkable? Obviously if it's just a rain catch, it wouldn't be, but look. There's some sort of thought-out process to all this," he said, fascinated with the construct.

"And you would trust whatever horrors made this device enough to drink from it?" Lanereth scornfully replied, looking around uneasily.

"Look," he said, ignoring her tone, "what do you suppose

those stones on the pool floor are? Could they be purifiers? I wonder if even hellspawn could stomach acid. Maybe even *they* require some sort of clarity to their water to survive."

"And if it is acid and we drink, what then? I'm already spent from that healing earlier. I can't do that again so soon. My body's not yet recovered," she argued, not happy with her companion's fascination with the strange substance, drawing them so close to such a massive hive city.

"And if we don't try, then this—" he said, grabbing his flask from his vest Lanereth wore, "—is all we have left to drink. How long will we stay alive without water, saren?" he asked, somewhat put out with the amount of opposition she was showing on the subject.

"Here, lets finish this water off first before I test this pool. Drink up," he ordered, uncapping the flask, handing it over to her.

She did not look happy, but she did drink half of the water, and couldn't help but let out a refreshing sigh, the water soothing greatly her burned throat. She handed the rest over to Malagar, who relished the drink, enjoying it almost as much as Lanereth had.

Leaving the flask on the side of the pool's ledge, he lowered a finger to the surface of the water, dipping a tip into the liquid, waiting to feel the sting of acid to let him know to pull away.

There was no sting.

He dipped his whole hand in and swirled it around.

"Feels like cool, clean water," he said smiling, looking to Lanereth who, for the first time, seemed somewhat hopeful in their prospects.

Dipping the flask into the water, filling it to the brim, he brought it up to his nose, sniffing it, then trickling a bit in his mouth, swishing it around for a moment, Lanereth frozen in suspense as he gulped the swig down.

"Water," Malagar said, smiling as he took another drink from the flask, handing it to Lanereth again.

She accepted the tin hesitantly, but watching the man, seeing no obvious pain from drinking the substance, gave her confidence and she tested it with a sip, tasting it first.

It did taste like water upon first analysis, and she took another gulp as Malagar looked back to the pool, reaching in, grabbing one of the black and white stones that sat along the bottom of the pool, pulling them up.

He lay the two objects out as Lanereth finished the flask, handing it back over to him as she inspected what he had plucked from the pool.

"This white one seems like some chalky stone," she said, flipping it over in her hand, placing it back along the pool's edge as Malagar inspected the black material.

"Some type of charcoal maybe?" he guessed, hefting it, contemplating the object. "It's denser than charcoal though. Not sure."

"Well I guess you were right. Perhaps whatever created this catch somehow found out how to convert this acid rain into drinkable water," Lanereth admitted, grabbing the two stones, pocketing them in the leather jerkin she wore.

"Good idea," Malagar agreed, scooping up another flask, downing one whole before refilling it one last time, capping it and handing it back over to Lanereth to put away.

"The fog's gone," Lanereth idly said, looking back the way they had come, the two looking out over the vista before them, showing them a better picture of where exactly they were in the landscape they had been blindly traversing.

They seemed to be a on a flat-top, the edge a mile or so further out, dropping off, overlooking a massive thicket of red interwoven structures, looking grotesquely similar to entrails. There was another plateau far across the way, and what looked like a land bridge that led along to it which Malagar, with his better eyesight, could see.

The mountain they were on continued even higher past the city sprawl, spiking up high into the dingy yellow sky. Strange towers and formations were littered along its jutting cliffs, showing to Lanereth and Malagar that indeed the place they traversed seemed far from barren of inhabitance.

Barely had they been granted the time to soak in the scene before their gaze lowered back to the dwellings they had been eyeing so cautiously at the start, movement catching their eyes.

Eyes in the dark of the entrances were staring down, gleaming in the rusty yellow light that flickered off of their gaze as they watched the two strangers drinking from their water supply.

Hundreds of eyes peeked out from the dark of the cocoons, waiting in anticipation as Malagar and Lanereth took a step back. Lanereth took in a startled, sharp breath as she noticed little figures standing still, watching them from all around, some even on the ground relatively close to them, which must have snuck up on them as they had been gorging themselves with drink.

"Praven?" Malagar asked, confused with the small, ashen figure's presence in the distant lands.

"Those aren't praven," Lanereth whispered, dread thick on her voice. "Those are greyoldor."

As if in reaction to the name spoken aloud, the ones closest to her hissed out, their sunken eyes and mummified mouths widening as they jittered closer to the pair which had been raiding their water source.

"Run," Malagar said, nudging Lanereth behind him, facing the little demon children to keep them at bay while Lanereth did as commanded and sprinted away from the hellish cocoon city network.

The three closest greyoldors lunged towards Malagar, teeth sharp and promising to shred any flesh they latched onto.

Though they were fast, Malagar's fists moved deftly to intercept the little malnourished creatures, slamming one aside, kicking another in the gut, and grabbing the other by the wrist, spinning around with it, launching it back into the water well behind them.

The rest of the greyoldors hopped in a frenzy, the action setting off the whole alcove nearby, many springing down out of their cocoons, rushing in at Malagar's position.

The move had bought Lanereth a precious few seconds to get some distance from the horde, and now Malagar turned and sprinted to catch up to the fleeing saren.

"To the bridge!" Malagar yelled ahead, Lanereth correcting course to make for the land bridge far ahead of them, the fog lightly rolling back in as the pursuing blood-thirsty squabble skipped along behind them, slowly closing the gap.

Malagar made his way up beside Lanereth just as a fog cloud

drifted through, slowing them slightly, the path ahead becoming more obscure, their breathing becoming labored as the air peppered their lungs with harmful fumes.

Greyoldors bounded through the mist in hot pursuit of their prey, catching up quickly as Malagar snatched Lanereth's hand, turning her around to defend themselves against the horde before being overrun.

"Your amulet," Malagar called out, transitioning into a defensive stance, watching as a dozen or so little figures in the mist skittered about in a tight perimeter around them.

Malagar calmed his breath, exhaling slowly, raising his hands in a defensive stance as he kept eyes forward, watching and listening for the figures that irritably jumped all about them, threatening to lunge in at any moment.

Claws reached for Lanereth at her side, and she stepped back just as Malagar smashed the backside of his gauntleted hand into the little corrupted praven's skull, tumbling it back into the obscuring fog.

The violent assault set the rest of the greyoldors into a frenzy, all in the surrounding cloud skipping in at the two as Lanereth took her necklace off, holding it in her hand, snatching a lunging greyoldor by the wrist and slapping the talisman to its chest as it wriggled and writhed, screeching horribly as smoke issued from the metal's touch.

A quick snap of Malagar's foot kept the creature to his right at bay, but as three greyoldors to his left bounded in on him, he had to step back, giving up ground that left Lanereth vulnerable, which the little devils quickly took note of, two of the assaulters leaping for her now instead of Malagar.

Lanereth was tackled by two small bodies, toppling her over on the hard, ashen stone, the two greyoldors clawing at her ferociously, quickly leaving gashes along her arms just as Malagar slammed his foot into the side of one's head, dropping it unconscious as he snatched up the other one and tossed it into the fog.

No sooner had he gotten them off Lanereth than three more leapt onto his side and shoulders, causing him to stumble and fall, balling up his defenses around his neck and face as the little claws and teeth began to rip into his arms above his gauntlets, splattering blood everywhere along the white rock beneath him.

A blur of fur and illusions slammed into the three figures atop Malagar, knocking them momentarily senseless, giving Malagar a moment to collect himself after the onslaught that had quickly left him badly battered.

Looking over his shoulder, he saw Wyld. The touch of the Seam had expanded, almost covering half of her body now, flickering it in and out of existence, the other corporal part of her badly scarred and burned from the caustic environment they had been subject to.

She was feral, heaving; a wild thing that looked upon the small greyoldor as prey. She gave them no time to recover.

She grabbed the nearest one by the neck and bit into its throat, ripping the life from it as it dropped, pouncing on top of the other two, slashing with her much larger claws into the chest of the little creatures, leaving deep gouges that began to show bone white, their ribs being exposed within moments of the assault.

Lanereth and Malagar stood up, eyeing the wild kaith as she turned, bounding back past the two, slapping another approaching greyoldor so hard across the face, that the two could clearly hear its neck snapping as it then proceeded to slide across the ashen floor.

"Wyld!" Malagar called, extremely happy to see his old friend, but as a dozen more childlike figures hopped through the fog towards them, he grabbed her bloody wrist, hesitating for a moment as she snapped her deadly gaze upon him.

She considered the man for a moment, and Malagar was instantly uneasy as she scanned him, deciding if he were friend or foe as the shadows in the mist came closer and closer.

Her eyes narrowed slightly, and Malagar knew her well enough to see some reason had come back to her just then in the midst of her bloodlust.

"We need to get to the bridge," he called out, starting the charge in the direction he hoped the land bridge was in, Lanereth running to keep up, and Wyld turning from the horde of greyoldors closing in on them just as they started to clearly come into view through the fog.

Just as Lanereth began to tire from the full-on sprint, Malagar stiffly held an arm to her chest, stopping her just before bounding blindly off the cliff's edge into a bottomless depth.

Quickly looking around in the fog, he pointed to her right, and she could see not but a hundred feet or so along the ledge jutted out a bridge of rock that continued on towards the amber light of the angry sun they had yet to see clearly through all the clouds and haze.

Calling back to Wyld to watch out for the ledge, Lanereth led the three towards the entrance of the land bridge, the greyoldors still chasing behind, slowly catching up to the group, and this time, in greater numbers, dozens joining the chase by that point.

Lanereth stumbled out onto the ledged bridge that jutted out over a drop that was thousands of feet down, the clouds clearing up the further along the bridge they ran.

Malagar caught Lanereth just before she stumbled dangerously close to the bridge's edge, guiding her to crouch further back, Wyld catching up now to the two, taking a rest to reassess how close the greyoldors were to catching up to them.

Along the line of fog at the base of the bridge stood dozens of greyoldors, standing in silence, watching the group from the shroud of mist that lined the ledge of the plateau.

Blood dripped from all three, staining the ash-white stone, Malagar helping Lanereth up as they scanned the scene before them.

The fog rolled down a sharp cliffside into a valley that stretched out into the distant haze of blood-red mist, miles and miles of endless tangles of large, red thickets, gently pulsating as though the network of vines wasn't just a bramble, but something more...alive.

Above it all was a slit in the sky, and both Malagar and Lanereth only blinked in confusion at the surreal sight, the rend in space boggling them at first.

Shadows, images of entities stood on the other side, looming hundreds of feet tall, giants among another plane of existence far off in the tear in space.

They could not turn away, and they watched as the gods in the rift shuffled wispily through the red nebulous world beyond the one they inhabited.

A slumped figure, shrouded in bending light and shadow, stood still, the other titans flickering about it. They could not see its features, but Malagar and Lanereth could feel its attention, and they trembled as they watched, naked before its vision, their presence beholden to the god in the sky that looked down upon their diminutive lives.

A flash across the plateau on the other side of the land bridge snapped the two from their shock. What appeared as daylight split the tinge of perpetual atmospheric haze, shining like a beacon miles in the distance.

"Move," Wyld ordered, the two gazing at the light several moments before snapping out of their daze, wiping tears from their eyes. If they had been weeping from the horrible vision of the god above them, or just having a reaction to the acidic air, they couldn't tell, but they obeyed the kaith's order, and they both got to their feet and managed to stumble along as Wyld jogged ahead, leading the two as her Seam scars split and fractured, then reknitted themselves over and over again.

Looking back the way they had come, Malagar no longer saw shapes in the fog bank, all greyoldors having dispersed, leaving him to wonder if the whole encounter with the little terrors had been nothing but a feverish dream, the slashes along his upper arms dismissing that possibility as soon as it had entered his head.

They doggedly ran along the mile-long bridge, and as they made their way towards the other side of it, flecks of ash began to flutter across their path, a gentle breeze of soot falling down upon them as they stepped out of a land of acidic rain and into a blizzard of ash.

20

THE DEAD HOST

Thousands marched tirelessly forward, guided by a giant shrouded figure, lumbering south down along the land bridge that spanned several miles wide from each side of the ravines that bordered it.

Four figures stood directly in line with the massive host, waiting for the army to come to them, led by the shrouded giant, antlers slightly smoking in the sunlight as it loped towards its master.

It came to a halt, kneeling before Sha'oul as he stood, scarred, armor broken, with his head raw and fleshy. Even though he seemed beaten down, he stood tall, his presence still commanding fear and respect from those that followed him.

"Lunt," Sha'oul called, looking over the large mess of rags that kneeled before him. "You have done well to carry out my orders."

The vast army of the dead stood, motionless as the desert winds played with the pestilence-ridden body of troops.

Lunt let out a stag's grunt in recognition.

112

"We have new orders from Telenth."

At the mention of the one they all served, and feared, the wendigo looked up, meeting eyes with his temporary master, the one that he was tethered to in this new realm.

"We make for the ruins of an old ritual site to the west of here. There we await word from the Ashen One."

The creature bowed its head in obedience, accepting the command before Sha'oul turned and began to lead the army forward on its endless march through the scorching desert.

"What of this man that follows at your heels?" Denloth asked as the day grew long, night slowly coming as they continued their march. He had been wary of how he looked upon them ever since first meeting him.

"He is my dog," the large man huffed, not terribly interested in the matter as he had grown tired after the long day's hike, still attempting to recover from the wounds he had suffered at the hands of his enemies the day prior.

"He looks at you with wicked eyes. I am surprised you trust him so readily," Denloth mentioned, eyeing the man that walked close behind them.

Sha'oul gave a humored chortle, looking back for a moment to consider the nomad.

"I know who's control he is under, and there is little hope of him breaking free from that leash."

The two walked a bit further before Denloth repeated, "Those eyes...," still uneasy with his master's unconcerned demeanor to the man.

Nomad's bloody eyes shot to Denloth now, watching him like a hawk, unblinking, his eyes dried from the desert winds.

"What...do you plan to do with him?" Denloth asked, doubly concerned as the man's dead eyes locked onto him, refusing to leave him.

Sha'oul looked to the man once more, giving Denloth's question honest consideration before answering, "He once destroyed nearly a hundred arisen before my warlock came to stop him."

He allowed that fact to sink in before continuing. "In combat, he was mighty in life. In death, I suspect he will be a vital part of the war that is about to take place. I feel a struggle within him. He is only newly turned, but our lord's influence embeds itself in his mind deeper and deeper by the day. He will become a husk, a puppet of our lord. A vehicle to carry out our lord's designs here in Una, until he is no longer needed."

"A swordsman is weak. Constrained to the weaknesses of the flesh and primitive tools of war," Denloth argued, discounting the faith Sha'oul seemed to place in a warrior's might.

"Surely manipulation of the hexweave is a superior asset to utilize."

"It was a brute that cut in half my former warlock—" he contended, silencing Denloth. "—Simple muscle, raw and focused. Do not underestimate the strength of sinew, or the skill of a master of the blade."

Denloth looked to the man once more, shaking his head of the subject, seeing he was not helping his master to see his reasonings.

His feet ached, and long had been the last two days, and though he seemed in better condition to continue the march than his master, he begged the question, "How far are these ruins?"

"A day, maybe two," Sha'oul answered shortly.

"And when will we take rest?" Denloth pressed, hoping to have time to recover his flagging step.

"The dead do not need rest. We march until we arrive. Then the real work begins," he answered.

Denloth's head slunk at the news, knowing that the dreary march had only just begun its torturous play with the man, the cool night air doing little to ease the throb of how many miles still lay between them and any sort of respite.

21

UNDER THE MOON'S GAZE

The light of Kale, the green moon, shown down through the canyon's lip as Yozo and Jezebel dragged Fin, Alva, and Revna out on the steps to the temple.

Breathing in the fresh air, glad to be out of the old temple's oppressive darkness, Yozo looked over Fin while Jezebel began to perform a healing on Revna, rousing her from unconsciousness.

Jezebel fell back, collapsing after expending all the energy she had to share with her priestess, lying on her back, breathing shallow breaths, the stars in the sky swirling in her vision as she struggled to stay awake.

"Jez!" Revna called as she came to find Jezebel collapsed by her side.

She repositioned her, holding her head on her lap, the saren's silver hair spread wildly across her robes. There was blood coming from her neckline, though it was too dark for Revna to get a good look at the wound to tell how serious it was.

She brought out an amulet and began chanting prayers to Sareth for aid.

Yozo looked to Revna as a faint light began to form around the amulet, a neat glow reaching out to touch Jezebel's forehead, forcing a gasp of air from the dying saren.

Eyes fluttering, she sat up, feeling her neck where the slash had been. Finding the cut healed, she looked to Revna and embraced her briefly, looking to Alva who was resting beside them, though much worse for wear then any of them, blood staining the tabard along her midsection.

"Alva," the priestess called, placing a hand along her face. The saren's skin had grown worryingly cold.

She began her prayer once more, the amulet glowing fainter this time, but still noticeable. A light rested upon the wounded saren knight, and she too breathed in the breath of life, sitting up immediately, looking frantically about her as she took in her new surroundings.

Jezebel patted her on the back, smiling that their goddess had deemed to answer their prayers with two healings.

"Saren," Yozo called, kneeling beside Fin who had not roused once since Yozo had picked him up back in the temple, his arm grotesquely positioned, indicating a clean break.

Revna needed no further prompting, and she came over at once, inspecting the man who had quite possibly saved what remained of the diminished band.

"I can't tell if he draws breath," she whispered, worried at how cold his skin was.

She began whispering a prayer, holding her amulet close to the man's chest. All waited for the cold silver medallion to glow.

The prayer continued a time longer before Revna put the amulet down, reaching out a hand, placing it on Fin's chest.

She flinched and released from him, glancing back to the other two sarens with a look of concern.

"He is slipping, and Sareth has already provided what aid she can this night," she said, turning to Yozo, adding, "and none of us are in a state to perform a healing of this caliber without risk to our own lives."

"This man must not die," Yozo said, a crack of concern entering his voice for the first time that night.

"You are sarens! I've heard—*seen*—the legends of healing your people possess. Surely you can do something for him!"

"I will die for him," Alva said, getting up to stand on shaky footing.

"You're awful at healings," Jezebel chided, standing beside her to help steady her.

"If anyone should perform a healing, it's me," she added, smiling as she helped her battle sister over to the rest of the group circling Fin's body.

"No. It's my duty as a priestess. This is my jurisdiction. The burden falls upon me," Revna said, silencing the two.

"Come, support me," she ordered, the two kneeling down next to her, wrapping an arm around her as she rested before her engagement with Fin.

"If I am to slip into our mother's arms this night, I want to be delivered to her in the hands of my sisters," she reverently said, Jezebel and Alva squeezing her in love and support as she prepared herself for the task.

Yozo gave her space, watching as she steadied her breathing, resting a hand once more on Fin's still chest and began to open herself up to the death aura that hung over him like a grave shroud.

He had been leaving, even as she reached out for him, his organs having been smashed so badly by the violent blasts and impacts that they were slowly shutting down, returning to lifeless matter within him.

She latched on to his spirit, urged its return, and began to draw life from her essence and filled what voids she could within his physical self, working on knitting together vital functions to a sustainable place.

The healing sapped her quickly, and the two saren knights at her side had to hold her as she withered under the constraints. They could see she would die soon.

Without communicating on the matter, both began to perform a healing on the priestess, all lending their life force, siphoning it through each other to give aid to Revna.

Revna returned, sitting up as she received the burst of energy from her sisters, finishing the healing on Fin, mending his broken arm just as she released her hand from him, falling back into the arms of Jezebel and Alva who caught her.

Fin sat up, coughing violently as breath came to him. His eyes were wide, looking to Yozo, who looked as if he watched a ghost, then looking to the three saren who kneeled next to him.

"I was dead, wasn't I?" he asked, looking around at everyone watching him, smiling.

"I caught you, just as you were leaving," Revna tiredly said, smiling warmly that their efforts had paid off, and that she was still there to enjoy the moment.

Fin smiled back, wanting to embrace everyone, thankful to be alive, but having to lay back down, extremely spent from the traumatic night.

"I'm glad to see you all," he said, accepting the pillow of cloth Yozo placed under his head as he caught his breath.

"Where are the rest?" he asked, attempting to get back up to look around for the others.

Their smiles faded, and Fin knew the answer as the weight of the defeat began to sink in.

"We were not meant to fight him," Fin whispered, eyes now skyward, gazing at Kale's green light.

The momentary silence was broken by Revna who said, "No, I think we were—though we may not fully understand the reasoning of this night now. Sareth would not have ordered this assault without a purpose."

The mood lifted somewhat until Yozo broke the quiet of the night.

"That purpose will not bring back your sisters. The cost was great, regardless."

"This is true," Alva agreed, though not as defeated as Yozo in her resolution, adding, "and we will mourn their brave ends. But this night, let us be thankful that there are a few of us left alive to carry on the fight."

The group rested a moment in the desert night's light breeze, collecting their thoughts, recovering from the traumas of the day.

Yozo stood up and disappeared back into the shadows of the temple without a word.

22

THE PATHS AHEAD

Their rest had been fitful, reflecting over the allies that still lived, each looking to each other in the light of the moon, sharing in each other's sorrow, having born witness to so many of their comrades ended in the most violent of ways. When they were able to nap for an hour or two, they often jolted awake from the aches and flashes of memories of the previous day.

It had been a day they would not soon forget, and they knew they would have a great deal of trauma to sort through, even years down the road from the event.

Yozo had come back from the shadows of the temple an hour after he had left. Everyone assumed he had checked for survivors, seeing how he was the only member of the group without injury and able to make the trek back into the darkness. He had returned only with a staff and a strange dagger enshrouded in illusion that Yozo was handling carefully, clearly aware that what he held was no typical knife.

He said not a word as he handed Revna the staff that she had dropped deep in the temple when she had gone unconscious, the saren graciously accepting the sleek white pole.

With the rising of the pink sun, the group began to slowly stretch out, gathering their things, the sarens coming together for their morning prayers.

Yozo had handed over the obscure dagger carefully, saying nothing about the rare weapon, but his eyes lingered on it as it disappeared from view as Fin tucked it in a fold of his outfit.

Fin thanked the man for retrieving it, speaking quietly to Yozo, asking of details of what had happened after the explosion that had knocked him cold. Yozo described shortly the events that followed after Fin had gone unconscious and how both Denloth and Sha'oul had made an escape after that point.

Revna finished her prayer, dropping Alva and Jezebel's hands and gathered with the two men to discuss what was next to come.

"Few would have been as brave as you two standing against an Avatar of Telenth. Sareth recognizes your valor."

Fin nodded his head slightly, moving past the pleasantries, but Yozo's eyebrows furrowed at the remark.

"If that were true, she would have healed Fin last night instead of forcing you to do it," he said, an edge on his voice that clearly had been building the night through.

"Was she even in there with us while we were getting slaughtered?" he pressed, wanting to say more, but figuring that his point was made seeing how taken aback the priestess was by the remark.

"Even Sareth cannot simply irradicate any and all evils that ever walk Una. Her power, like all the gods, is connected to the faith of her followers. We can do but what we can do.

"Yes, we failed last night. We lost many loved ones at the hands of a wretch, but we only truly fail if we cease to make the attempt. His vile presence in this realm will not stand, and Sareth will continue to bless our mission.

"I have seen his defeat in vision. Sha'oul's days on Una are numbered."

Revna's speech rallied the other's hopes for a moment before Yozo mumbled out, "And so are ours. So are everyone's."

121

"Do you mean to give up the hunt?" Fin asked plainly, stopping Yozo's brooding in his tracks, the question forcing Yozo to look away down the canyon for a moment, considering the simple question.

"Malagar had vowed to kill Denloth, or die trying, as we all vowed. Most are dead. We are not. Nothing about that vow has changed for me. I'm seeing this to the end. Denloth, and his master, they need to be stopped, Yozo. There's going to be losses, but it's like Revna said, if we stop now, then yeah, why did we even try in the first place?"

Fin's words were uncontested and Yozo remained silent, but Fin wasn't having his friend's ambiguous loyalties this time. He needed a solid answer from the man on if he was committed to the cause.

"Do you respect Malagar's vow, or are you turning your back on them? Choose now. Remain by our side in this fight, or walk out of this canyon alone. Whatever choice you make, make it with conviction—and I don't want to see that conviction waver from here on out if you remain with us."

Yozo snapped back to Fin, staring him in the eyes, inches from his face, frustrated with the man he had mixed feelings towards, frustrated with the goddess that seemed to allow her children to be brutally slain, and frustrated at himself for not having the unwavering credo that everyone around him seemed to easily hold.

"The only companions I have known these last few years were just murdered before my eyes. What do I have left to fight for? Nomad is out of my reach, those I was coming to know are dead; I step, and tragedy befalls me everywhere I roam—"

"I'm still alive, Yozo," Fin said, cutting into his rant. "Revna, Alva, Jezebel, they're all still alive. We're united to a just cause that'll bind us far beyond these short days of war. You've saved my life. In battle, you are the most reliable person I know. It's outside of the fight that you struggle. You must decide if you are committed to this fight, but I fear that if you leave now, untethered from a purpose again, you'll wander land after land, searching for something that you could have had, right here, right now. A cause to give your present focus, to make right your past, and a future with friends that care for you enough to fight, and die, alongside you in battle."

Yozo stepped back, closing his eyes, aswirl with emotions and responses that he worked at calming. The man with all the daggers and the old brawler had always had a way of disarming his fury.

"How could we possibly hope to strike Sha'oul again now that our surprise is blown and with only five of us?" Yozo sighed out.

"Well, that's what we need to discuss. I have some ideas, though we'd be splitting up," Fin said in an easier tone, seeing that Yozo had softened, coming back to the group for the time being.

"Go ahead," Revna prompted, curious as to what Fin had in mind.

Fin nodded, launching into the plan he had been mulling over since he had woken up. "It's clear now no strike force is going to have a reasonable shot at Sha'oul or Denloth, especially now that an assassination has already been attempted. They'll likely be tighter with their guard.

"It's been too long since I've checked in with Sultan Metus in the Plainstate. He's sure to help if I can get him the information of the arisen army's size and location. On horseback I can be at the borders within a day, to the capital, two, at the latest, three. If I return with an army, we may have a chance at facing the arisen threat head on."

"What of us then?" Alva asked.

Fin nodded, continuing with his plan. "There is a fort west of here. The Tarigannie people are skeptical of foreigners, but perhaps you can bring news of the arisen army on the move in the area. They're stubborn, but they're not lazy. They will send scouts if a report of a nearby threat is announced. Once they validate the information, they can send word to Rochata-Ung of the invasion force and with the aid of both the Plainstate and Tarigannie, we may have a chance at meeting Sha'oul directly on the battlefield."

"Let's hope our horses are still tethered to the shrubs back at camp," Jezebel said, everyone looking to Revna who stroked her soft chin in thought of Fin's scheme.

"Yozo," she said, grabbing the man's attention, "what did you see when you returned to the temple's interior? I must know for certain."

Yozo's expression was grim, shaking his head as he said, "This is indeed their final resting place. None survived within."

"At a later date, the monastery will pilgrimage here and properly put their remains to rest. Until then," Revna said, gripping her white staff, holding it up as it began to glow faintly, "Sareth, protect these grounds from any whom seek to defile it. Keep it shrouded from all passersby until thy children may reclaim the remains of their sisters."

The staff glowed bright, and then blinked out, and they all could feel a quiet fall upon the temple steps.

"I accept your plan, Fin, and we will raise the alert in Tarigannie. I hope to meet you again on the battlefield once we have gathered our armies to the cause," she said hopefully, the other two knights standing stoically at her side, a show of resolution.

"And what of me?" Yozo asked, stepping up, Fin looking to the man with a smirk.

"Though I wouldn't mind the company on the road, I think it would be best if you traveled with Revna. Tarigannie can be an unforgiving country. If Fort Wellspring does not welcome you with open arms, I'd rather you be with them in case something were to happen. Is that agreeable?" he asked, looking to the two groups.

"That is acceptable," Revna agreed, "but watch your tongue when speaking of Sareth as you were. I can only overlook blasphemy for so long and not have a bad taste in my mouth about you. She is our light, and even if you do not follow her personally, please have the decency to respect those who do."

Yozo looked rather abashed at the reprimand, bowing slightly, apologizing for the offense he had caused.

Fin slung an arm around both Yozo and Revna, breaking the awkward tension between the two, looking up the cliff they had come down from.

"We'd better get to work on getting up that canyon wall. We've got a long day of riding ahead of us."

23
TOTEMS AND SPIRES

The ash fell thicker, slowing their pace as they trudged in the direction of the rays of light they had glimpsed earlier from the bridge. They didn't know if they were headed to salvation, or to their doom, but both Malagar and Lanereth had felt something of hope in the light all those miles ahead of them.

"The ash had coated their ripped-up arms, and for the most part, the bleeding had stopped. Lanereth had no energy to heal them of their lacerations. The sting of agitated flesh was a constant reminder to them that all this was no nightmare that they'd soon wake up from. They were living in an actual hell; a place neither of them ever dreamed of visiting.

Lanereth hacked up blood-specked phlegm, bending over to cough through a raw-throated episode. Malagar soothed her back as he looked around the ash cloud they were in, hoping no creatures lurked just out of sight.

Wyld had followed them. She drifted out of sight from time to time, but generally was around. Malagar worried over his long-time companion. He had known her for years, and the Seam scar she wore, that continued to grow, seemed to be untethering her sanity, bit by bit. He did not know for how long they would be able to rely on her.

The kaith was fixed on something ahead, and as Malagar helped Lanereth up from her knees, the two of them walked forward, curious as to what Wyld had such interest in.

A massive figure stood motionless before them as they made their way closer to Wyld, and they hesitated at first, ready to bolt, but Wyld was not on alert, and Malagar trusted her instincts more than anyone.

Twenty-foot tall before them loomed a spike jutting out of the ground, adorned in bone, covered in ash, dried blood lining the cracks between corpses, many which Malagar could identify as greyoldor, the other corpses being foreign to him.

"An effigy?" Malagar asked in a worried tone, the sight of mangled limbs so horribly tacked to the structure caused him to hope that whatever had made the scarecrow, wasn't close by.

"Perhaps this is why those greyoldors didn't follow past the bridge," Lanereth hoarsely whispered, her skin taking on an unhealthy yellowish tone.

Moving past the towering structure, fresh ashfall padding their footsteps, more communal crucifixes came into view, each seeming to hold a certain number of fresh bodies along its spire.

"Sareth help us," Lanereth gloomily uttered as the haggard group of half-clothed, badly injured outlanders made their way through the fields of corpse trees.

A shrill screech high above split the hush of the ash fall, large wings flapping slowly over them in the clouds as the unseen winged beast flew past them to some destination ahead.

Crouched by a crucifix, the three huddled, waiting for the winged predator to pass by before Malagar broke the silence once more.

"Its wingspan—sounded massive," he said, trembling as he considered if it had been wisdom to enter this new land that the greyoldors had refused to follow them into.

"There are horrors here I hope we do not have the displeasure to discover," Lanereth whispered, trembling as she wrapped her arms around her cold body.

Wyld began to prowl once more, and Malagar gently tugged on Lanereth to keep moving, worrying for her, seeing that she was looking worse as time wore on.

He reached in her vest, taking what scant rations he had stored away in his jerkin, and gave them to her, indicating for her to eat.

She looked at him hesitantly at first, but he kept his eyes on Wyld. He knew she was the one that needed the energy. Though his stomach was shrunken from hunger, their time in the distant realm at that point running long now, he was no stranger to fasting. He knew how long he could go without food and how to handle functioning without sustenance; and, by the looks of it, especially after her first healing, Lanereth had become much more exhausted over the course of their damnation.

She ate the mix of dried crackers, berries, nuts, cheese, and meats, savoring every salted morsel as they made their way through the ashen fields, Wyld keeping them at a slow but steady pace through the endless grey that surrounded them on all sides.

Though it had been hours since passing the morbid effigy towers, the group had kept diligent about their march. They had not heard or seen any further signs of life, but the ash fall had begun to lessen slightly, and in the distance, they could see more silhouettes of structures up ahead, though these structures loomed much greater than the totems they had passed earlier. These seemed like actual buildings, hundreds of feet high, stretching well up into the thick clouds above.

"The Fallen Towers," Wyld said, breaking her usual silence.

Malagar and Lanereth looked to the kaith, many questions coming to mind, the ominous structure before them bespeaking of countless horrible fates sealed away in its otherworldly cinder and bone walls.

"The Fallen Towers? You speak like you know this place, Wyld," Malagar probed, not sure how in the hells she would know of the structures they had come up upon.

"Kaiths have not forgotten, though man might have. Man is very forgetful, but kaiths...we remember all the way back to the end of the New Dawn, when man brought many others here for the first time, and the last time, to try to conquer the God of Ash."

"The New Dawn?" Lanereth whispered, considering Wyld's words now more seriously. "That was part of the First Age, tens of thousands of years ago. There's not much written of that time in the record."

"As I said, man forgets easily, even with his books. Kaith remembers through memory and the spoken word. A history we keep close to us in our blood, and here, my people suffered, as did man and all those who crusaded in this hell, though remnants of that war seem to still linger as you saw with the structures above the greyoldor nests."

"Then what are these fallen towers, Wyld? What's in them?" Malagar pressed, both him and Lanereth looking to the structures that loomed silent and lifeless ahead of them.

Wyld stared blankly, reflecting on the stories of the past that had been passed down to her from endless generations before her. She spoke from a mental distance that Malagar knew not whether it came from a deep pit of reflection, or from a disconnect from the Seam that invaded her mind.

"Kaith never stepped foot close enough to find out. Those who fell in battle were taken there. Men as well. None fared worse than the praven though. Of all the praven who entered from the Spire of Hope, none returned. All were taken. The Fallen Towers were their tomb, more so than any other kin of Una."

"That perhaps explains the origin of the greyoldors. We saw they live here still, and after tens of thousands of years in this hell...," Lanereth wheezed, hunched over, holding onto Malagar's arm as the three beheld the silent towers.

"What a horrible fate," she whispered as they all reflected on the long, painful history of the place.

Wyld flinched suddenly, and Malagar could see Seam scars widen along Wyld's face, cutting jaggedly into her flesh right before their eyes.

A sharp crack of thunder sounded behind them, and in the distance, they began to hear rainfall, though, through the ash, they still couldn't see it.

"We need shelter," Lanereth said franticly, the trauma fresh upon her patchy scalp and skin sending a wave of fear and anxiety throughout her shaky frame.

Wyld had already taken off, bolting for one of the tall towers closest to them.

"Come on," Malagar said, pulling Lanereth forward, holding her close as they stumbled along through the ash, the dampening roar of rain rushing quickly towards them.

The massive spike of a tower in front of them promised them both safety, and doom, the pocked shear walls rising high into the sky, a forty-foot open doorway at the base of the building leading into darkness beyond.

They were close; not but a few hundred feet from the entrance now, but as Malagar glanced behind them at the now deafening wall of rain that cut into the ash cloud they had been trekking through, he could see they would be overtaken within moments. He spurred forward frantically, practically dragging Lanereth with him.

"Run, Lanereth, damn it!" he yelled, but as much as she struggled to keep up, the continued exhaustion from her healing threatened to drown her in the dark of unconsciousness, her eyes fluttering, trying to stay functioning as long as she possibly could.

Malagar dug deep within for the strength they needed just then. He snatched Lanereth up and hoisted her over his shoulder, taking off in a dead sprint towards Wyld who was just making it to the archway of the ash-bleached tower.

He could hear nothing but the flood of acid rain behind him now—not even his own breath or his pounding heart. The stinging mist stung his nostrils as he heaved breath after breath of acid vapor.

The shadow of the archway shrouded them just as the sheet of rainfall sliced down behind them like a guillotine, angrily hissing on their heels as Malagar slowed within the cover of the dark tower to collapse atop Lanereth who had fallen unconscious.

He heaved, trying to recover, but he had pushed too hard.

Darkness overcame him.

24

THE FORGOTTEN NIGHTMARES

Malagar startled awake, breathing in deep as his eyes shot open.

"That's not Wyld," were the first words he heard Lanereth whisper to him as he sat up, looking to a lone figure further in the chamber entrance to the tower.

Malagar held Lanereth's hand. She was cold, and shivering still, but seemingly in better shape than last he had looked upon her. She was deeply concerned though with the figure that stood facing them, just far enough in the shadows to be out of sight to get a clear understanding for what might be watching them.

"How—long has it been there?" he asked, struggling to jog his brain back into consciousness from slumber.

"I don't know. I just woke up a minute ago," she whispered, her eyes never leaving the figure.

The thing took a step forward, and another, slowly, stalking forward with intent.

Malagar scrambled to his feet, pulling his gauntlets tight along his forearms, ready for the thing to get close enough to strike.

Out of the many rills along the corridor's walls bolted Wyld, slamming into the creature, ferociously ripping into the thing's chest with her claws as she clamped down on its neck, snapping its spine quickly, the fight leaving it at once.

She stood there, hunched over what looked like a greyoldor's corpse, looking ferally at the two who watched in startled hesitance, not knowing if they were going to be next in the kaith's sights as she tossed the lifeless body to the side and looked down the dark tunnels that weaved deep into the lightless towers.

"Eat," they heard her call back to them over her shoulder as she disappeared into the shadows once more.

They waited to see if she would return for a minute before staring disgustingly at the mutilated creature further in the hallway, the sight of it churning their stomachs, and turned to consider the rain outside. It was coming down hard as ever, and luckily, or by design, the entrance was sloped to keep the acidic runoff flowing out around its base, keeping them elevated and dry.

"The water," Malagar softly said, motioning to the flask of water they had saved from the cistern. "Let's have a drink and fill it up while there's rain."

Lanereth sluggishly flipped open the pouch and complied, drinking from the flask as ordered, handing it over after she had drank half, Malagar finishing off the remainder before stepping cautiously up to the entrance of the tower and carefully collected runoff from the side of a rock that acted as a spigot, quickly refilling the flask.

"The stones," Malagar gestured, holding a hand out for Lanereth to hand him the black and white stones they had collected earlier that they hoped would act as water purifiers.

He plopped them both into the container and set it aside for the time being, taking a seat next to Lanereth, who already had sat down, leaning against the tower's arch for support, looking horribly ragged.

"How are you holding up?" he asked, Lanereth not even bothering to answer, breathing lightly, resting against the wall as the thunderous rain poured down just outside of their reach.

She winced in pain slightly, the constant discomfort of the environment they were in slowly eating away at her ability to ward off despair.

He picked her hand up, squeezing it lightly to let her know he was there for her, and the sign did seem to comfort her slightly, her features relaxing a bit.

"Where are we running to?" she murmured, her voice barely audible.

Malagar considered the question. They had seen the light of day off in the distance. For him, that was sign enough to investigate. They had no other leads, so other than laying down to die, what else could they do?

"We may yet find hope at daybreak," he said, squeezing her hand once more, then getting up to search the shadows for Wyld.

Lanereth rested, slumbering for the first time since their arrival, and her sleep was deep. They had no indicator of time there, but Malagar knew their visit had spanned days at that point. Exhaustion was setting in for all of them.

Malagar searched the corridor for an hour while the rain continued to pour down outside, drowning out all other sounds. The patterned channels within the walls cast shadows so black that he feared to search them, so he kept mostly to the center of the hallways, fearing any moment something might materialize just within the cloak of darkness that surrounded him on all sides.

He found no signs of Wyld, nor of anything else. Perhaps the kaith was seeing to it that nothing else bothered them.

After a fruitless surveillance, he returned to the entryway, finding Lanereth in deep sleep where he had left her, joining her in sleep by her side.

All was black, and he slumbered without dream or notion.

The flap of wings and a horrendous screech roused them, sending them scurrying back to an inlet along the walls further in the tower's entrance, seeking a hiding place as they listened for the flying creature as it swooped closer, filling the tower's archway with a forceful gust of ashen wind.

It landed above them in the tower, the ground and walls trembling slightly as the beast stomped down on a ledge many floors above them.

They stayed glued to the rivulet in the wall, not moving, listening for the creature's path and direction high above them.

After a time, it seemed to settle, and the two eased up slightly, but as Lanereth was about to speak, Malagar held his hand to her mouth.

Large human-like figures, completely hairless and grey with sunken steel-blue eyes that glinted in the shadow of the tower, slunk in through the archway, silently searching the interior as they entered.

The two froze. They were in one of the shadow places Malagar had avoided, and he did not know how far the crack in the wall went back, or if anything was maliciously stalking them from behind. His only hope was that the creatures could not see them now in the veil of darkness.

Thirteen in all, they skulked in, passing the two by, the lead grey man coming across the greyoldor Wyld had slain.

The thirteen moved eerily silent. If Malagar and Lanereth had closed their eyes, they would have no idea a small troop shared the room with them.

The lead grey man picked up the greyoldor's corpse, tilting its head in thought for a moment. It opened its mouth, showing its jagged teeth as it bit into the limp thing's neck, causing the weight of the head to snap off its unsupported spine, making a sickening thud as it smacked into the floor.

Another grey man picked up the discarded head, slowly munching into its face as the others continued on into the darkness of the corridor, not as interested in the find as the first two were. They slowly followed as their pack began to leave them behind, silently slipping into the shadows.

Minutes went by before Malagar dared to move, grabbing Lanereth's hand, leading them to the archway. Snatching up their water flask, they scanned the perimeter outside.

The rains had washed away much of the haze that had accumulated throughout the day before, and the ash had cleared in the wake of the storm. They could see the glimmer of light they had beheld earlier that had acted as their destination. It shown faintly now, flickering oddly, but its golden rays continued to flirt with their hopes regardless.

They had been close to other structures, smaller than the tower they were in. The tent-like formations stretched around out of their view behind the tower.

The two looked back into the dark hall, wondering what Wyld's fate would be, but knowing they could not help her even if they dared enter further in to look for her. Stepping out onto the ash plains once more, they followed the tower's perimeter to get a better look at the strange structures that had been just out of sight.

A network of cave-like stone structures stretched on along the endless plateau, paths weaving through the chaos, and they could make out small figures moving through the streets. It was some type of city, and though they were too far away for Lanereth to clearly make out what creatures were residing within its limits, Malagar's keen eyes showed him the truth of the matter.

"What do you see down there?" Lanereth asked, knowing he had the better eyesight.

"Nothing good," he answered, watching a moment longer before adding, "That creature we first saw, the large horned one that you burned. Many of those, and other beasts. Skinless oxen, or something like it. Things with large heads, scorched black. Much of it in shadow. It's too far for me to make out."

He studied the masses closer, looking at forming patterns of creatures moving in one direction. "Looks like they're forming up. Many are headed towards the light."

The account did not put Lanereth's mind at ease.

"We should stay far away from that city. It is damned," he whispered, eyes looking fixedly upon the torment and depraved acts unfolding before his eyes that were blind to his companion.

"What place isn't damned in this hell?" she replied, but agreed silently, having no desire to go anywhere near the stretch of hell hovels.

"The light is beyond though," he puzzled, looking to the flickering golden light at the top of a rise at the end of the plateau miles away.

"You can't make out what that light is?" Lanereth asked, hoping that he had some insight as to what the odd glimmer was in the distance before they placed any more hope in its destination.

"No," he answered somewhat frustrated by the beacon's obscurity, rubbing his eyes, "it's too blinding. Nothing about it is clear. In fact, everything directly around it seems stuck in some sort of warp. We'll have to get closer."

Lanereth looked to the fringes of the city where the ash fields became too uneven to be built upon. Pointing to the network of crags along its borders, she said, "If we can't go through the city, then we must go around. See the cracks in the ash shelf over there along the city's edge? That may keep us out of sight of any pit spawn. It circles around to the side of it all. It might make the trek to the light more difficult, but I am not going anywhere near that camp of defiled."

Malagar looked closely at the trench she had indicated. He could see that they would be well hidden from any eyes of the city, but what dwelled in the trench could be just as frightening as what was above it.

"That may work. It does seem to lead roughly to the light. Perhaps there will even be some overhangs or caves in there in case another rain comes. If a downpour like the one that just passed by caught us in the open...there'd be nothing left of us within a minute of exposure."

He looked back to the direction they had come from, wondering if Wyld would be able to find her way out and catch up with them at some point. She had a predator's nose and was the best tracker he knew. If she were still alive within the tower's dark walls, he didn't doubt that she could find them if she wished to, but she had made him uneasy the last few days with the Seam scar clearly jostling her attachment to reality.

Looking to the sky, trying to determine if the clouds rolling in were rain or ash clouds, he stepped out of the shadow of the tower looming over them. Lanereth watched the same clouds and gave a short prayer to Sareth that if it was rain, they might have a swift end in a downpour, and not a drawn-out erosion of flesh from a constant, light sprinkle as there was no refuge for the next mile or two of their journey.

Part Three: War on the Winds

25
EYES ALONG THE WALL

The horses had remained at camp, though slightly agitated by the long neglect and lack of water, but once they had been fed and watered, the group had made quick goodbyes, Fin heading off east to the Plainstate, and Yozo, Alva, Jezebel, and Revna trotting off west to the fort that stood many miles down the dusty trail.

They had followed Fin's instructions, and the road had made the path simple enough. They had seen no sign of any other travelers along the highway that whole day, but towards evening, on the horizon they had seen the early glow of a structure, signs of activity present as they rode closer to it as the night came on.

The four trotted up to the front gate, its walls reaching twenty-foot-high, portholes and parapets allowing the occasional gate guard to peek down on the approaching gang.

They waited at the gate of the large fort for a minute before the small side door unlocked and an armed soldier stepped out.

"Few come from Dolinger Crags these days," the older man gruffed, eyeing the four closer, adding, "Fewer still be foreigners.

138

What's yer business here? This ain't no tourist destination."

"This is a military fort, is it not?" Revna asked.

The man looked to the woman high on her horse, offering a simple, "Yeah."

"Do you patrol the countryside? Have your scouts reported signs of invading armies?" she asked.

The man gave her a sideways look, not liking where his gate shift was headed already.

"Say what you got to say, miss. Who are you four and why are you talking about invading armies?"

Revna looked to the fort where quite a few soldiers had begun to peak over the wall to gaze at the group, particularly interested in three platinum blonde women who were idling at the gate.

"We are sarens from the Jeenyre monastery far to the north. We came hunting an army of arisen that was headed for the Tarigannie region. They're here now, and we just suffered a defeat. We came to give warning. You may be Tarigannie's only hope in stopping them now."

The man closed his eyes and raised his eyebrows, unsure of what he just heard. Waving to a man up on the wall, he waved for the gate door to be opened.

Yozo moved closer to Revna, eyeing all those watching them from the wall.

"I don't like this. We gave them the warning. We don't need to enter those gates," he whispered, seeing the same callous, dead eyes in the soldiers that he had become accustomed to throughout the region whenever he strolled into any given town.

Revna looked to Yozo, unaware until then how uncomfortable the man had gotten with the situation, offhandedly replying, "We can't just tell a gate guard and go. We need to speak with the captain if anything is to actually be done."

"You don't see how those men on the walls or in the portholes look upon us? Upon *you*?" Yozo pressed, the doors finally opening as the gate guard waved them forward.

"This is our task, Yozo," she said, exasperated with the man, ending the sudden debate, leading the other in through the small gate to enter the open court, two stable boys coming out of the stalls to handle their mounts as they dismounted.

"If what yer saying is true, Cap Durmont will be wanting to speak with ya personally. Follow me if you will," the old gate guard said, leading them past a well and awning into the shade of a set of rooms and narrow hallways deep within the large fort's interior.

The stairway lined with torches blackened the walls they passed through, leading to a waiting room, a somewhat more elaborate set of double doors on the far wall with a few simpler, smaller doors flanking it.

The old guard knocked on the large door, cocking his head close to listen for a reply.

"Come," called a strong voice from within, prompting him to open the door, issuing the small group inside, Yozo at the back of the line keeping an eye behind them, untrusting of any passing resident.

The room was modestly spacious, a large, well-used table at its center with chairs lining the walls closest to them, shelves and chests cluttering the outer edges of the room on the other side of it. At the desk sat a young man, shorn hair with ebony skin, darker than most from the region. The dark tattoos he had along his collarbone and neckline were barely discernable, but the subtle patterned effect, along with his golden eyes, caused the sarens, and even Yozo, to hesitate when he put down the ledger he had been looking over to consider the group.

The old guard cleared his voice. "This lot said there's an army of arisen roaming the countryside. Figured it best they spoke with you 'bout that, sir."

The captain nodded his head to the old man, looking to the others, eyeing them one by one, spending a considerable amount of time looking Yozo over before saying, "Very well. This is no small report you bring to my fort. I would have details of the news you bring, but first, explain to me who you are and why I should listen. It is obvious none of you hail from Tarigannie," he said sitting back in his chair, fingers intertwined in wait for their response.

"It is clear that neither are you. Does it matter where we are from?" Jezebel said, a hint of defensiveness in her tone, getting a stern eye from Revna who clearly disapproved of the candid woman's answer.

Durmont held Jezebel's gaze until she looked off to the side, irritated by her own overreaction, but too proud to walk back the statement.

The man smiled slightly, waiting a moment longer before replying to the slight spurn. "Where I come from, one takes pride in who they are, who their *people* are. To hide one's birthplace disrespects those generations whom you have to thank for being here today. So tell me, are you ashamed of those that raised you enough to hide it from me?"

As he spoke, his words were measured, though not sluggish. Sharp, though not aggressive. They knew they had to tread carefully with their words with the captain.

"We have no reason to hide who we are or where we're from," Revna said, glancing disapprovingly at Jezebel a moment before continuing. "My name is Revna. This is Alva, and Jezebel. We are saren from the Jeenyre monastery, here in Tarigannie following up on reports of an arisen threat along the Tarigannie border."

"And this man," Durmont asked, eyeing Yozo intensely.

Revna looked to their companion, prompting him to speak for himself.

Yozo side-eyed the others, clearly not comfortable in the closed-door room or the fort in general.

"Yozo. I come from far to the east."

"And your reason for being with these saren?" the captain coaxed.

"I have vowed to kill those heading the arisen army. These saren share the same vow," he huffed, hoping to be done with the interrogation.

He seemed satisfied with the reply and returned to Revna's remark.

"Why investigate a threat on our borders? They are *our* borders, after all, not yours. Do you think us incapable of watching over our lands?"

She did not like the sharp turns in tone and calculated assumptions in their motives the man employed at every juncture of conversation. She considered her answer before speaking, making sure there were no holes he could poke through in her response.

"Evil knows no borders, and neither does our commitment to fight it. We were given a vision from Sareth herself of a great evil stirring here, and we came to answer the call of duty."

"Indeed," the shrewd man readily agreed, nodding his head as he sat up in his chair, once more changing the direction of the conversation.

"Now then, this is *who* and *why* you are here. You say the arisen army is indeed in our lands. If that is true, where might we find them?"

Revna was about to start with the encounter at the old temple deep in the canyon, but stopped herself, knowing to mention the temple would be to invite others to know of its location, and she did not want military poking around at the burial ground of her fallen sisters.

"Our band had been surveying the arisen army east of here in the crags for days now, waiting for the opportunity to strike. Their leaders were exposed yesterday, and we rushed them. They escaped...and many of our sisters died fighting Sha'oul, the army's warlord. He left, and so did his army. We do not know where they are now, but they were headed out of the north side of the canyon yesterday last we knew."

The captain had listened intently, letting her story sink in before asking, "And how many are in this warlord's army? Are they all the risen dead?"

Yozo was the one to answer, knowing out of all of them, he was the one with the most experience at that point with the enemy force. "All are arisen, though not all are human. They have many rotted beasts in their ranks—large abominations. Their numbers are great, perhaps three thousand. Four thousand at most."

The man stroked his smooth chin, calculating while the others waited for a response.

"And how did you even happen upon this warlord's name? We have heard rumors of arisen in past months, but even with our network, little information has been delivered."

Yozo hesitated, considering how to avert explaining the

turncoat arisen Dubix to the captain.

"A friend, Dubix, had been following the arisen lord for much longer than us. He gave us the warlord's name."

"And what happened to this...*Dubix*?" the captain quizzed.

"He died fighting Sha'oul's forces at my side," Yozo simply offered.

I am sorry to hear that," Durmont sincerely offered, pausing a moment to take in Yozo's information before asking, "What size of force was your contingent?"

"Eleven sarens and five in Yozo's crew. We joined forces along the canyon before planning the attack," Revna responded.

"Are you all that survived?" he asked, his tone sympathetic to his suspected answer.

"One other that is not with us survived. He's gone to neighboring states to ask for aid and to warn them of the threat."

"Eighteen against thousands. I commend your bravery. Truly, you have it if your story is an honest one," he said, his voice one of reverence as he reflected upon the account.

"I cannot contend with thousands of hell spawn with the strength of Fort Wellspring alone. We'll need to send word to Rochata-Ung and Gunnison if this is true. There's a standing militia in Gunnison that would help to bolster our numbers, and the army of Rochata-Ung is known throughout the Southern Sands. Together we should be able to eliminate this threat."

Revna's relief was visible as her posture eased up at the declaration.

"But," he continued, "before any of that is executed, we'll need to verify your claims, which I will do with all haste. I would appreciate your cooperation while I do so. After all, if this report turns out to be true, then none understand this enemy better than you. Would you be opposed to extending your stay with us until I have my scouts track and validate this army?"

Yozo stiffened at the request, seeing it clearly as an order they could not refuse, and even Revna was back on guard with the man as she hesitantly answered, "We would hate to take up room in a military fort. I know how busy they can be. We would do fine camping outside the walls so as not to get in the way of operations."

The smile and pause caused a moment of worry amongst all in the group, but all eased up when Durmont said, "As you wish. Our gates are open to you if you need supplies or change your mind. We have rooms to spare. I would caution against leaving the area without checking in with me first, however. You are a source of intelligence. I cannot have you leaving before we resolve this presage you have brought to our doors."

"Our mission was to warn Tarigannie of the threat. If you will take the warning seriously, and send word to the Rochata-Ung army, then we will be happy to camp close by and provide aid and information when needed for the foreseeable future," she agreed, now slightly sharing Yozo's distrust of the fort and those within.

"Good. I will send scouting parties out within the hour to scour the land north and eastward. Within a day we should have our reports. I may call upon you from time to time. Until then, we will see to your horses and see that you are resupplied to make your stay on our perimeters as pleasant as possible."

The captain looked to the old gate guard and ordered, "Scars, see that Revna and her crew are resupplied with food and drink before seeing them outside the gates to set up their camp."

"Yes sir," the guard said, snapping a salute before seeing the crew out of the room and back down the stairs, grabbing two young pages that idled near the well on break, sending them this way and that to gather supplies for the visitors.

"I see you've been bloodied. You all seem fit enough and in good health. Any of ya need looking over from our medic?" he asked, drawing some water from the well as a few guards all along the walls on duty stared unashamedly at the small company, causing them all a good deal of unease at the odd amount of attention they were receiving.

"No, we're fine, just tired from the travel," Alva answered for the group.

"If ya need cleaning, we don't have no oasis nearby. We have to sponge bathe here. I'll see that ya get extra water fer that," he said, trying to help as best he could, feeling the awkward air about the group, wanting to be done with them and on with his uneventful shift.

"Lance, there ya are boy. Got the victuals?" he asked, taking the sacks of foodstuffs from the page, handing it over to Yozo who slung it around his back, bowing in thanks.

Lance, carry this pitcher for them out the gate, will ya? Garret, you too," he said, motioning for both the hands to follow him with the jugs of water to the gate as he went to unlock it.

Scars saw them out into the night's welcoming sands, Yozo and the others grateful they had not been held captive within the fort walls, the eyes of the soldiers following them all the way to the dune a hundred yards off where they had decided to set up camp for the night.

26
ARISEN ALONG THE HIGHWAY

"Men on the horizon," the skulking wendigo croaked out, kneeling before his master as he reported the sighting of Tarigannie scouts riding along the moonlit crest in the distance.

"How many?" Sha'oul asked, uninterested in the news, his whole focus remaining on the task that lay ahead of him at the forgotten ruins they were destined for.

"Five," the hunched-over demon answered.

"Denloth," Sha'oul called, grabbing the attention of his exhausted traveling companion before he had passed too far ahead.

"Send your Oathbound to take care of them. We don't need reports spreading of our location just yet," he said as he scanned the horizon to see the small figures far over the dunes to their south.

"Yes, my lord," he managed, catching his breath long enough

to order the blood-soaked knight to his side, whispering commands close to its skinless face, pointing the direction the scouts were in.

Denloth stood back as the Oathbound streaked through the Seam, ripping apart the dimensions and reality they inhabited, passing through a slipstream of other dimensions, closing the gap of a mile between them and the scouts within a few seconds.

They had only been deployed that evening, coming upon the arisen army Captain Durmont had sent them to find a little after midnight.

The host was a sight none had seen in their military career. Thousands of various sized living dead marched listlessly forward across the dunes. It was a sight they wondered once reported if they'd be believed. The arisen were but myths to most, but seeing the horde of dead walking with their own eyes caused them to stare at the sight in silence, not even speaking between themselves as they took in the direness of the scene.

Without warning, a strange rippling and fraction of the air around them preceded a thunderous snap as a knight from a nightmare plunged into the midst of them, hooking and ripping off the head of the lead scout with its khopesh quicker than any could react.

None had their swords at ready, and as they went to draw their weapons, the Oathbound was already slashing into the back of the scout closest to him, sending the horse off running over the dunes as its rider fell, reaching for its split-open back before the Oathbound brought down its blade into the man's skull to finish his struggle.

The other three turned to run, but the Oathbound fell into the Seam, heatwaves angrily vibrating around it as it opened another Seam rift above one of the mounted men, plowing into him with its full-plate armor banging the man off the mount mid-gallop.

The two fell down the crest of the dune the scout had been riding along, tumbling over and over as they both attempted to right themselves.

The scout was up first, looking around for his scimitar he had been holding before the bloody skulled knight rose from the sands, grabbing for a curved knife, having lost his khopesh in the tumble.

The man turned to run, giving up on the hope of finding his weapon, but just as he began his retreat, the Oathbound chucked the knife at the man, the blade thudding deep in the center of his back, causing the scout to arch backwards in pain, falling over to his side as he spasmed, his muscle straps completely severed, his spine sending a torrent of pain to his brain as he let out short screams, trying to find a position that didn't blast his brain with excruciating anguish as the dark knight walked over.

It grabbed the handle in the man's back and slid it out, causing the man to let out an elongated scream, the knight placing the blade to the man's neck as he slit the voice from his throat, drowning it in a gurgle of blood before the scout slumped over dead.

The Oathbound looked up to where the other riders had been. They were nowhere to be found. They had long fled the scene with terror nipping at their heels.

It had failed its master's command.

27
THE SCOUTS RETURN

"Should have never entered that fort," Yozo murmured as he ate morning breakfast in the sarens' company.

They all shared a seat on a canvas sitting area they had spread out under the few ghost gum trees that speckled the rocky dunes, providing them a bit of shade as they awaited the scouts' return.

"The food that we're eating is thanks to them. We were out of water, need I remind you. If we hadn't had entered the fort and told Captain Durmont himself of the arisen army, do you think Scars would have done anything with the report? What would we have done to feed and water our horses? They'd be dying of thirst right now, along with us," Revna rebutted, tired of Yozo's constant attitude of negativity and pessimism.

"At least our horses would still be in *our* possession," he mumbled, finishing up his rations of flatbread and dried mutton.

"Our dead horses would be ours; yes, that is true, Yozo," Jezebel answered, put out by the man's persistence to kick against the route they had taken.

Clearly seeing that he was outnumbered in his view, he brushed his hands clean of crumbs, grabbed a clay mug of water and returned to brood in his tent, out of the sun.

The three saren gave understanding looks of frustration between themselves of the man they traveled with.

"What do you think became of Lanereth?" Alva softly asked, looking to her meal as she slowly picked at it.

Revna and Jezebel turned to the youngest of them, looking to notice the reasoning behind the solemn mood she had been in the whole morning.

"Yes, Lanereth. I have been thinking of her as well," Revna said, looking out across the orange sands of the dunes that stretched out for what seemed like forever.

"We know Sha'oul worships the Lord of Ash, and so seeing the rift they opened in the temple, the probable bet is that that rift led to the Planes of Ash. It surely did not look like any landscape I have read about here in Una."

"The Planes of Ash...," Alva ominously echoed, considering the implications of Lanereth being sent there.

"Would there be any hope of escape if that were the case?" Jezebel asked, wondering the same thing Alva was too afraid to voice.

"Surely there is hope. There is always hope—but of how it is possible to open a rift back to Una in such a plane...I would not know anything about that," the priestess admitted as the three of them sat quietly contemplating the plight of their teacher.

"Hey," Jezebel distractedly said, pointing the others' attention to the dunes close by, looking to the horizon as two riders came galloping over the last of the dunes in a straight line for the fort.

"Those are the scouts that left yesterday," Alva muttered, the three saren getting up from their breakfast picnic, gathering their things as Yozo came out of his tent at the sound of the commotion.

"Looks like two of the scouts have returned. It looks urgent. They may have found the arisen already," Revna announced, catching Yozo up.

"Already? That would mean the army is close," he said, his previous ill-temperament quickly dissipating under the news.

"Yes, they must have been on the move this whole time to have gotten so far," she agreed, adding, "Grab your travel gear. If we are needed for the road, I want us to be ready to ride at once."

Within a few minutes, the four had geared up, packed some travel rations, and filled their canteens, setting out for the fort just over the small dune separating them.

They ran to the gate, seeing that it was still open for the two riders who beat them to the fort, entering behind just as the new gate guard closed and locked the gate with a large iron bar behind them.

"Arisen—" one of the scouts gasped as he dismounted, the stable boy taking the lathered horse to the watering trough promptly.

"—Army of 'em. Where's the captain?" he bellowed, even as Durmont came down the stairs, out into the open court, Scars at his side.

"Captain," the scout promptly saluted, the other scout falling in line behind his senior.

Durmont acknowledged the men and ordered, "Report. Where are the other three in your scouting party?"

There had gathered a good number of soldiers in the courtyard, more filing in from the barracks. Revna and her crew were on the inside of the quickly crowded circle, waiting to hear the scout's findings.

"Sir, yes sir," the scout stammered, collecting himself for a brief moment before explaining. "We came upon the arisen army soon after full night. We barely had a chance to survey them before...a demon flashed into our ranks."

Though the court was packed now, everyone held their breath, listening for the news they had all been gossiping over the last night about.

"Demon?" Durmont questioned.

The soldier struggled, trying to explain himself. "It was some sort of knight—a bloody skull. It seemed to jump between places, disappearing and reappearing. He killed Haadee, László, and Akin within moments. We stood no chance. Ubaid and I retreated. Galloped our horses all night to get back."

At that, some in the crowd softly cursed, and a murmur rose

before Durmont quieted his men, raising a hand for silence.

"Those that die under my command do not go unavenged. You all know that. An attack from any nation, any people...any cult, be they backed by gods, good or ill, will be answered and will cower before us to answer for the blood they have spilled on our ground."

The court was silent once more, drawn in by their quiet leader's firm declaration, Durmont looking over the crowd of soldiers as he assessed the mood of his men, ending his scan on Revna, holding her eyes a few moments before continuing.

"These saren risked their lives to deliver us news of this arisen army marching freely within our borders. Our scouts have also paid the price to deliver us the confirmation of the threat that we now know is real. We will send riders to Rochata-Ung and Gunnison to call for support. And we will answer this cult of corpses with steel and death. This day, we prepare for war."

A low murmur rippled through the crowd at his declarations.

"Chiefs, scouts, in my command room in five. Revna and company included if you would," he ended, lingering on the priestess momentarily before returning up the stairs he had come down from.

There was a mixed reaction from the soldiers filing into the yard. Most had been roused by the captain's word, excited that their generally peaceful military terms were about to become a lot more lively, and profitable, if the fort detachment did end up answering the call to war first in the region, but the cheers for the call to arms was subdued by most of the veterans who had already seen their fair share of battle, intimately knowing the horrors that were soon to come if they did end up engaging with a force of "demons" as the scout had put it.

The court began to clear, most moving to their quarters to pack their belongings, preparing for deployment and orders. Revna motioned for her companions to follow, and they, along with a few other officers the captain had called for, made their way back up the fort steps leading to the waiting room outside of the captain's command room.

After a few minutes of idly waiting with the other officers amidst hushed whispers, Scars came out of the double doored room, issuing everyone in the waiting room to come inside, the command room filling up quickly with the five chiefs, two scouts, and Revna's crew.

Scars closed the door behind the last scout to enter and squeezed his way around the chief's and Revna's group to stand at Durmont's side. After everyone was settled, the captain stood from his chair to address his officers.

All began with a salute upon standing and the shuffling about the room quieted as Durmont cleared his throat preparing to speak.

He looked to the lead scout and asked quietly, "How large are their ranks?"

"It was dark. Only the moonlight shown our way, but from what I could gather, the host was two thousand strong. Possibly more, but as I noted, the conditions made getting an accurate count... difficult," the scout stuttered out, obviously not used to issuing reports directly to the captain in front of the leading body of officers under tense circumstances.

"Can you confirm this?" Durmont asked, looking to the other scout that stood at the very back of the room by the doors.

"Yes, sir. Could have been closer to three thousand, but it was indeed hard to make out exact numbers," the other scout confirmed.

"What direction was the host moving?" the captain asked.

"West," both scouts answered at once.

"And you say there's closer to four thousand?" Durmont asked, looking to Yozo, Yozo nodding in affirmation.

"Having an exact count on their numbers would be helpful, but as you say you've been following them for a while, I'll trust your estimation," Durmont said to Yozo, going on to add, "Regardless of how many thousands, it is a number larger than my three hundred men could handle on the open plains. We will need aid from the rest of Tarigannie. We may be able to enlist another hundred or so men from Gunnison along with horses and supplies. They have standing orders to cooperate with us in times of war. It should not be too difficult to raise a militia within a day or two.

"Rochata on the other hand, though I respect the military's

leadership, their High Judges tend to get in the way at the worst times. They cannot refuse aid to a threat like this, but I wouldn't put it past them to skimp on the size of the reinforcement detachment they send."

"Lőrinc," Durmont called to one of the chiefs standing at attention, awaiting his captain's orders.

"I'll have no general officer take this task. I need you to entreaty the state to send aid. Make sure they understand the severity of the threat. You are best in dealing with bureaucrats. Send word that Fort Wellspring calls for a detachment capable of meeting the threat of an army of four thousand or they will have arisen running through their streets within the week.

"Take your pick of a stallion, see that you ride with all haste. Is that clear?"

The chief saluted and confirmed the order.

"I will see to your platoon. Take a companion with you. I don't care who it is, but set out within the hour. You are dismissed."

Another salute and Lőrinc saw himself out of the room.

"Kaylic, see to it that Gunnison is rallied. Send one of your officers to herald the news," Durmont said, looking to another chief.

"It will be done, Captain," Kaylic saluted.

"Now, those are our allies, let us discuss tactics in the meantime while we wait for reinforcements."

"Your crew has fought this enemy once before. If you choose to fight with us, I will see to it that Tarigannie compensates your heroisms. You shall have your pick of favors," he said to Revna.

Revna looked to her fellow saren and answered, "We would hunt this evil alone if we had to. Sareth deems his elimination, and we shall carry out her will. We will stand by you in this war."

Durmont had seen displays of courage from many soldiers through his time as captain—many that were willing to lay down their life for a greater cause. Endless respect he had for those who were wholly devoted to their course. That kind of conviction never ceased to impress him.

"Let us hope this *Sareth* watches over you," he calmly replied, though from the casualties from the saren's last encounter did little to bolster his confidence in the unknown deity.

28
THE RUINS OF SOLSTICE

"More men along the highway," Lunt offered, bowing again before the arisen lord.

"How many this time?" Sha'oul asked, once more showing little interest in the report.

"They are keeping well hidden. Ten perhaps. Their numbers could be more," the hunched over beast croaked.

"Bah," the large man dismissed, waving the news off. "The ruins are within sight. It matters not if a scouting party happens upon us now."

Denloth heaved, trying to keep up, sweating terribly under the heat of the Tarigannie sun, having been on the constant march for days now. He wondered if the two scouts that had gotten away had sent word to nearby outposts. If it was his Oathbound that slipped up, he knew that Sha'oul would have *him* pay for it, and he knew his master was not in the mood to forgive missteps.

Large curved needles of stone shot high into the sky, providing a dramatic landmark for all travelers along the road to Rochata-

Ung from the southern towns. Few lingered upon the old historical site, it being common knowledge that little remained other than crumbling strange structures along with a pair of spires curving into the sky that could be seen from miles around.

The spires came closer into view as the dead army trudged forward through the dunes. They marched, up and over sand dune after sand dune, until the last one between them and their destination was behind them. Sha'oul was the first to step into the large clearing at the center of the ruins, remaining empty but for him, looking around, inspecting the long-forgotten place, seeing that the ages had not been kind to the expansive remains of the significant religious site Sha'oul knew it once to be.

At his age, knowledge more easily slipped through his grasp the further back his memory spanned, but he had remembered early in life, before his augmentations and hunt for immortality and power had firmly set its hooks in him, he had visited this exact place. Back then, hundreds of years ago, the far-reaching network of structures had been mostly standing, the old people that once inhabited the region having a reverence for historical locations, but now, it was clear it had been vandalized and abused by common passersby.

None of that mattered in the end, other than the slightest tinge of disdain for man in general and their disregard for anything that did not directly affect them.

The only thing he and his god cared for at the location was the curved spires that had withstood the weather of time, looming over the bones of the former structures that once stood below it.

"Denloth. Lunt. Come," Sha'oul barked, the two hurrying to their leader's command.

"This was once a great hub. Long forgotten magicks powered this gate to various places across Una, so it was said. Even in my early days, it was only known as a distant legend.

"The Ashen One would have us perform a great ritual here. He will help us repurpose it to open a great rift directly to the Planes of Ash."

"How long will this repurposing take? The Tariganniens know of our position now. We may not have much time before the nation is upon us," Denloth questioned, still worried about the failure of his Oathbound earlier the previous night.

"The sooner the Tariganniens come, the sooner the ritual may begin. Through the desert haze Telenth has shown me how the rift may be activated.

"As Telenth has spent many souls in the building of his great Hell Gate, so too must souls be offered up here in Una to help power the rift. A great deal of blood and essence must be rendered for this ritual to be successful.

"The blood bead we have used to commune with our lord in the past will be the link between worlds, and the transfer of souls will be the catalyst used to initiate the rite to open the passage between realms.

"There will be an endless host awaiting on the other side—your brothers and sisters, Lunt—ready to ravage this world, reaping the spoils for the good of our god. All to blood, and blood to ash."

"All to blood, and blood to ash," the others droned in reflexive response, offering the prayer that all would soon offer once the land had been dominated and controlled by those few who would be left to survive in submission to their god.

29

THE EXPERIMENT OF EXTENDED SIGHT

"Cycle the watch," Kissa said to Naldurn, sending her Shadow off to pick six new scouts to relieve their comrades from duty along the dunes.

The day had come and gone, and all had been ordered to stay put, those few haltia that they did have in their company helping to keep a better eye on the surrounding highways far to the west and south, watching for activity along the roads which had remained clear and quiet.

"Do you think Rochata will pursue? We still have no report of movement north, west, or to the south of us. I had half expected that if they were in pursuit, that we would see some sign of them today," Kissa quietly asked of Hathos as he stood encircled by his centurions.

Hathos was quiet in thought, mulling over the same problem he had been working on all day, deciding on when to move out, and where to move to. No matter how long he tackled the subject, he could make no firm plans without also knowing the locations of those that pursued them and those they were pursuing.

"Gather Reza and her company. Henarus also," he announced at length, waiting for Kissa to rush to retrieve the large group.

Filtering in through the makeshift camp, Reza and the others made their way to the widening circle of leading officers, all waiting to see why Hathos had called them forth.

He did not keep them waiting for long. Once Henarus and his priest showed up, Hathos addressed them all, getting right to the point.

"Some of you I know very little about, and that goes with knowing the full extent of your abilities and potential. I need help, and I'm hoping one of you may hold a set of skills useful to giving me needed information."

Hathos' gaze turned to Zaren, the old enchanter that Hathos knew Sultan Metus had thought highly of.

"Master Zebulon. It is my understanding that you are an enchanter. Is that correct?"

Zaren grumpily nodded his approval of the assessment, Jadu wearily by his side, the desert heat having sapped him of his usual spunk, lingering through the day in the unforgiving dunes.

"Is it within your powers to scry?" Hathos probed.

The old man laughed, thrusting his open hands forward, exclaiming, "Does it look like I'm carrying a crystal ball with me? No. Scrying is an enchantment that requires many things, all of which would take much too long to go into here."

Hathos disliked the old man already. He continued, seeing what he could get out of the group.

"Prophet Henarus. Are you capable of sight beyond our current limitations? Haltia can see ten, thirteen miles at most it seems, much further than most of our sight here, but is there a way you can help them focus that sight further?"

Henarus brought a hand up to his jaw, reflecting on the idea, at length answering honestly, "I don't know. I can petition Hassome. Perhaps further clarity may be granted, but even then, he cannot bend light. The haltia that is touched with the focus of

Hassome would still only be able to see what is visible from their location. In other words, they wouldn't be able to see around mountains or tall dunes that obstruct the path of sight, regardless of how far-reaching their sight can be extended."

"Bending light—" Jadu mumbled, rolling the phrase over again and again on his tongue.

The prattling of the enchanter's apprentice halted the group's conversation, everyone eventually eyeing the little praven as he began pacing, stamping around in the dusty sandbank he was standing in.

"Jadu, settle yourself," Reza scolded harshly at the little annoyance, but to everyone's surprise, Zaren held up a hand to her, placing a silencing finger to his lips, quietly ordering all to not interrupt the heavy contemplation Jadu was obliviously engaged in.

"If light could bend, well then, perhaps we could see through what it was bent around. Yes, yes. That study was interesting, even my professors were too dim to understand my thesis, but that's beside the point. With extended vision, and warping light's path, one could see, well, around mountains if one had the sight to see that far. Possible we could exaggerate some of these heatwaves to do the trick. Shouldn't be too hard I suppose."

All had begun to listen to Jadu's rantings more closely, seeing that there was a possibility that the small praven might be on to a solution to the problem they all faced, though as to the details of his plan, they were all completely lost.

"You want to see farther than you should?" Zaren asked in a quiet and cryptic tone, snatching back everyone's attention. "I could help you see things you search for in ten different ways, but weaving the hex comes with a price, and for this cause, I would not risk it—myself.

"You do have Jadu, however. I'm excited to see how he tackles the problem. He is the reason I am even here with this godforsaken company. He needs real problems to solve, not the fabricated tests I've been putting him through all these months in the classroom and in studies. He may be able to help you, but—" Zaren paused, holding up a warning finger, "he is no master of the weave just yet. Proceed with caution. He may fail you—

extravagantly."

"Failing is part of the process. It's the key ingredient in the path to success," Jadu quipped, joining in the conversation now having thought through his calculations to a satisfied extent.

All in the large group hesitated to ask how the junior enchanter intended to help them, speculating they might regret utilizing the strange pair's aid.

Hathos gently cleared his throat, grabbing Jadu's attention.

"You can make it so that we can see beyond these dunes?"

Jadu held a finger in the air, opening his mouth to speak, but then recalled the thought. Folding his arms and bowing his head, he muttered, "Pretty sure," looking up to the group, exclaiming, "One can always make the attempt! Without the initial effort, nothing would ever progress."

Hathos looked to all members in the group, looking for validation for proceeding with Jadu's mysterious methods—no one offered it.

"Very well, what do you need for this...experiment?" he asked, feeling more unsure of the plan the longer it was discussed.

"The Hassome man—"

"—Prophet Henarus," Reza corrected

"Yes, yes. The prophet of Hassome. If he can indeed extend vision with his blessings, then he will be key to the procedure.

"Next, a haltia. Their vision is a remarkable innovation of nature. Their lenses are pristine—lovely ocular specimens they are. Using a haltia as our subject will net the greatest results.

"Lastly, myself! I won't bother running through the details of what plans I have in mind, but suffice it to say, if we position our haltia subject atop a tall dune during the main heat of day, with me at their side to weave the hex, then an altered vision should be granted."

Few were convinced, least of all Hathos, but Cavok, the large, quiet man Hathos barely knew, spoke up, vouching for the small one.

"Doesn't sound near as dangerous as his usual antics. Usually gets the job done. I'd give him a shot at it. Low risk, high reward—easy trade."

Hathos considered the stoic man's words, adjusting in place, slightly uncomfortable, at length agreeing. "The hour grows long. You said you require the heat of midday? Are you saying we need to wait for the returning sun tomorrow?"

"That would be favorable, yes," Jadu concurred, nodding his head vigorously.

"By then we may not need supernatural sight...," Hathos grumbled, slicking the sweat off his smooth dome, frustrated at the runaround.

"Well, if we still have not spotted any activity by then, we have his scheme as a backup," Arie suggested, trying to offer relief to the strained mood amidst the group.

Though none seconded the notion, Hathos only giving a slight nod to the whole thing, he called for all to return to their post and to continue their holding plan as before.

"If we still see no sign of arisen or Rochata by noonday tomorrow, we ride south. With or without Tarigannie's forces in tow, we need to find that damned force and put an end to it."

Throughout the night, Shadows came and went, scouts reporting nothing new as they returned late into the morning hours.

Hathos had not slept well that night, and it showed in his dealings with reports, his tone more terse than usual.

Kissa spoke, keeping her voice low in the quiet of the blistering morning heat.

"But why would we not see them make a move to follow? At this point, if they were to pursue, there should be some sign of trackers or scouts at the very least."

Hathos replied softly back, his nemes headdress protecting him from the scorching sun that shown down upon them.

"We have two enchanters, one that said he could easily extend sight, and even a student that seems sure he can as well. You think Rochata, as large and powerful as they are, don't also have those skilled enough with the hexweave to gain insight on our position? Perhaps they make no move on us because they see we hold here."

Crossing his arms, looking to the praven that held what little hope they had left of getting some clarity on their enemy's positions, he admitted, "I don't know. Perhaps it is that—perhaps it is not. Regardless, we need to let this *Jadu* make his attempt he's been talking up. With luck, he will come through for us."

Kissa continued to listen to Hathos' line of reasoning until he asked, "Have you a haltia that is willing to volunteer to work with him?"

She looked uneasily to her superior, turning to inspect the eccentric one immersed in his notes.

"I will volunteer. If there is harm to come from being associated with this endeavor, I will take the risk. I won't buck it to those that serve under me."

Hathos did not seemed pleased by the decision but could not argue that he would not have made the same choice if he were in her position.

The two walked over to the praven, ready to see if he would indeed be able to make good on the results he had promised the evening before.

Jadu had been busily preparing for his experiment, engrossed in a few travel books and pads that he flipped through, scribbling stray notes here and there, more entertained than he had been throughout the majority of their trek so far.

"Jadu, are you ready?" Hathos asked, the military man's size and presence greatly overshadowing Jadu's small frame, though if Jadu was intimidated by the looming presence, he showed no trace of it.

"All should be in order, yes. The sun is high; the air—scorching. I am ready," he chattered out.

"Then let us gather Henarus," Hathos answered, looking for the prophet as he spoke.

"And Reza," Jadu threw in.

Hathos looked back to the praven, asking concernedly, "Why Reza?"

Jadu replied in a quick string of words. "For her healing ability, of course. Just in case something goes wrong. Always risks, you know, when trying anything new and experimental. Just want to have her there as a precaution. Surely we won't need her, but...we should bring her."

Hathos looked to Kissa, the two sharing a worried look before ordering the praven to grab his things and to meet them up on the highest dune just to the north of them.

Within half an hour, Hathos and Kissa, along with Reza, Henarus, and his priest, Josiah, sluggishly made their way up the steep, sandy dune, the heat of the desert sun making the trek truly miserable.

Jadu and Zaren awaited there, Jadu holding forth a tome before him, excited to begin the experiment, the old enchanter less so.

"Considerable effort is required for performing such a spell. A great deal of concentration. I'm wondering, Henarus, might I receive a blessing from your priest as you pray over our haltia here?" Jadu queried, motioning to Kissa.

"I can do that," Josiah agreed, speaking for himself.

"Good. Now then, I'll need the haltia to stand here at the peak," Jadu began.

"My name is Kissa, little praven," Kissa chided, giving him a glance that would have put the worry of death in anyone else, but Jadu brushed it off, correcting himself.

"Kissa. Never heard a name like yours," he said, continuing with his instructions after the slight interruption.

"Priest—" Jadu started.

"—Josiah," the man corrected. Jadu waved him off, quite over the menial details the group was being so picky with.

"You'll be praying over me, *hopefully* helping with my clarity of thought...if there is anything to your religious convictions and power. I've sure heard enough to be hesitant to doubt it's all myths."

Pointing to Henarus, he said, "Prophet, you will be praying over Kissa here to increase her tremendous vision."

He then looked back to Reza, adding, "You be ready to help if something goes wrong."

Reza scowled at the recklessness she had come to expect of the man, but he was on to Hathos before Reza could contest.

"Sir...you just stand back, you don't really even need to be here."

"Zaren...," he started, deciding at the last moment to skip giving any orders to his mentor, opening his book back up as he held it up.

"Okay. I'll take care of the rest once the blessings are upon us. Ready to start when you two are, followers of Hassome."

With that, everyone thoroughly ruffled and slightly confused as to what exactly was about to happen, Henarus looked to Josiah, both nodding their head, holding hands over both Kissa and Jadu's head.

"Ah!" Jadu yelped, waving his hands frantically, all worried that something had already gone awry.

"Almost forgot," he said, fishing around in his robes, producing a pair of smoky glasses, handing them to Kissa, ordering, "Wear these over your eyes...just as a precaution. Wouldn't want 'em to burn out of your skull!"

She flippantly snatched the shades from the junior enchanter, putting them on as Henarus and Josiah took a deep breath, placing hands on their heads once again.

The chanting echoed in unison, the hymn of faith weaving with each other to create a strangely soothing sound. The men's voices quickly reverenced all there, and even though the majority of the blessing was being bestowed upon Kissa and Jadu, the others began to feel the effects of the blessing as well.

All in the circle began to feel a oneness—a peacefulness that stilled the tumultuous thoughts and feelings that had just moments ago, cluttered the mind.

Everything seemed more crisp, not just thought, but physical sensations as well—heightened to their peak.

Kissa's sight was expanded, all the haze along the atmosphere clearing, the tones becoming more vibrant, shapes in the distance having more depth and contrast to them; and as her lenses continued to focus, she could see further into the distance, seeing far across the desert plains to the mountain ranges days away from them.

Jadu sped up—*if that was even possible*. He flipped wildly through his spell book, dropped it, and produced a notebook within an instant, chattering senselessly as he looked blankly forward, churning calculations over on his tongue before snapping his fingers, going silent.

Plucking a wand from his sleeve, holding it high in the air, his large robe cuffs falling down over his face, he chanted incoherent word after word, the ground around them beginning to shake.

A burning hot gust of wind rushed out in all directions, followed by a cold blast up above it, rippling flat the heatwaves flaring in the distance. The ripples soon turned to waves in the air, growing taller as they traveled from crest to trough.

The distortions in the air grew, warping the view from their vantage point, bending their sight far above the surrounding dunes, allowing them to see up and over many of the obstructions blocking their sight from view.

Kissa turned slowly, scanning the warped horizons, awestruck at the sight before her, seeing through the warped lens the region tens-of-miles in all directions.

Jadu trembled, his wand glowing angrily as he continued blasting forth waves of scalding and chilled winds.

A hand patted his trembling shoulder, Zaren looking down on his pupil with a warning eye to watch his exertion with the spell.

Whipping the wand around in a growing circle, he cut the spell off, the tip of the wooden stick sizzling and hissing from the heat as Jadu fell to his knees, breathing heavily as he attempted to steady the swirling world around him.

"I could see the arisen, and the Rochatan army," Kissa breathed, still overwhelmed by the sights she had taken in and the rush of the blessing that had briefly been bestowed upon her.

Jadu only half heard the announcement as he plummeted limply to the burning sands at the peak of the dune.

30

THE SULLEN CANYON

Dust swirled as Malagar touched down on the canyon floor. The shelf they had dropped down from was high. There was no return for them. He hoped they would eventually find a path out at the end of the canyon's run.

Helping to catch Lanereth as she lowered from the shelf, he looked around their surroundings as she righted herself.

The canyon stretched on for a hundred yards or so before weaving around the bend. It was roughly thirty-feet deep, just enough to make it difficult to find an exit, most of the ledges and walls jagged and vertical, very few slopes issuing down into the crack in the ground.

There were black and orange vines of some sort, flat-topped mushrooms fanning out from them, covering the ground and walls.

Malagar was starving. It had been days since he had eaten. It was the same for Lanereth, save for the trail rations she had just had before the tower. His mouth salivated at the sight of the fungus that resembled the closest thing to food they had seen the entire time in the hellscape.

He plucked one from a vine, it creepily recoiling slightly at the motion. He stepped back, waiting, watching the vine to ensure that it wasn't going to attack him.

"Don't eat that!" Lanereth scolded, keeping her eyes cautiously on the vine as she stepped closer to him.

"We're dead eventually if we don't eat," was his simple reply, gnawing off the leathery cap that flapped slightly upon touch, testing it in his mouth for a bit, chewing laboriously before swallowing.

He went for more, snatching off cap after cap, shoving them in Lanereth's hands, ordering her to store some in the leather pockets as he wrestled the tangle of vines that sluggishly jumped and retracted from the assault.

"Eat," Malagar issued as Lanereth looked to the writhing vine, stripped of its fruit. She trembled, holding up a cap, sniffing its leathery surface.

Looking to Malagar, who continued feasting upon the strange fungus, she took a nibble, having to chew hard to tear a bite from it.

"Just eat," he said, as he helped stuff more caps into her pockets. "If they're poison, we're dead. If we don't eat them, we're dead. One death is quicker, that's all. If they're edible, then we may have a chance at surviving a bit longer, perhaps long enough to find a way out of this hell."

She had stopped chewing as he spoke, and the hopelessness of it all seemed to weigh heavier on her then than ever.

"Can there possibly be a way out of this hell?" she asked, swallowing the disgusting fruit down as it wriggled inside her throat weakly.

"There was a way in—" Malagar answered, holding another cap up for her to take.

After a moment, his words lifting her slightly, she took the sorry excuse for food and bit hard into it, chewing angrily, the two moving on from the living vine.

Ash had begun to fall later that day, and the ravine began to show signs of development. Bones were scattered, some morphing in with the ashen rock along the walls and floor, and face-sized nodes stuck out of the walls as if looking at them, watching those who entered.

They had not liked the looks of their new surroundings, much preferring the benign network of vines they had passed through earlier, but the canyon walls were high, and Malagar knew that the canyon's end led around the city, and if they were to get out prematurely, they'd come up dangerously close to the residence of the twisted civilization. They needed to see it through and stick to the safer route.

Around a bend in the canyon marked a drastic change in tone. The walls bled a dark, red sap, weeping out pores like the canyon itself was sick, trying to expel toxins.

Faces, torn in agony of all different creatures slowly pushed at the rock face as though it were a heavy sheet. The slow scratching of claws and bone on rock quietly sounded through the whole canyon.

Entrails pumped through holes in the wall, creating a living network of vines and membranes that grew into the cracks and floor of the canyon.

"I don't want to go through there," Lanereth whispered, eyes locked on the horror before her, completely exhausted at that point of it all, not hiding her fear of the corridor in the least.

Malagar looked just as uneasy as she did, but he had seen how close the canyon ran to the city.

"If we surface, and even one of those demons find us...," he left off, knowing there was little chance of them outrunning or hiding from such a gathering of the malevolent giants.

They looked down the hell corridor a moment longer, frozen in place, neither wanting to move a step further.

"It looks like it ends further up," Malagar hopefully suggested, pointing to the weaving trail a hundred yards further up the canyon, the faces upon the walls there remaining stationary and looking less defined, returning to the nondescript rock nodes they had just passed, the ooze and vines lightening as well.

"You first, then," Lanereth said, waiting for Malagar to set foot on the bloodstained floors.

He looked to both walls, watching for reactions from both directions as he stepped into the red canyon.

He tread softly, the slick, spongy surface he walked upon sticking to his boots as he walked deeper into the nightmare, but he kept pace, and remained focused ahead, keeping aware of his periphery as the faces and hands reached out for him on either side.

Seeing that she was getting left behind, Lanereth started forward, following Malagar's footsteps, the sappy, congealed blood squelching beneath her as she moved to catch up.

Her senses were pulsating, and at first, she was not sure whether she was panicking or if something was wrong; if the place they had stepped foot in was actually assaulting her mind.

The squelch and scratching grew louder in her ears, and Malagar, who was only a few steps ahead, began to blur in and out of her sight. The red along the walls began to flow together, sickening her and throwing off her balance.

She wavered and stumbled before catching herself. She stood in place for a moment to make sure she righted herself before moving on, watching as Malagar continued forward steadfastly, seemingly unaffected by the waves of disorientation she was withstanding.

"Mal...," she slurred out, holding a hand up for aid, but none came. He kept onwards, as if in a trance, walking forward like a machine, disappearing out of her blurred vision.

She stumbled forward, forcing herself to take sluggish steps, each requiring a monumental effort, more so than the one before. The noise in her ears of the cries of the stone faces, the sloshing of her boots, and the scratching at the walls writhing around in her brain louder and louder, were driving her mad, setting a flaming itch in her skull that caused her to gasp for breath.

There was a shade behind her, she *felt* more than *saw*. Eyes, sullen, mournful—hateful—bearing down on her, hovering just inches over her shoulder.

It easily kept up with her debilitated pace. She struggled for breath, jerkily taking steps, inching her way forward as she let out short coughs and whimpers.

The shroud floated closer, strands, black vines, and misshapen bones reaching out, creeping closer to her unprotected head.

She felt its chill presence, the penetration of its eyes digging into her, weakening her.

She could see Malagar again, only for a moment, and she saw there was a cloak following him as well, tethered behind him, reaching for him.

She didn't want to turn and face hers. She didn't want to look into those eyes she knew were there, waiting to snare her in complete despair.

She reached a trembling hand up to her chest, gripping her pendant. It was warm. The only warmth she had now.

She slowly turned around, pendant in hand, shoving it out to the horror of souls, and all the chaos of the walls shrunk as Lanereth held it forth.

The shade retracted its claws. Its eyes that at first lanced through Lanereth in an overwhelming wave of fatigue, broke its gaze, not being able to hold its lock on the woman in the face of the relic, looking down to the ground and floating off before dissipating into the haze of the ashfall.

The debilitating aura from the shade suddenly drained from her mind and body like a plug had been pulled, emptying her of the neurotic effect.

She struggled forward, drained from the experience, but in control of her senses once more. She moved in on the shade that hung over Malagar, like a death shroud latched onto his flagging body as it slowly marched forward.

Holding up her amulet, she pressed it towards the chilling mantle. It gently recoiled from them, floating away into the shadows, causing Malagar to stop his march and turn to see Lanereth standing there before him.

"Go, we're almost there," she prompted, her voice weak and struggling.

He wrapped an arm around her for support and the two hobbled out of the red-slick corridor and back into the ashen canyon that bore no faces.

31

REPOSITION AND PREPARE

Reza walked into the circle of friends that tended to Jadu, who lay atop a bedspread, Cavok holding up a palm frond for shade as Terra prayed over him as he snoozed comfortably.

Zaren stood by, unconcerned at his student's condition, having declared that he'd be fine with some rest and that he just overexerted himself in the spell. That didn't allay everyone else's concerns for him, even Reza.

"How's he doing?" she asked, nudging her way in between Cavok and Arie.

Terra ended her prayer, looking up to the saren and shrugged her shoulders, replying, "Elendium does not answer my prayer of health, so I assume he is, as master Zaren said, 'just tuckered.'"

Reza looked upon the comfortably dozing praven for a moment, her worries over him subsiding, then announced to the group the news she had come to deliver.

"Hathos wants everyone packed and ready to ride within the

hour. Whatever Jadu and Henarus did up there worked, and Kissa claims to know the location of not just the arisen army, but multiple Tarigannie forces on the move across the region. We're going to need to relocate."

"Where's the arisen army?" Arie asked.

"Close by, actually. Just south of us, not even a half day's ride. They did not take the highway, they march along the skirts of the dunes. Once Kissa's sight was augmented, she was quickly able to spot them. The force is large. More than what we'll be able to consider contending with. We will require the Tarigannie forces if we hope to win," Reza reported.

"So then, where are the Tarigannie forces?" Cavok asked, tossing the frond as Jadu sleepily snorted, sitting up, stretching out as he came to.

"There's a few. A small force comes from the fort south of us. They already seem aware of the arisen army and are positioned nearby.

"Then there's two coming from Rochata-Ung. A cavalry unit, a bit larger of a force than the one that collected the prisoners from us the other day. They're positioned northeast of us further up the dunes.

"The second is an infantry unit. That one's the large one. A thousand to two thousand soldiers. They're marching on the road south to Daloth's Ribs. My guess is they are attempting to cut us off, surrounding us from behind, and with Fort Wellspring south of us, I suppose they were in no hurry as we'd come upon the fort and been intercepted if we had continued south.

"There's also a mounted force crossing the Dolinger Crags," she explained, looking once again to Jadu who had been rubbing his eyes sleepily.

"So, the experiment worked?" the praven asked, standing up wobbly.

"Indeed, my young one," Zaren answered for her, giving a crooked, slight smirk of pride at his performance that day. "Your marriage of science and enchantment is, dare I say, impressive at times."

Jadu smiled at the praise, and all present gave him the moment, knowing how rare a thing it was for Zaren to be giving compliments.

"So where are we headed?" Cavok asked after the pause.

"Yes," Reza grunted, shifting in place, getting back to the matter at hand. "Hathos believes that Rochata-Ung's forces needs to see the arisen army for themselves, so we're going to have to get somewhat close to Sha'oul's force. We'll move to the dune's edge and trail them from a distance. The infantry force should intersect the force regardless as they come south, but the cavalry, they're the ones I worry will not believe us on our word of the looming threat. They'll need to see the arisen army for themselves, and so, if they want to engage us, we have to be close enough to the arisen army to force them to behold the enemy within their borders."

The plan sunk in with everyone for a moment before Arie whispered, "We near the end of all of this."

Her words lingered for a moment, all coming to terms that war was inevitable at that point, and they were currently just at the edge of the storm.

"Good," Cavok gruffed. "I'm ready to smash that sonofabitch arisen's face in for all the trouble he's put us through. We might finally get Nomad back."

"Let's hope he's reclaimable," Reza distantly said, the slightest tremble of hope in her voice for the outcome.

"Ready up," she said, coming back to the moment. "Only a few miles left to our journey."

32
ALONG THE RIDGES

"Eighty men, all passing Daloth's Ribs now. Paari, the officer I sent to collect them, rode ahead to report that they should be here before nightfall," Kaylic whispered, sneaking up next to Durmont, Jezebel, and the scout that was on duty watching the ruins far across the highway.

They had a good vantage point from their camp, and along the crests they had stationed sentries, keeping low and out of sight, watching the activity of the dead army as the days wore on, very little activity ever occurring amidst the totem-like figures that stood along the outskirts of the site.

"Supplies?" Durmont asked, hoping that the neighboring town had been kind enough to send as much aid as they could.

"They're all on horseback, though they only brought a few ten tethered. Some food and drink, though no spare weapons. They brought what they will use for battle, nothing more," Kaylic answered.

Durmont gazed over the still scene down in the valley a

moment longer in reflection of the report, tapping Jezebel on the shoulder as they backed out of the perch, leaving the sentry there to keep watch.

"Now we wait for Lõrinc to return with, hopefully, a force worthy of facing that necropolis down there," he said to the both of them, making their way back to the army's camp tucked in the foothills of the sloping mountain range.

"What if they do not send enough troops?" Jezebel asked, seeing the mere three hundred fort soldiers camped amongst the boulders at the base of the hills, knowing Durmont's men, coupled with the eighty villagers on their way up from the closest town to the south would make little impact on the formidable horde that was stationed not but two miles east of them, nothing but a small ridge hiding them from view.

"If they don't send enough to openly confront the arisen..." he paused, mulling over the options he had been giving thought to the last few days, "then we will wait for them to make the first move and react. If they don't, then I will return to Rochata myself. Let's hope I do not have to do that. Heads would roll along the judges' floor at their dereliction of duty."

"Speak of the devil," Kaylic exclaimed, looking to the camp, seeing a horseman ride in through the back canyons from the highway. "I do believe that's Lõrinc."

Durmont hastened back to camp with Kaylic and Jezebel close behind, the three smiling to see that it was the chief, returned from his mission, the captain desperate for updates and news on the hopeful Rochatan support.

"Tell me you bring good news," Durmont entreated, helping the man down from his horse, handing the reins to Kaylic to deal with as he guided Lõrinc with Jezebel into camp.

The chief's expression told of good news even before he replied. Though he seemed exhausted from the long journey, he returned the smile that hinted at success as he gave a reply.

"I didn't even make it to Rochata before I intercepted an infantry battalion—a large one—close to two thousand. I spoke with the lead colonel. They were headed south chasing a Plainstate threat. It seems other states have been active as of late in our region. Not sure if that other faction is truly a hindrance or help, but I briefed them on the arisen threat and of our current situation, and they plan to continue south along the highway to inspect for themselves. They will send liaisons once they're here later tonight. We should be able to begin coordinating a strategy of attack."

Durmont kept a stern face during the report, asking, "Two thousand you say? We will still need more than that I fear to face them head on. I've been studying their army. There's an assortment of horrors within their ranks, large beasts, ferocious looking. They have done well to keep hidden mostly, but we've spotted them in the shadows from time to time. Their force is no simple matter of outnumbering. We will need a strategical advantage if we hope to level them."

Lõrinc knocked back gulps of water from his canteen, nodding his head as he wiped his mouth with his sleeve.

"There's another detachment of cavalry east of them in the dunes. They're chasing the Plainstate company. We might be able to get word to them to join in on the effort as well. They should be closing in daily in our direction," Lõrinc replied, catching his breath before adding, "With what the sarens were saying about having come here to face this threat, I wouldn't be surprised if that company our men are chasing are here for the exact same purpose. If that's the case, they too would be potential allies to this extermination."

"That...is better. Still, we'll be outnumbered if our numbers are correct. But that is good to hear. We'll need to send riders out promptly to begin a network for this effort. Without communication, it seems we hold the disadvantage in a confrontation as it stands."

"Give the word and I will send riders to all parties to begin coordinations," Lõrinc said, Jezebel adding, "We will help with the Plainstate communications."

The two looked at her, Durmont calculating how wise that was for them to trust the relatively unknown group to take on such a pivotal task. If they botched it, and the Plainstate became hostile with them, that would be an additional problem they did not need to be dealing with at the present.

"Yozo, the man with us, and the others we had teamed up

with to fight the arisen the first time, they have ties to the Plainstate. If luck serves us, then perhaps they even know this mysterious detachment your men are chasing. Yozo is a good rider, unmatched in combat. He could act as our diplomat," Jezebel explained.

"Perhaps that is best," Durmont approved, agreeing to both suggestions.

"We'll proceed as such. See that our riders are out of camp as soon as possible. We have given our enemy too much time to prepare already. Let's see that they are given no further advantage."

33
THE MOUTH OF HELL

Rain lightly drizzled along the canyon's brim, and from their location at the edge of the rise, they had a good view of the surrounding terrain.

Safely under a low, but wide, canopy of leathery mushroom tops that overhung the cliff wall they huddled against, Malagar scanned the movement of the various demons that were migrating from the city to the shining light that had also drawn them forth.

There was a draw in such light in a place as this. It was a sign of something different, of potential change and hope. He wondered if even the wretches of this vile place constantly hungered for the chance of change, the potential for hope—anything to grant them more than what they had here in this hell. The draw to escape its sullen atmosphere ever gnawing at them.

They sipped from the flask of slightly acidic water as they rested, gnawing on some of the leathery fruits they had pocketed further back, not wanting to agitate the mushrooms they currently were using as shelter by attempting to snack on them as well.

"They move to the light," he noted, pointing to the thousands of distant dots that moved in herds up the sloping shelf towards the beacon at the edge of the plateau.

"Then we'll need to keep close to those rocks along the edge of the shelf to stay hidden if we dare hope to get close to whatever that light is," Lanereth said between mouthfuls of mushroom fruit.

"We are getting closer…," Malagar distantly mentioned, looking with squinted eyes at the blinding light that was now only a few miles from them.

"Can you see what it might be yet?" Lanereth asked, holding up her hand to shield the light that shown down from the rise above them.

"It's a monument of some sort. I can make tall statues out. The light is coming from some sort of structure. Hard to say. I can't see much detail with how blinding it is," he said, looking away, rubbing his eyes from staring at the blinding light for too long.

"Even at a slow pace, that distance is maybe a day away," Lanereth said wistfully, worried what possible hope they might cling to after that if they arrived at the light to find no lead to their liberation from the realm.

"Yeah, seems about the way of it. Hopefully we don't run into any more specters…," he added, leaving the thought to linger, both still not having yet discussed the living nightmare they had trudged through earlier in the canyon. That was a trauma undoubtedly they would need to unpack and work through some other time, if they ever had the privilege of focusing on anything but survival. Until then, they both seemed to think it best to leave that event forgotten and behind them.

"Hope Wyld finds her way," Lanereth said, looking back to the towers in the distance, the ash and rain tumultuously mixing to create a muddy swirl of foul weather, obscuring all but the closest structures.

"I do too," he added, looking back for a moment, before testing a hand out from under the mushroom canopy, finding that the rains had passed them by.

"Well, it's not far now. We'd better get to that light before the masses down there do. You ready?" he asked, offering her a hand up from the uneven rocks they had been resting on.

She accepted his hand, though had no answer for him. She was afraid to place too much hope in the light.

The day had been relatively calm, the hike through the boulders being difficult at times, but with no further rain showers, and no other creature sightings, it was simply a scramble through most of the day that they had to undertake, and that was a struggle they both did not mind, especially now that their bellies were filled with food and drink.

The closer they came to the beacon along the rise, the clearer they could see the statues around it, though, they did not know if that was a good thing.

The light ripped into existence from within a framework of bone. An archway of massive proportions, hundreds of feet high, held together with ivory belonging to every size of creature imaginable, formulated a gate that was undergoing some sort of action that warped the fabric of reality before their eyes, churning over and over on itself, attempting to stabilize.

The statues loomed a hundred feet high, and sat upon thrones, robed in rippling cloth made of a substance similar to the faces in the wall they had passed earlier, souls bound within, slowly morphing through its creases, silently screaming, ever searching for a way out.

Luckily, they could only see the backs of the figures. Even then, they avoided eye contact with the looming monuments, afraid to look too long at the shadowy cowls.

The horde of pit spawn had been slow to the monuments, even *they* seeming to fear the line of statues that looked down upon the path leading to the light. For the time being, they were at bay, and the two made their way around the rock fields to the side of the huge structure that shown forth its golden light across the hellish land.

Malagar froze at the edge of the outcropping, turning to see Wyld quietly making her way through the last of the boulders to set paw out into the clearing, walking up to the base of the structure.

"Wyld!" Malagar urgently whispered.

The kaith didn't seem to hear his warning voice, and her Seam scar flared along the small remaining part of her corporeal body.

They looked down the path to the hellish creatures lining up along the rows of statues to see if any had taken note of Wyld as she strolled out towards the base of the gate. All were in a trance, standing silently, swaying erratically, staring straight ahead. The strange image sent a chill down their spine.

Malagar sprinted out after her, Lanereth following reluctantly behind, running up the old steps to the mouth of the gate. The massive arch of bone had lattices tacked to its side and base which stretched all the way up its several hundred feet, old structures looming over them, threatening to topple on top of them at any moment.

Wyld entered one of the hovels of bone, huddling with arms around her knees while looking to the ground, rocking back and forth.

Malagar and Lanereth caught up, kneeling beside her, Malagar gently touching the only part of her arm that still remained fully in their realm, the rest of her fading, flickering between places.

His forearm burned, a memory of the bite she had given him weeks ago reminding him of the sting of the Seam he had often felt. It seemed to be inexorably tied to his fate, and he wondered, was his destiny going to look similar to Wyld's?

"I don't know how much longer she's going to be with us, Lanereth. Regardless of if we find a way out of this hell or not. Wyld's existence is...becoming less sound."

Lanereth could hear the worry in her companion's voice. He cared greatly for the kaith, she could tell. And though she had sympathy for her, she knew of nothing she could do to help, even with the direct aid of Sareth.

The Seam was a place of confusion, unknowns, and danger, even for the gods themselves. It was potentially one of the only things that could wipe their immortal presences from the planes of Wanderlust permanently; and because of that, none but reckless mortals flirted with it.

She looked up to the mouth of the gate above them as light strobed down over the countryside, flashing brighter, tendrils of warped dimensional matter reaching out to latch on to the frame of bones around it.

The sunlight splashed into the alcove of bones they were in, illuminating them, warming them like the Tarigannie sun used to do, flooding them with distant memories of their past lives in Una, when they had been in a land that still made sense, that had more than endless suffering and pain—a land they had sought so hard to return to.

The rift inched open, widening every passing minute. The three sat there, surrounded by bones on all sides, waiting for whatever was to come with the rift's completion.

With the warm rays that flowed down like light from the heavens basking them, Lanereth laid herself out flat on the ground, completely exhausted, feeling numb and oddly enough, at peace, even though her body was wrecked.

A tear ran down her cheek as she smiled, gladly awaiting what was to come through that gate, knowing comfortably that nothing—no other realm—could possibly be worse than the one they were currently in.

34
THE NIGHT RIDER

Yozo rode east, just north of the ruins the arisen camped at. He could see the dust of a large host making their way towards him along the highway. Surely that was the brigade of soldiers the captain had told him about.

They had been desperate for him to make the connection with the Plainstate force. He knew the sultan and his band had made plans to be here, and though he had his opinions about the sultan, he didn't doubt for a moment their motives were aligned with the Tariganniens and were here to wipe out the arisen.

The last scout to ride at his side, the one destined for Rochata-Ung's cavalry unit, turned to look his way, saluting after making eye contact, then riding off into the dunes as the sun began to set, casting orange hues along the ridges as the cool blue shadows slowly overtook the warm colors of day.

He had been swept up in a war of nations; a war of worlds really. For years, his drive and enemy were clear—simple. Kazuhiro Kasaru, the one the people of this nation had known as *Nomad*, had left his life in ruins, and he had vowed to exact vengeance upon him for it. But what had that brought him? All those years hunting the man only seemed to keep the wounds of his past and his misery fresh and burning brighter than ever. He grew tired of the pain, the miserable solitude, the depression of it all. He hadn't cared if he was dead or living for most of his travels, only that Hiro received punishment at his hand one day.

Things, for the first time in years, felt...different now. *He* felt different. There were others that knew him, if only for a short time, but Fin...he did not wish to displease the man. Him and Matt had helped him, spoke with him as though he were a person, not like all others who saw him as a rat foreigner, a vagabond, no consideration given to him.

He had received beatings, spat upon, jailed for simply walking a street. He despised people—but this group he had fallen in with, did seem to have a bond, and he could feel that they were extending their hand to him. He just hoped that all the damage that he had received throughout the years of being on the road would not cause him to ruin their invitation. He struggled with his own self-destructive faults, and he didn't know how much his companions could take of his pessimism and aversions. Their convictions were so sure, while his were tender—hesitant.

He knew one thing, though. He trusted Fin and Malagar—the sarens too, though they had shorter tempers with him. They were invested in this cause to put an end to Sha'oul, and so he would fight for that cause as well. It was, perhaps, the first unselfish thing he had pledged himself to in a long while, ever since Hiro had....

He snapped his horses reins sharply, spurring it on over a dune. The night was coming on, and if he were to find the Plainstate contingent, he would need to hasten his flight.

"Naldurn sent word of a lone rider headed our way from the west. She'll be seeing him into camp soon," Kissa interrupted, running up to Hathos who had been discussing tactics with Reza, the rest of the camp generally already bedded for the night.

"A terms agent from Rochata perhaps?" Reza suggested, clipping her sword and strapping some of her armor back on as she motioned for Gale and Jasper to her side as they followed Kissa and Hathos to the front lines to meet the scout and rider at the edge of camp.

The moon had well been on its path across the night sky by that point, and the group struggled to make out the silhouettes of the riders as they made their way over ridge after ridge.

"Jasper, Gale. Keep sharp. See that our *guest* behaves themselves."

"Oh, I'll make sure of that," Kissa said, stringing her bow as they waited for the riders to descend the last ridge and gallop the stretch of open desert to their location.

"Is that...," Reza mouthed in disbelief, staring hard at the man Naldurn rode up with at her side.

"I don't believe this," she muttered, drawing a questioning gaze from all others.

She had no time to explain as the two rode up to the group, taking the lead as she knew no one else knew the man but her.

"Yozo? What are you doing here?" she asked, baffled by the surprise appearance of the man she had least suspected to see that night. "If you're looking for Nomad, he's not here. He left our company many days ago."

"No, I've given up that hunt—for now at least. There's more important matters at hand."

Reza stepped closer, motioning for Kissa to lower her bow. "What could possibly be more important to you than snatching Hiro?" she questioned as the man dismounted, Naldurn eyeing him cautiously.

Yozo considered the question, giving his response some thought before answering sincerely. "The people of this land are in danger, and they are finally waking up to realize it. I...have decided to join the resistance against Sha'oul. If left unchecked, his force will bring about a great deal of destruction, suffering, and death among many nations."

Reza looked hard at the man, her trust in his words wary. "You have never seemed one to worry for others, and you have let us down in the past, Yozo, so forgive me if I don't immediately trust you on the matter."

"I understand. You are not wrong to consider me anything but an enemy; but Fin and Matt...they changed my mind on many things—helped me see how empty my life would continue to become if I did not cease my pursuit of Hiro. I am trying to follow a new path.

"Whether you choose to believe me or not is another matter, however. I come bearing news from the captain of the Tarigannie fort south of here."

"Wait, Fin? When were you with Finian?" Reza quizzed, cutting off Hathos who had looked as though he were going to ask a question as soon as the Tarigannie forces were mentioned.

"We had been traveling together for the last few weeks, fighting the arisen. We parted ways not but a few days ago. He was heading to the Plainstate to gather forces to help combat Sha'oul and his army," Yozo answered plainly.

"Thank the gods he's alive," Reza offered a thankful prayer, quizzing the man again before Hathos had a chance to ask about the Tarigannie forces.

"How did you meet up with Fin? He went to recruit a friend and we haven't heard from him since. I've been worried sick over him. What happened?"

"It is a long story, Reza. What I can say tonight is that I have traveled with your companion, Fin, for some time now. We met up with some sarens seeking Sha'oul's destruction. We were defeated. Many casualties, but I carried on with him and a few of the surviving sarens and joined up with the company at Fort Wellspring. Once our report of the arisen army checked out, they took us on, and we've been providing aid and information as we've tracked Sha'oul until now.

"I'm here tonight to offer an alliance to you and your company. It is clear we are all here for the same purpose; to eradicate the arisen army, and I will vouch for your band as I've been in your councils. I know your motives are well placed.

"I will relay this to Captain Durmont. With the two Rochatan companies to the west and east of us, Durmont's men, and yours, we may stand a fighting chance at mounting an assault on the force on the morrow."

"Wait," she held out a hand, holding off Hathos' attempt at getting a word in. "You ride with saren? Where are they from?"

"Yes...," Yozo hesitated, knowing Reza shared blood with his recent companions, not enjoying the idea of being the one to deliver the news that their force had been badly decimated by Sha'oul. "A saren High Priest named Lanereth led our charge. Eleven in her group they numbered before our battle with Sha'oul. Three they number now. I am sorry, but many fell by his hand and the claws of his minions."

"Lanereth...," Reza fretted, trembling slightly at her fears coming true that the sarens in question were that of her own order.

"And what three saren do you still ride with, Yozo?"

Yozo could tell Reza was affected by the news. His tone was mournful as he made known the list of saren that survived the slaughter in the temple.

"Revna, Jezebel, and Alva remain with us."

Seeing her turn away, hiding the tears that began to well up in her eyes, he added, "Though Lanereth's fate is not necessarily sealed. She was whisked away in a rift to the Planes of Ash. There is no telling what has become of her from there."

"Sareth save her," she whispered before taking a few steps away from the group, needing some space to recollect herself and to take in the news.

Hathos watched her for a moment, hoping she was able to come to terms with the announcement, but knowing there were matters at hand that he needed to discuss with the spokesman.

"You are saying that the Tarigannie military is wanting to ally with us to aid in an attack on the arisen army tomorrow?" he asked.

"That's the short of it. Yes. Captain Durmont is proceeding under the assumption that you are here to face Sha'oul. He sent riders to the Rochatan armies to spread the word of the alliance and of the plans for an attack on the morrow. Revna will send a flare into the heavens sometime after noonday. Look for the sign from the ridge along the east of the ruins. That will be the sign that all riders have returned and all companies have agreed to the plan.

"At that time, you and Rochata's cavalry will enter the ruins where Sha'oul hides from the east. Fort Wellspring will split, attacking both north and south ends of the ruins, and Rochata's infantry unit will drive in from the west.

"We're outnumbered still, the arisen army numbers close to four thousand. Together we only number three thousand," Yozo answered, explaining the orders he had been given.

"Why press the attack if we're outmanned? You said the arisen are holed up in the ruins. Couldn't we request the full might of the Rochatan military to ensure our victory?" Hathos drilled the man, concerned with their odds and strategy.

Yozo nodded his head in understanding, explaining, "The warlord is at work within the ruins. Some ritual is being performed, and Durmont does not think we have much time to wait. He does not wish to allow the enemy further time for their preparations and rites. Call it a gut feeling, but I have seen the ritual glow of runes along the two tall pillars at night, and it does bespeak power; a power that if we let continue in its dark construction, may become too much for even a sizeable number of reinforcements to answer. Durmont believes we need to make our move tomorrow."

Hathos thought on the man's reasonings, looking to Jasper as he sorted through his options. "I guess we don't have the privilege of talking this through with this *Durmont*, do we."

Yozo didn't answer, Hathos eventually reluctantly agreeing to the terms laid before him. "If Tarigannie rides to face the arisen on the morrow's evening, then the Plainstate will join the effort— and may the hearts of all the men and women, and all the gods that we follow, be stronger than the hate that binds our enemy to their cause."

Yozo bowed, honoring the Hyperium primus' words and answer, returning to his horse just as Arie and Cavok showed up from the shadows of the night, Arie with a look of surprise, and Cavok with a glare that promised death to the man if the two had happened to be alone in the dunes that night.

Yozo met the man's glare but showed no recognition of the feud between the two, snapping on his horse's reins, turning it off into a gallop back the way he had come, disappearing over the dunes as quickly as he had arrived.

Hathos took note of the two that had approached, looking to

Reza as she returned to them after Yozo's departure.

"We got what we were hoping for. The Tarigannie military will fight alongside us, though, the numbers of the arisen force do concern me. This will be no easy war to win," he spoke aloud to all present.

Metus met the eyes of each there, gauging their readiness to the cause they had signed on to.

"Get some rest tonight. Tomorrow we prepare for battle. Tomorrow we go to war with the spawn of hell."

35
THE LAST DAY FOR MANY

"The blood-red glow of dark magic set the monoliths alight all night, Captain," Scars announced, Durmont and Revna listening to the man as he saluted, reporting of the watchers' findings through the previous night's shift.

"Any sight of the riders we sent out?" he asked, knowing the probable answer, expecting that word would have been delivered promptly if they had returned.

"Nothing yet, but we've been on the lookout for 'em," the veteran soldier replied.

"More rituals last night then," Durmont mused, rubbing the stubble along his jaw, looking to Revna for her thoughts on the matter, gauging how much of a concern it was for her.

"I saw the pillar lights for myself. They are planning something, and it does look worrying. I don't know why he's chosen these ruins in particular to camp at, but it looks like those pillars have something to do with it.

"Telenth is a lord of the Deep Hells. His rites are nothing to scoff at. If his avatar establishes a foothold of evil among those ruins, there is no telling what may come of his efforts. They could be catastrophic," she offered.

The captain heeded her words, agreeing with her. "That is what concerns me. Few in Tarigannie are superstitious, but they also do not come from a place that deals with the supernatural all that often. I know the horrors that lie beneath our feet where Hell awaits to open its maw and swallow us. I do not know of this *Telenth*, but know of devils like him. Show any sign of hesitation to the advances of a devil and you will see Hell spread into the realm of man faster than man can contend with. We must strike this day, or I fear what will come from those ruins in the night."

"Scars, Captain," a man hailed, running up to the group, looking as though he carried urgent news.

Durmont and the others looked to the watchman, waiting for his report.

"Your companion, my lady, looks to be returning across the highway. Should be here within the moment," he offered, catching his breath.

"Go and meet him. See him to us," Durmont ordered, sending the man running off after a quick salute.

"If Yozo has returned, then my rider northbound for the infantry unit should be returning soon. We may need to wait a bit longer for the rider destined to connect with the cavalry unit to make his way back. He would have had to travel farther than both the other riders," Durmont considered as they waited for Yozo to make his way to them.

"How visible will your flare be? It must be seen from miles around during the light of day," the captain asked of the priestess.

"Sareth rarely holds shut simple spells such as that. If she does not heed my cry, it will be a sign that our path is one she does not condone," the saren offered, though her answer did not seem to please the calculating man.

They looked to Yozo as he ran up to them, the scout taking his exhausted, lathered horse to water once he had arrived.

"I know the company from the Plainstate. I spoke with them last night and gave them your orders, Captain," Yozo tiredly announced, trying to stretch out his aching legs as he made his way to the three.

"You vouch for their commitment to this war then? We can depend on them?" Durmont asked, demanding a firm answer from him.

"Yes, I vouch for them," Yozo easily said. "They are committed more than anyone I know to the extermination of the arisen. They will be ready to ride by this evening, approaching from the west of the ruins."

"That is good," the captain softly spoke, looking over the crest of the dune that stood between them and their enemy entrenched within the ruins.

"We will need all the help we can get. We will hit them hard from all sides. With no ramparts to stop us, the ruins should offer little haven for their numbers." He stopped to look over the scene off in the distance where they'd be charging to mere hours from then.

"Revna, Yozo," he softly spoke, grabbing the two's attention. "Will your band still be riding with us into battle this evening?"

The two looked slightly confused by the question, figuring it was apparent they would be riding by their side that night, but affirmed then and there that they would fight along with the company in the coming war.

Durmont smiled, looking to the two. "I have a feeling I need you in this battle. I don't often have premonitions, but something about this fight tells me we are in desperate need of a god, and Tarigannie forsook their god a long time ago. It is my hope Sareth watches over us this night."

"It is my hope as well," Revna whispered.

The four of them watched the unmoving army of dead a few minutes longer, wondering how many lives would be lost along the fallen ruins that evening, knowing the count would be high, even if a victory was theirs to claim.

36
FLAGS UNFURLED

The sun had long since begun its descent to the horizon, and Hathos, along with the rest of the Hyperium, were mounted and awaiting the signal that was promised would come in the western sky to signal the charge.

"Horsemen approaching," a voice called from the rear of the company, causing all to turn to see the Rochatan cavalry head towards them at a casual gallop.

The horses seemed to stretch along the dunes for miles, hundreds of stomping feet angrily trying to find purchase in the soft sand under hoof, making the large shape of the army look like a giant centipede carpeting its way slowly across the bright-orange sands.

Hathos turned to eye all his centurions.

"Naldurn, Eilan, keep watch of the western skies for the signal. Kissa, eyes on the negotiations. If things go poorly...order the men to retreat. Tau, Undine, with me."

The three men split off from the rest of the Hyperium, rushing ahead. By the time the large company of horsemen slowed to a halt, only a dune away from them, and the Saadir and his seven chiefs came forward, the Hyperium leaders were already almost to them, Hathos keeping as much distance between the opposing force and his troop as possible.

The two groups of leaders cautiously approached each other, an older gentleman, dressed in crisp Rochatan military garb, took lead, riding up to Hathos, looking down snidely upon the man. He could see from the start, negotiations were not going to be easily navigated.

"I am talking with the captain of the band known as the Hyperium, I presume?"

Hathos nodded, agreeing with the man even though he had undervalued his proper title, not caring to mince words at that time with one already in a displeasurable mood, issuing a quiet, "You assume correct. And who are you?"

"Saadir, Captain of Horse. You are responsible for the recent reduction of men under my command," the man abruptly announced, placing the onus of blame firmly upon the opposing leader.

"We...," Hathos began, wanting to state the facts of the matter, that they were simply defending themselves from Set's merciless assault, but he knew that would get them nowhere, opting to go another route with his answer. "We were attacked, and we defended. Yes, it was by our hands that they are now dead."

"A crime that will not be forgotten after our current engagement, I assure you," the tightlipped man declared, eyeing both Tau and Undine as he let the threat linger.

"But we have other matters before both of us now," he continued, collecting his passions before tersely asking, "You received the communique last night of the temporary alliance?"

Hathos nodded his affirmation.

"Though I protest on principle to the idea of an alliance with an enemy of the state, I will serve where duty calls, and Captain Durmont declares it so."

Hathos sat in his saddle silent, knowing the captain shared rank with Durmont and could simply protest the orders if he wished.

His calculation must have showed in his features, as Saadir further explained shortly, "Captain Durmont is not one to issue orders or make military moves without reason, his record is impeccable. If he deems this alliance a necessity, then it is a necessity."

Hathos simply continued to hold eye contact with the captain, allowing him to continue, having nothing to say to the man.

"Do you agree to a temporary truce between troops?" the captain asked.

"Yes. When the flare is seen in the western sky, we ride to overtake the ruins and kill Sha'oul," Hathos firmly agreed.

The captain eyed the western mountain front, letting a gust along the dunes play itself out a bit before again speaking.

"We will ride at your side this day—but not by personal choice," the captain sneered tightly, putting an abrupt end to their communications as he, along with his chiefs, headed back to their divisions.

Hathos watched the men leave, grateful they did not have to deal with the large force just then. Though the captain had a vendetta against him and his men, he did get the sense that a truce would be honored, at least during the battle. Where that left them afterwards...he would need to deal with hostilities and diplomacy once the arisen threat had been taken care of and his mission completed.

Turning back to his company, the three men rode at a fast clip, the sun slowly making its way towards the mountains in front of them.

"Primus! Look!" Tau shouted as they rode, pointing to a spot low in the sky, a burning white light crackling along the mountain range, hanging in the air as it sparkled brilliantly, showering the range with pops and sparks of phosphorescent light.

Though they were each battle tested—undisputed veterans of war—the sight of the light, the signal flare that marked their charge, sent chills down their spine, their heartbeat shooting up as they rushed back to their divisions in preparation of the charge.

"What of the talks?" Kissa asked as Hathos rode back into formation.

"Our allyship is secured, at least until this is all over," Hathos quickly explained, both of them looking to the flare in the sky.

"It seems it is time," she said, her tone reverent, respecting the moment that marked the final chapter in so many men and women's lives come the evening of battle.

"That it is. See to your post. I'll have word with the Hyperium shortly before we charge," he replied, looking down the line of his company, ensuring all were ready to move out.

It pained him to see such a diminished Hyperium, roughly half remained with him, though they had Reza's small company, and he suspected they would prove a hearty group and a pillar of reliance in battle.

He trotted out before the gathered company, raising his voice to reach all surrounding him in the light of the flare.

"This task that has been placed before us—some might consider impossible. But you are part of the Hyperium. We have overcome the impossible time and time again. We have proven ourselves; defied the odds; cheated death; and outwitted and outlasted our enemies. Never once has our company failed an assignment our sultan has commanded us to fulfil—and we will not fail this evening.

"Though our numbers are few in comparison to Sha'oul's, we will not flinch at the first blades crossing, and neither as the last blades cross. Their deaths plunge them to hell, while if our day does come this evening, we pass on to a place of refuge and eternal peace, to be with those great warriors that stood strong in their final hour. We will be with our gods, and our loved ones."

As he spoke, he saw the hope, determination, the readiness, and even the fear just below it all. He knew his men and women needed his assurance now more than ever. Never had they faced such a foreign foe, one so corrupted, one so evil.

He raised his sword and shouted, "Bannermen, ready our colors! All flags, unfurled! Ride now, in the name of our sultan! In the name of our people! In the name of our loved ones! Drive our enemy back into the ground from whence it came!"

A cheer erupted, and though their numbers were less than sixty, even the Rochatan horsemen that were on their way already to the ruins, turned in their saddles to view the war cries.

Black and gold banners came out, tied to light frames of a few of the companies' backs, the triangular flags flipping and snapping in the desert wind.

Hathos snapped the reins of his horse, charging forward, his leaders' dolingers digging into the clay-cracked ground, carving slices in it as they bounded forward, the Hyperium in a sprint over the few dunes that separated them from the ruins.

At the crest of the highest peak, he could see the battlefield. All Tarigannien contingents were converging, as planned. The ruins remained dark, a shadow cast upon it, but he could still see the vast horde within and stretching out beyond its borders.

The desert sun seemed in a hurry to lower below the mountain range to avoid the sight that was about to unfold along the Tarigannie sands, light already beginning to wane.

Shouts and battle cries echoed throughout the valley as all charged forth to meet their destiny.

Part Four: The Furnace of War

37

CLASH OF THE LIVING
AND THE DEAD

The arisen, once outside of the perimeter, slowly backpedaled, consolidating behind the city's boundaries. The Tarigannie horse riders rushed forward, just ahead of Hathos and his Hyperium, galloping in through the sections of downed wall and leaping over the low parts that still stood, breaching the perimeter of the forgotten ruins in chase of the scared foe.

A line formed, roughly stretching across the whole southern side of the ruins, and those arisen that had spears held them level, pointed at the riders that were about to run them down in a calm phalanx.

The riders collided ferociously with the line of the arisen dead. A few were violently ripped from their horses by the spears, others thrown to the sands as their mounts were skewered, but most plowed through the front line, battering down rows of walking dead, slashing and hacking into the soft skulls of those that were unprotected by armor.

The charge broke down the front lines in an impressive display of gore, the Rochatans slashing through the feeblest of front-lined arisen, diving their ranks deeper and deeper into the horde, but the momentum slowed as they started passing stranger, more lively arisen shoving through the other listless arisen to make their way to the riders.

The riders began to lose speed and mobility, the greatest assets to the cavalry unit, and as their pace slowed, more and more hungry dead tore their way into the ranks of the riders, beginning to rip them from their mounts.

The Hyperium heard the bloodcurdling screams, men and women getting ripped apart on the battlefield, but they kept their focus straight ahead on the two hundred walking dead that were clumped along the northeastern ruin walls.

Hathos ordered the charge, though when they arrived at the line, they glanced through, weaving back out of the fray after a strafing run, slicing the weak arisen down with impunity.

A few crossbow bolts from the Shield Company sunk into the arisen group to their left, aiding their struggling allies, the cavalry having a hard time brute-forcing their way through the ranks of the dead.

Hathos shouted orders to his company, watching as two hundred more horsemen rushed in a ways down the wall through an open spot along the ruin's border.

"Press the attack! We make to flank with Captain Durmont's men!" he yelled into the fray, seeing how instantly outnumbered the two hundred riders were as they charged into a horde of five hundred or so arisen, and not all were humans either. Some were mutated, others, creatures that looked straight out of hellish nightmares.

Dolinger's plowed into walls of standing flesh, easily ripping off limbs as they raked their way forward, their riders slashing and piercing with their spears and swords as they waded through the sluggish ranks, slowly making their way to the golden tabards of the Fort Wellspring soldiers.

Massive beasts burst through a line of shambling arisen, flinging corpses out into the crowd as they smashed through a wall along the mound that led up to the two pillars at the center of the ruins.

Three giant ape faces, deep in a state of decay, turned to the golden tabards of the soldiers of Gunnison and Fort Wellspring, the angry orange rays of the sun gleaming upon their armor, causing them to glow valiantly, seeming heaven-touched.

The apes rushed towards them, trampling and battering all arisen that were in their way.

"Shields, crossbows; Shadows, arrows; fire on those giants! Blood, press forward along the wall!" Hathos barked as the group as a whole fended off the walls of arisen along their left flank while the troops at the center of the group focused on firing upon the charging apes.

The arrows and bolts did land, but had little effect, the quills not even seeming to phase the massive juggernauts.

As the apes got closer to the group of two hundred riders, the men in golden thread began to take note, backing up their front line from the sluggish arisen to prepare for the hulks that charged towards them.

"Spearmen out front!" Scars ordered the Gunnison militia, the other chiefs yelling the same command to their Wellspring divisions behind them.

Spearpoints thrust through the front of the lines as soldiers rode up, having only moments to lead the point to their target as the first of the mountain apes smashed in, slapping the last of the arisen out of its way, ten spears tearing into its flank, chest, and head, ripping chunks off its side, gouging straight through, oozing black gore out onto the spearmen as they impaled it.

The giant slammed its club arm across the front line without regards to how badly it had been skewered, sending man and horse flying out of its way as it stumbled through the front line, the other two apes impacting the other line of awaiting spearmen with a similar devastating effect.

"Cease fire!" Hathos yelled, looking to Reza, seeing that they were not nimble enough a force to make it to the apes in time to help the broken line of allies.

"Reza—" Hathos started, but Reza was ahead of him, seeing the issue the fifty plus of them were having making headway through the ranks of the dead before them. She had an answer to the problem at the ready.

"Zaren, Jadu, Arie, Naldurn!" Reza shouted out, calling the four of them to her side against the ruin's walls away from the frontline.

"Zaren and Jadu, break through the gap in the wall ahead and make your way to the Tarigannie force. Deal with those apes or those riders will lose the north flank. Arie, Naldurn—protect them."

"Anything to get out of this crowded mess," Zaren griped, Jadu giving Reza a thumbs up as he sat behind his master, clutching onto his robes as the enchanter rode forward, Arie and Naldurn charging off to keep up.

"They'll handle it," Reza confirmed to Hathos, who seemed concerned for the small measure Reza had offered to solve the devastation happening fifty yards ahead of them, the apes having broken through the rider's line, scattering their formation as they slammed the ground around them, grabbing any fleshy contraption they could, ripping bone and limb apart as they hungrily sought more meat to rend.

He did not have time to second guess Reza's actions as a rumbling from the ground around them staggered everyone to a halt.

"Sinkhole!" some of the frontline Blood troops called out, everyone stepping back as the ground fell in on itself in front of them, the sand swallowing up the dead they had been engaged with.

"Back! Fall back!" Undine ordered, their front line of dolingers back-treading as the hole widened, a large, desiccated worm mouth breaching the sands, plucking a mounted Blood soldier and their dolinger from the front line, swallowing them whole as it returned to the liquid sand beneath.

"Waste worms!" came shouts from the Blood Company, the new development forcing Hathos to change his immediate plans of coming to the aid of their allies up ahead, to pushing up the slope of the ruins to the center sprawl of buildings that cluttered about the central pillars.

"Up the slopes! Press past the dead! Into the rubble!" he ordered over the chaos of the opening sinkholes forming closer and closer to them, threatening to engulf the whole attachment.

The Blood soldiers took more risks, slamming the dead down, slashing through their ranks hastily as the rearguard attempted to help, firing arrows and bolts into the crowd ahead, shining spears sticking into the arisen that got past the Blood line.

They were in the thick of the horde, but the old streets ahead looked to offer them some hope as the scathing corpses that crowded the outer perimeter thinned out amidst the rubble of the old ruin's many buildings.

The dolingers had kept most of them up high and safe from the clutches of the dead as those that got close were sure to be received by sword, spear, and shield from the riders, or the claws and teeth of the mounts they rode.

A few had fallen though, and the dead were quick to swarm to the downed Blood riders, ending them quickly in a ripping torrent of grabbing hands and gnashing teeth. To dismount to help a fallen comrade would have sealed both soldier's fate, and the company moved quickly through the sea of bodies, slaying when possible as they made their way onto the sand-covered cobblestone paths, fallen portions of walls and debris littering the way, making it difficult for them to traverse as Hathos led the group into the husk of a larger structure that gave them at least two walls to place their backs to as they regrouped.

"Shields, take the front line and give the Bloods aid! Shadows, up on walls, fire at will! Find me Sha'oul!" Hathos yelled over the snarl and bark of the dolingers ripping the arisen that rushed in at the company's rear guard, waving for his company leaders to come to him for further orders as the rest of the soldiers got to work at their duties.

"Henarus, a blessing upon my scouts' eyes. We need to find Sha'oul and end all this. We stand little chance winning this battle any other way," Hathos entreated of the prophet, the holy man nodding readily, ordering his priest to speak a blessing upon the leaders as he took care of the scouts along the walls.

A droning chant began as both men began a prayer, reaching

out their hands that glowed a light blue, chanting words that were lost in the din of war as Hathos continued to call out orders, the blessing of Hassome beginning to clear out the exhaustion and chaos that had been mounting since the start of it all, sharpening everyone's thoughts and perception of the scene around them.

Hathos, looking to Reza, asked in a much calmer tone, "Once we locate Sha'oul, will you be able to lead the assault? The Hyperium will secure the perimeter for you. We'll hold the line for your strike force. Take whomever you need to get the job done."

Reza, who herself now felt the calming presence of Hassome, immediately called out, "Gale, Jasper, Eilan, Kissa, Cavok, Terra, Henarus, all with me. We end Sha'oul as soon as he shows himself to us."

The pillars that loomed high above them flashed, the runes that were painted in blood along the stones flashing a bright red, so bright that it caused all to recoil momentarily as a rumble of shockwaves crackled through the husks of the buildings the group was bunkered against, shaking the rickety structure, threatening to collapse it all along the soldiers huddled by it.

There was a momentary hush along the battlefield, but the arisen paid the blast no attention, continuing to press the attack on their momentarily stunned victims, ripping shields and weapons from their grasp as they began to break through the line the Shields had formed.

"Hell hounds!" one of the scouts called from the wall top as a pack of arisen dolingers bounded around the corner, taking one look at the Hyperium's improvised bunker and leapt in at the Shields that turned to face the new horror.

The Hyperium dolingers had been prepped for war, and reacted in kind, rearing up, snapping their maws down at the charging, unliving doppelgangers, wrapping up in a heap of flailing claws and teeth, most of the Shields jumping off spryly before getting smashed by the beasts' ferocious clash.

One arisen dolinger squeezed through the line, entering a group of Shadow soldiers, swiping two off their mounts with its large, rotten paw, following them to the ground with its yellow, black teeth, chomping into them viciously, crushing ribs and limbs before other Hyperium dolingers could run it down.

Their mounts were on the stray hound quick, tearing it apart as two more arisen dolingers scaled the low wall, knocking the scouts off and sending them running as the dog-like horses jumped into the fray.

Pandemonium began to set in as their ranks were broken, the arisen dolingers ferociously wreaking havoc as the Hyperium troops retaliated, sticking them with spears and slashing them with their scimitars.

"Dismount!" Hathos ordered, seeing that arisen dolingers were going to rip them apart if they did not soon deal with them, or retreat from the slaughter box they were holed up in.

The troops dismounted quickly, the front line holding the walking dead back, siccing the dog-like mounts into the horde, and dismembering those arisen that were unfortunate enough to get in their path.

The dolingers inside the building's walls were becoming too unwieldy to handle, and as their riders dismounted and sent them in to attack the arisen dolingers, they happily obeyed, barks and horrid snarls making it hard for everyone to hear the orders being shouted out to the company.

The few horses that had survived thus far into the night, now ran off into the ruined streets, searching frantically for a way out of the battlefield.

The dolingers had given them some breathing room, and Hathos along with all the company command shouted for a withdrawal from the building, leading the troops out into the streets.

The scouts that had been on the walls rushed to him, giving him their reports of the battlefield and the figure they had seen atop the hill in the center of the ruins as the group slashed through standing corpses in the street, chopping through the weak resistance as they headed for the glowing monoliths that began to spark with red energy.

"Jadu!" the old enchanter shouted back to the praven as they galloped through the break in the wall with Arie and Naldurn at their sides. "You know all those spells that I yelled at you for wrecking every training hall and room you studied in?"

"The fiery explosive ones?" Jadu squeaked back, hugging Zaren tightly around the waist as they galloped.

"You're free to play around with them here on those big monkeys. In fact, the more explosive, the better," Zaren croaked loudly.

They rode up behind the struggling band of golden tabard riders, the men frantically scurrying out of the way of the flailing gorillas as they reached for the unfortunate soldiers that happened to get too close, snatching their long spears from them, yanking them from their horses, stomping on those that fell to the ground.

"Alright, think I've got a spell suitable for this; though, all those men close by will need a good bath afterwards," Jadu announced, turning around in the saddle to face the battle, his back flat against Zaren's for support as he produced his yew wand.

He shot his wrist forward, revealing a stone-scarab bracelet. The various gemstones the scarabs were carved from held a slight fuzzy glow to them, and as he tapped his wand point to a red one, he slowly extracted the glow from the stone, transferring it to the tip of his wand, holding it aloft, chittering strange runic words into it as he held it up, pointing it to the front-and-center ape.

A flicker of black and red shrapnel shot forth from the wand, whizzing angrily towards the beast, sizzling into the ape's chest.

Those men close to the beast paused for a moment, not sure what the flickering red streak had been or what it signified, but the arisen mountain gorilla did not seem phased by the sizzling ember that burned within his chest cavity as it flung its club arms out at the jabbing spears again, reaching for another victim to tear and trample. Jadu, however, was finishing his incantation, drawing intricate tracers in the air with his wand, snapping his finger at once, jabbing through the sigil to break the tapestry of light.

As the illusionary symbol shattered, an explosion combusted within the giant's chest, ripping its structure violently apart, sending bone and black gore everywhere. So explosive was the blast, that many nearby horses and riders were knocked to the ground, wounded and stunned, everyone looking with ringing ears to the momentarily standing pair of gorilla legs, its upper half completely scattered across the battlefield.

"That'll do, looks like," Jadu mumbled, working with the other two gemstones along his bracelet, repeating the same process before shooting both shards into the other two gorillas.

This time, the company made a full retreat before the blast went off, though the gorilla bits still managed to make impact on many an unfortunate rider as arms, heads, and chunks of rib racks went flying through the air, ripping apart – at least for a moment – the advancing front line of the dead, long enough for the bloodied riders who still had their wits about them, to charge, taking advantage of the foes that had been laid prone, stabbing and hacking at the undefending mob.

"Where to next, boss?" Jadu quipped, flipping back around in the saddle, leaving Arie and Naldurn completely flabbergasted as Zaren scanned for tougher foes along the enemy front.

"Not a challenge enough for ya, huh?" Zaren mumbled just as the pillars in the center of the ruins flashed to life, runic symbology flaring angrily along the structures.

"Hit the pillar closest to us with that spell," Zaren ordered, studying the writ along the structure, trying to decipher its meaning as Jadu turned in his saddle once more, mentioning, "Last one I got for this spell without channeling it raw."

"Get ready for your real test, boy," the old man whispered, barely audible to Jadu as he rested against the hunched over master enchanter.

Few times had the enchanter actually spooked him with words, but the ominous tone and rattle in his voice certainly caused him to hesitate as he began formulating his next missile towards the odd lit-up structure.

<hr />

They were getting closer to the center of the ruins, which gave them some view of the battlefield. The view, however, was not an inspiring one. All companies were struggling, especially the horse riders led by Saadir, which looked as though over half his attachment had been overrun by vicious dead that had surrounded and separated them, the fight continuing in small, hopeless pockets that proceeded to shrink moment by moment.

The small attachments led by Captain Durmont were holding the perimeters of the ruins along the broken walls. They had not made much progress, but they had not become surrounded either, and their numbers looked healthy still, though the destruction the apes had caused along the northern front had been noticeable, and though Zaren and Jadu had apparently taken care of the threat, their numbers had been reduced.

The two-thousand-man infantry unit at the west entrance to the ruins had been lain low, hundreds of fresh bodies laid torn apart along the ruins' former gate yard. Two massive centipede-like golems of flesh, wickedly writhed and thrashed amongst the troops, its cavernous maws engorging itself upon the flesh of the living as it slithered through the troop's ranks, snatching up all within reach. Those that were engaged with the two abominations, were dealing with armored arisen hulks, much larger than most men, towering over their child-sized opponents, smashing through lines of defense with crude rods and oversized choppers, badly battering the western force as their numbers dwindled before Hathos' eyes.

He knew from the scene before him that they would not be victorious this day if they did not find Sha'oul and dispatch the army at its head, having seen the tides of war too many times to even have hope of a victory any other way at that point. So much blood had been spilt already, and the sun was beginning to set. They would soon be left in the dark of the night to finish the fight—left in the shadows to slowly die, one company at a time.

A blast impacted the pillar closest to them, sending a rumbling shockwave through the rubble and ground around them, rocks pocking off, impacting both arisen and Hyperium alike, everyone heading for cover as they tried to assess what had just happened.

Along the mound at the top of the cracked steps leading up to the monument flashed another light, this one a brilliant white, matter along the hill warping in shape as ripples of reality flared slightly before returning to normal.

209

"What was that?" Naldurn shouted over the drum of battle happening in all corners of the ruins around them, looking to Hathos who still stared looking to the anomaly that had patched back up as quickly as it had occurred.

He did not answer her directly, but he shouted to his troops, "We make for the center of the monument! Once there, we secure its perimeter," ordering all companies forward as they began the press once again up the hill on foot.

"Reza!" he shouted to the saren who had her longsword out, slashing into the walking dead that rushed at their right flank, slamming into the line of Blood soldiers she was with. Falling back, she heeded Hathos' call.

"If we find Sha'oul up there, I leave him to you and your crew. Good luck," he told her just as the front line cut a path through the arisen's line that had been blocking them from the mound's platform in the center, the company spilling through the gap as the remaining Blood and Shield soldiers held it open for them to make their way through.

"Form a line!" Hathos shouted to his companies, over and over, till they ran along the platform at the top of the hill, smashing back arisen that came running to them as soon as they took note of them.

The last rays of sun shone long across the desert scene beyond them to the east, and though the ruins looked dire, the horse riders of Saadir all but drowned out by the brute arisen that picked them apart, a line of dolingers ran over the nearest dunes from the southeast carrying colors Hathos knew well.

The Plainstate had arrived in force.

Just as his heart took hope, the pillars pulsated, energy crackling behind them from curved pillar to curved pillar, a constant arch wicking between the two.

The platform was just out of sight, but Hathos had seen Reza and her comrades make their way up the broken ledge. They alone could see what dark machinations transpired above the fray. The sight of reinforcements from his homeland was reassuring, as he knew their seven-hundred-man battalion would do much to help even the battlefield, but as a series of pops and strange explosions sounded along the northern front with the constant hiss and warbled buzz screaming in his ear from just overhead along the red pillars, he knew the tides of war still did not favor them.

He watched as his men slowly were pressed for ground, some being pulled into the horde, their armor and weapons pulled from them, then their limbs, then their faces.

Josiah came to him, seeing his deliberation, quickly praying with hands of blue, reaching out to lay his hands upon the Hyperium Primus.

"Hassome bless you with sight, clarity, and focus to deliver your men safe from harm this day and guide them in the chaos of battle at this time, that good may be the ultimate victor."

He closed his eyes through the prayer, and though short, when he opened them again to look upon the scene, his eyes glowed with conviction.

They would hold the line for Reza, and Reza would deal with whatever awaited them along the hilltop platform.

He rushed to three Blood soldiers who were being overrun, slashing with precision at the dead that groped at their tired sword swings, Hathos decapitating the ones that had begun to pull a soldier down.

"Up, man!" he yelled, hacking through the arms that reached for them both, giving the soldiers time enough to recenter their small formation before Hathos sprinted away to the next group of Shields and Shadows, shouting down the line for Tau and Undine to hold the line at all costs.

"Let no dead reach that platform!" he shouted, his voice going hoarse as he picked up a discarded spear, slashing and prodding the dead that rushed the mound, pressing against the line of Hyperium with all the mass of hundreds of bodies.

The sun was down now, and the horrors of the night had begun in full.

38
TEST OF WILLS

"That trick will cost you dearly," Denloth scathed, even as he walked through a Seam rift, materializing with his Oathbound before the enchanter and his apprentice.

"A Seam walker," Zaren whispered, noting the strange choice of hexweave expertise their opponent had chosen.

He lifted Jadu by his robes, depositing him on the ground to stand before his opponent.

"You beat him in a duel, and you will be a master enchanter, young Jadu," Zaren said, looking down on the praven who looked up, a little taken aback by the sudden change in his master's tone.

"If you fail—you die. This is no class. No test. Focus. Remember what you have learned at my side."

No sooner had Jadu turned back to face the deathly man than he had pointed at the praven, sending the skeletal knight running to him.

An arrow whizzed through the air, exploding into the knight's skull, shattering it in a spray of slick blood.

Everyone turned to Arie, Naldurn by her side with saber

drawn.

"Deal with them. The praven is mine," Denloth hissed, beyond frustrated by the second-rate group that had almost ruined his master's plans by collapsing the obelisks before the rift could stabilize.

The Oathbound reformed its skull, blood coating it in thick gobs, its bloody eye sockets turning to look at the two haltia, acquiring its new targets.

It ran towards them at surprising speeds. Arie nocked another arrow, loosing it once more at its skull. It phased out of existence at once, the arrow whistling harmlessly past, leaving the two women looking around frantically for their foe.

In a blink, the knight warped back into being behind Naldurn, curved dagger in hand, stabbing it through her jerkin, ripping it out of her side, thrusting in once more.

She leapt forward before the second blow could land, but blood spattered the sands as she haggardly turned to face the death knight.

Arie turned and loosed the arrow she had at ready, but the shot skipped harmlessly off the knight's armor as it lunged in for her with its thick knife cocked and ready to snap forward.

It made a thrust, Arie using her bow to block the blade, jumping up, spinning with the press of the knight, and kicked it squarely in the back of the skull, sending a spray of blood along the ground in front of it as it fell to all fours.

Naldurn lunged, screaming in pain and fury, smashing through the thing's congealed blood head with her saber, dropping it to the ground, but no sooner had it been leveled than it began to reform, this time a pearlescent sheen began to glow across its sickly forming skull, the space around it fractioning, sharding over and in on itself.

Naldurn brought up her saber to smash the thing's skull once more, but its gauntleted hand latched onto her leg, and before the sword could land, the space around the two warped and slowed.

Arie watched as the image of the two combatants slowly drifted sideways, reset, then drifted again, diamond fractals turning bits and pieces of them inwards and out before the two flickered, and blinked out of existence.

"Naldurn!" Arie shouted, searching frantically for her companion, but the space she had last occupied remained void, other than the pool of blood that she had left behind along the sands.

Bolts of crackling energy split the stark air between Denloth and Jadu, the sizzle slashing into the outheld wand tip Jadu shot forth to absorb the force, each tendril of purple energy hissing as it was sucked up into the focal point.

Jadu flicked smoke from the stick's end, trying to cool it down before revealing his scarab bracelet, chanting softly, pulling forth yellow light from the tiger's eye gemstone, swirling in circles the gritty light before abruptly slicing through the dusty glow with his wand towards his dueling partner.

A burst of sand flacked through the air between them, generating a full-on sandstorm in a cone in front of him.

Buying himself some time, Jadu pulled out a small, leatherbound book, hastily flipping to a set of pages. He read out loud speedily through the text, the runes on the page glittering as he rushed through the incantation just as the sandstorm began to dissipate.

Spectral skulls and anguished faces danced about Denloth, sucking in the simple spell until the winds had died out, the sand blown out behind the spectral faces in piles as the dark robed figure began menacingly striding towards the small praven.

Jerking his hand out, a long, black withered staff materialized from the smoke, Denloth gripping it angrily.

Multiple pages burned into ash from his tome, Jadu's eyes locked now on Denloth who strode his way, glaring at the praven, waiting to see what else the little trickster had up his sleeve to throw at him.

Pink slivers of glass crystallized in the air above Jadu, splintering out into needle sharp spikes. A line of crystals flung forward, showering Denloth in hot glass, but as the man held his staff in front of him, smoke emitted in a thin wall on either side of him, deflecting the pink glass that shot towards him until the last missile had been flung.

Jadu finished up with his reading, and already strange things had begun to take foot as he snapped his book closed, tucking it back in his folds.

Denloth pitched left involuntarily, his dark robes tugging at him, yanking left and right, attempting to bind him up. He tried to steady himself, but the bewitched clothes wrapped around his head, throwing him to the ground.

Jadu pulled another sparkling orb from his bracelet, blue electrical arcs pricking him as it was drawn from its tourmaline home. He winced as he held the stone lightning in the air above him, shooting it towards the man who had been wrapped up in his own robes.

The bolt arced, spanning the distance within a fraction of a second, blasting into the bundle of cloth, causing the man on the ground to go limp, along with the once animated robes.

He did not wait to see if Denloth had been finished by the blast, immediately preparing a counter spell in case the spellcaster was to answer him back. He chanted, marking lines in the air before him, establishing an invisible grid in front of him to net any incoming spells.

Denloth twitched to life, sitting up, shooting the praven a glare of absolute loathing as electricity arced all about his body, his eyes still aglow from the charge.

He stood up, his gait somewhat stiff, his robes smoking, and he snapped his staff point at Jadu, patterns in the sand cutting into the fabric of space in the area, gravity shifting this way and that as the ground became the sky, and the sky became a void, tumbling Jadu this way and that.

"I don't have a counter for that!" Jadu grumbled as he flipped head over heels in space, losing hold of his ineffectual spell shield. This was no magic he had studied.

He smacked his wand to the last gemstone he held a spell in, pulling a silver glow from the quartzite stone, tracing a triangle around him as he stuck the wand tip to his chest. He righted himself as he began to float in air, looking for his opponent in the confusing split between half-realms.

A sizzling streak of hot metal ripped past him, singeing his arm and burning a hole through his robes as it flew by.

He turned and barely maneuvered under another bolt of molten steel, seeing Denloth producing a line of flaming rods before him.

Jadu's silver aura pulsated, and he shot forward, floating towards the man, wand leading the way, beginning to glow.

Another bolt ripped by him from an odd angle, and Jadu weaved in his path, not sure where exactly the man was actually firing from, the warped reality throwing off his perception greatly.

He ripped off a trinket from his necklace, draining it for raw hexweave, channeling it into a spell, lines of runic ribbons flowing forth from his wand tip, another bolt of molten steel being batted away from him as the ribbons sprung to life, spinning around the tip of his wand, a slashing set of hex blades blazing through the void as he slammed into Denloth, the blades slicing into his robes, wrapping around the man as the warp released its clutch on their reality.

They both fell to the ground in a bloody, tangled heap, but Jadu was quick to spring back, yanking his runic tethers free from the warlock, slashing him to the bone as the thin bands sliced through the man's body like paper-thin sheets of metal.

Denloth screamed in pain, his flesh having been corkscrew-unraveled, leaving him without the use of his legs as chunks of muscle and flesh peeled off his bones, falling to the sands.

Zaren, who had been watching the duel the whole time from his horse, after seeing the results of the last spell, trotted his horse further from the two, turning his mount back around at a good distance to watch the duel from a safer vantage point. Jadu began busily chanting another spell, drawing symbols in front of Denloth, ignoring his opponent's cries of pain.

Denloth gripped his staff tight, blood seeping into its cracks as it began to glow a burnt umber. Lifting it skyward, black shale slabs shot from the ground all around Jadu, and small, spectral tethers shot out from the formation, shooting into him, the hooked barbs piercing his skin, holding him tight in place.

Jadu tried to ignore the web of hooks that was painfully binding him, finishing spell he had begun, shouting the finishing line in his incantation as a blast of searing white light

216

shot forth from his wand towards Denloth.

The blinding light engulfed the area where Denloth was, sizzling the sands, melting everything in the area, turning the desert's surface to glass.

The beam of light abruptly ended as Jadu's wand fractured and exploded, blasting him back, ripping him free of most of the barbed hooks that had penetrated the superior layer of his skin.

He stood up, shook by the explosion, hand burned to hell, feeling tenderly along his face and holding his side where patches of skin had been ripped loose.

He stooped over the shale slabs to see that a deep depression of glazed glass melted down the slope of the crater like thick honey. The heat from the blast point caused him to reflexively recoil behind the rocks, away from the intense heat.

Hunching down behind the stone slab, he began to tend to his flayed skin, a few of the hex chains still in him.

The space just outside of the rock formation warped, and a Seam rift deposited Denloth's mangled body out onto the sands.

Before Jadu could reach for his spell book, Denloth darkened the area around them as he slammed the butt of his staff against the stone, more hex chains shooting out from its ends into Jadu, these going deeper into his torso, stringing him up, yanking him to the center of the rock circle.

Denloth yelled, blood draining from his lacerated legs, his anguish and anger pressing his spell to other levels as the sand in the rock pit fell out. A torrent of flames came up, burning along the rock walls, black gusts of ashen heat rising up, scorching Jadu from below.

Demonic chants issued from within the hole. Hellfire and twisted limbs licked their way upwards to the suspended praven, his robes only doing so much to keep him from getting scorched.

He reached into his folds, producing his thin spell book, but as it came out, a streak of melted steel slammed into it, splashing molten metal across Jadu's hands and face, sizzling into his skin, a globule of metal eating through his left eye as it baked inside its socket.

He screamed out in pain, writhing in the hellish bindings as demonic claws and embery hands began reaching up from the hell pit towards him.

Denloth held his obsidian ring out, reaching for the praven, a dark tendril of energy impacting him, connecting the two life forces as Denloth began to drain aether from the small body to himself, his legs mending slowly as the life slipped from Jadu into Denloth.

Jadu's jaw went slack, and his body quickly withered as claws latched onto his ankles, yanking a few hooked barbs from his skin as he began to tear loose from his chains.

He threw a hand into his robes, grabbing whatever he could find within, pulling forth a bulbed, corked bottle, flinging it directly at the warlock's surprised face, it shattering as it impacted his skull.

The green contents within slimed the man's face and robes, a light green flame sparking to life as soon as it made contact with the air, the ghastly fire carpeting the glue-like surface as Denloth's draining tether released, opening his mouth in horror as the substance quickly began to eat away all surface materials, robes, hair, skin.

He dropped his staff, holding his black ring aloft, glowing a bright magenta as the Seam began to warp around him, diamonds in time cutting the reality that locked his anguish in place.

Jadu reached for the warlock's black staff that lay against the rocks, grabbing hold of it as he began chanting a spell of levitation.

The hellish hands retreated, and the sands filled in the pit as Jadu ripped free from the remaining hex ties, leaving him badly bloodied and mutilated as he touched down outside of the shale prison.

He caught one last glimpse with his one good eye the final images of Denloth's white skull, eaten all the way to the bone, flicker one last time before the Seam swallowed him up to a distant plane of existence.

Jadu crouched down on all fours, attempting to stay conscious through the pain of his injuries as Zaren rode back over to his student, dismounting, putting a hand on the small praven's back, causing him to wince in pain at first.

He spoke quiet words over the man, a warm, white glow

easing over him, and Jadu relaxed, slumping to the side in a peaceful slumber.

"What was that? It took Naldurn to wherever it disappeared to," Arie called to Zaren, coming to him for answers as she rushed over to their location.

"Will he be alright?" she asked, kneeling down to see serious wounds speckled all along the praven's body.

Zaren stared blankly, deep in reflection over his pupil's amazing progress through the short months he had trained him. Impressed he was with the man's ingenuity, and proud in his victory over such a powerful warlock.

"Naldurn, Denloth, and his minion, all warped into the Seam. There is no way to know of their fate now. The Seam is a void that few can freely travel—not even I understand its paths.

"I would not hold hope for your companion. The Seam is likely her final resting place," Zaren said in a restful voice, bending down to scoop Jadu up in his arms.

"As for this one. I'll see to it that he recovers," he said, looking to Arie.

"We've finished our task here. Your warlock is dead, or at least no longer a threat to you lot.

"Best of luck with Sha'oul. Though he is a powerful magus, Reza has proved herself resourceful in the past. The odds are not impossible that your band claims victory this night."

Arie was about to plead for Zaren to stay and help, but the sands gusted around him as he turned, forcing her to turn away from the sudden gale wind.

When she turned back with squinted eyes to continue her plea, she found the robed man and bloodied praven had vanished, leaving her a ways out from the ruins, none left in the attachment that she had traveled there with.

The night grew dark now and the sound of battle raged within the walls, the pillars at its center lit red with energy and red lightning.

She picked up her bow and gave the blood stain along the sands where Naldurn had last stood a mournful stare.

Nocking an arrow, she rushed back to the ruins to support the gold tabards in their fight.

39

TERRIBLE MIGHT ALONG THE LINES OF BATTLE

Yozo's curved blade slashed through the neck of a large arisen as it rushed at Revna, Alva and Jezebel flanking the two, keeping the sides clear as they pressed through an outcropping of enemies struggling to make their way into Captain Durmont's main troop.

They could see that the Rochatan foot soldiers at the east side of the ruins were having troubles, and the horsemen along the west side of the perimeter were hard to spot at that point, the arisen so thick there.

"Watch out!" Yozo yelled as he dodged out of the way of a charging, massive arisen, seemingly constructed of many bodies merged together.

His warning was enough to allow Revna time to rush to the side with Jezebel, but Alva slid to the ground, hacking into its shin as it rushed past towards the Fort Wellspring troops, toppling its large frame into the sand, soldiers at the front of the line taking the opportunity to chop into it with their weapons, dismembering it quickly.

"They're getting bigger," Yozo called back over his shoulder to the saren, Revna preparing a spell of light as Jezebel ran up to Yozo's side to help him contend against the next wave of arisen.

"Two more!" Yozo called out to Jezebel whose resolute stance told him she'd be by his side for this one.

The two hulks that lumbered towards them were larger than the last one, a good ten-feet tall each. They came in fast, their long strides bringing them to the puny combatants that stood in their way quickly.

A huge bone club swung in towards Jezebel, attempting to swat her out of the way, her shield smacking the side of it at the last second. She jumped to the side as she brought in her sword to cleanly chop into its heel, unraveling the tendons that held it together, causing it to stumble on the exposed bone stump. It turned then, realizing too late the threat that it had underestimated.

She stood ready for the fight with the goliath, loaded on her heels, ready to spring.

Yozo dodged to the side of the rampaging hulk, rushing in behind the charging arisen, jumping onto its back before it could get too far along.

It swung a hand back, trying to swat the nuisance that had latched onto it from behind, but came back with only a stump for an arm as Yozo cut through its wrist.

It spun around wildly, attempting to fling the man off of it, dizzying Yozo, but not succeeding in detaching the man from its shoulders.

Alva hacked into its stomach and thighs as it focused on the nuisance on its back, slowly losing control of its functioning body parts.

It flailed madly, frustrated with the two harrying swords, smacking its bone club all along the ground around it, slamming into Alva's shield arm, sending her flying, dazed and reeling, flinging Yozo off now as one twerk proved too violent for him to keep a good grip along the thing's fleshy muscles

Revna held her staff up, the tip glowing a bright white as it shot a beam of light into the monstrosity's face, burning through flesh as it backed away, holding its remaining hand and stump arm in front to block the burning light from eating through its skull.

Alva and Yozo recovered, rushing in, Alva slicing halfway through its hamstring, bending it backwards as bones cracked, the muscle no longer holding its weight. Yozo followed up with a slash that cut cleanly through the back of its neck as it came down, causing it to go limp instantly, nothing then but a massive heap of rotten flesh.

Jezebel jumped back, avoiding the club swing all together, knowing now that blocking with her shield was going to do little to blunt the massive blow.

She jumped and dodged once more as it lumbered on its stump leg towards her, swinging again, but overextending itself without a foot to balance on. It came down on a knee as she slashed into its club hand, causing it to drop the bone, snatching out at her.

It tore her shield from her arm as the other lacerated hand reached for her head, but she slashed it aside, cutting through the forearm. She batted it down with her blade, lunging at it in a gambit, moving in to swing at the thing's head.

Her sword slammed into the large, bloated cranium, but didn't quite crack through bone as she wound up for another smack, the thing's other hand coming in to restrain her before she got her second swing, the arm with the broken hand tightening around her waist as she attempted to flee.

She was bound up, and the goliath began to squeeze, crushing into her armor as it opened its mouth, about to bite into her head.

At the last moment, another beam of light lit into its exposed back, crackling the skin open instantly as it threw its victim away, turning to rush towards the source of light to snuff it out.

Yozo was there in a flash, slashing through its knee joint, toppling it to the ground as Alva came in immediately after, stabbing through the back of its skull, cracking open its head as ooze gurgled free from its fleshy shell.

A rush of arisen stumbled past the downed corpses, forcing

Yozo and the rest back to rejoin the main body of Durmont's troops as their right flank was hit hard by the press of walking corpses, more goliaths coming in from the back of the line to make their way towards the fight.

A creature, a huge rack of antlers dipping low, scooping up soldiers as it flung men behind enemy lines to get mauled by the arisen behind, tore through the frontline of troops joined by two titan flesh behemoths, each smashing past both infantry and mounted soldiers alike, flattening those who dared challenge their charge.

Riders rushed in through the southern front; not Durmont's men, or Rochatans, but another faction Yozo knew to be of the Plainstate.

Yozo smiled, suspecting it was the efforts of Fin that resulted in the timely arrival of the Plainstate's much needed reinforcements.

The right line was being bolstered by the riders, relieving Yozo and the saren from their positions to make their way through the front line, headed towards the large beasts that were sending soldiers flying, leveling a whole squadron of men with their massive club arms, each pincushioned with arrows, spears, and other shafts.

"Alva, Jez, take care of the one on the right. I'll handle the left," Yozo shouted, the two saren pushing through the line of men that were backing up away from the flesh golem's destructive arm span.

It grabbed for a soldier, gripping him tight suddenly, crunching ribs, then slammed him to the ground broken as it swiped for another soldier that had lunged too close on the attack.

It grabbed ahold of the soldier's sword, snapping the blade in its grasp as it lunged towards the unarmed man, scaring the line of men back a few steps as they gave ground.

A flutter of white lights hovered over the crowd, flitting towards the raging arisen, catching its attention just before the hovering lights pocked into its side, ripping holes in its skin as the thing recoiled, now aware of how dangerous the wispy lights were.

Alva and Jezebel broke through the line, one swinging at the front of its left leg, and the other at the back, both delivering solid blows with their blades to its supporting base, rotten sinew and muscle popping loose from its frame as the thing became off balance.

It frantically swung away at the lights that flickered about it, triggering the rest to explode, ripping its left arm up as it fell back to the ground.

The soldiers moved in all at once, sticking it in the head with spears, slashing at its limbs and core, Alva and Jezebel helping to lead the charge.

Yozo pushed through the line of horses that trotted worriedly back, giving space to the other goliath that had been gutting horses and their riders, ripping limbs free from their bodies brutally and with speed that made the front line hesitant to get close to, giving ground to the beast freely.

Yozo broke through the front line, surprising both sides, the men along horseback watching the lone man rush forward, the giant clapping its hands together in an attempt to snatch the small creature.

Yozo ducked under the tremendous hands that were half as large as he was, rolling forward through the thing's legs, barely dodging the arisen's shuffling feet as it attempted to see where the little one had gotten to.

The men on horseback rushed in with their spears and swords, jabbing and slicing through the torso of the behemoth as it looked for Fin who had made his way around to its side, sword slashing here and there.

It flailed, batting men off their mounts, smashing down with its club hands to crunch those unfortunate enough to be under its thick arms, sending some of the riders trotting back once more. A few kept on the press, however, and Yozo double-handed a cut at one of its arms as it wound up for a swing, slashing through most of its triceps, the bone cracking under pressure as it swung it once more at an unfortunate horse that lay on its side, smashing the animal's head in, its arm tearing off the rest of the way as the arisen recoiled it from the swing.

Men to its side worked its left flank as it struggled to balance itself, spears hooking into the bottom of its jaw as they shoved upwards at the giant's head, toppling it to the ground.

Yozo positioned himself overhead, chopping down onto its neck repeatedly, severing its head after the fourth blow, the thing going limp after that.

The men had no time to celebrate the giant's downfall as a rack of antlers charged into their blindside, ripping through horses and knocking riders to the ground.

Yozo scrambled out of its path as the demonstrable hell beast rushed in, letting out a horrendous roar, bloody claws slashing at all in front of it, ripping up horses en masse and battering the armored men aside.

Its white glowing eyes locked onto Yozo, an unchanging smile along its jagged-teethed mouth. It lurched towards him, hesitating for a moment as two daggers came thudding into the side of its neck and shoulder, sending it ducking, rushing in at Yozo faster as it tried to dodge the projectiles, keeping its eyes on its prey.

Yozo showed his sword to the beast's face as it came in, threatening to impale it, the wendigo rearing up as its bloody, long claws slashed out at the man deceptively fast for its size.

Yozo tumbled to the side, dodging the first set of claws, cutting through the tips of the second scratch, the bloody nubs still snagging on his clothes however, launching him through the air.

He hit the ground and rolled, shaking his head as someone helped to right him, sitting him up.

"First time I've seen you get bested," Fin greeted the man, surprised by Yozo's sloppiness on the battlefield that had almost cost the man his life.

"It's been a long night," was all he had to say back, springing back to his feet as he faced the charging hellspawn, rack down and coming to gore the two.

Fin drew a fan of daggers, taking one in his throwing hand, Yozo running up to meet the beast head on, cutting into the molting antler, shattering the right side of its horns with a loud crack, splinters of bone flying everywhere as Yozo spun around, slashing deep into its ramming shoulder, slicing open a gash all along its arm, flaying it open in a loose flap of skin as it rushed past the wickedly lethal man.

225

Dagger after dagger thudded into its skull, mouth, and neck as it tumbled into Fin, collapsing onto the man in its final charge.

Yozo rushed over to the downed monster, grabbing it by the antlers that remained intact, pulling its bulk off of Fin which had been crushed under the beast.

"God damn, that thing was more nimble than it looked," Fin grunted, helping to push his way out from under its torso, rolling to the side, catching his breath as he allowed Yozo to help him to his feet.

"You alright?" he asked, Fin limping as he stretched out his leg, wincing slightly.

He didn't have time to answer, drawing a dagger from his hip, tossing it over Yozo's shoulder at an incoming arisen, a new attachment arriving behind the hulks that were quickly being dealt with from Durmont's troops along with the sarens.

"I'll be alright," he said as the riders rode past them, pressing the new wave of arisen back.

"We need to get to the top of the ruins. That platform in the center," Fin said, pointing up the sand hill past the collapsed buildings. "That's where the real fight is going down, by the rift. I saw them when we were coming in."

Yozo nodded, needing no further explanation, helping Fin to walk off his limp as the two weaved around the main fight, making their way into the shadows of the side streets that led up to the hell rift.

40

THE RIFT OF THE DEEP HELLS

Reza's boot touched down along the hill's cracked platform as the last afterglow of the setting sun died off, the cool shades of periwinkle washing over the battlefield as a chill gust of wind swept away the heat of the desert day.

Gale and Jasper jumped up in front flanking her sides while Henarus, Kissa, Eilan, Cavok, and Terra followed behind to face the cowled lord and his minions that stood performing their rites along the platform, each holding blood ivory that acted as a conduction point for the arcs of red lightning that jumped from pillar to bone to pillar, creating an oval web of dark energy.

Sha'oul chanted, his demonic voice booming across the platform, and as he finished his final line, he looked down, smiling at Reza as he locked his wicked gaze upon the small saren he had once before shared the battlefield with.

Two arrows whizzed across the large platform, Eilan and Kissa firing without hesitation, shots aimed straight for Sha'oul's head, but both were stopped by a winding net of transparent tendrils that reached out for the tips before they could strike their intended target.

Reza bounded forward across the gap and all followed her lead, rushing past the spectral zealots that were kneeling, speaking in dark speech rites to a prayer to the ashen god.

"Kissa, Eilan, Gale, kill those cultists," Reza ordered, shouting above the crackle of energy that sparked above them.

Sha'oul pointed to Reza, and the cloaked figure at his side lifted his cowl, unveiling the face of one they all knew well.

Nomad unsheathed his sword, charging towards Reza with deadly intent in his blazing red eyes and ashen scarred face.

Reza raised her sword, though the conviction in her charge had all but died once Nomad had showed his face. Her sword hand weakened as she came to a halt. She knew she could not fight the man she had cared so much for—and so did he as he rushed ferociously at her, ready to take advantage of her weakness.

Cavok slammed into the charging man just as he was about to connect with Reza, the two flying off to the side of the platform as Nomad scrambled to get back to his feet, looking to the man who had held him captive only a few weeks earlier.

Cavok's expression was one of complete stoicism, even as Nomad's twisted features were that of pure hatred towards the man.

Nomad's sword cut in at Cavok in a flash, and bringing up his hand, his tattoos flaring to life, flashing a bright blue, Cavok caught the blade, his skin holding like steel against the razor-sharp edge that slid along his palm as Nomad recoiled.

His inked designs flared to light as the large man rushed in, slamming Nomad to the ground, barely dodging a stomp that cracked the stone beneath.

Nomad slashed an arc with his curved sword up at the man standing over him to give him room to recover. Cavok deflected the weak blow with his iron-skin arm, sending the attack wide. Cavok rushed in again, pressing Nomad with a kick to the stomach that sent him sprawling across the platform. He roared as he steadied himself only to see the large man upon him once more.

Gale slashed through the midsection of a specter, drawing a trail in the ghost's outline, the wight not seeming to have even noticed the man's presence.

He looked to Kissa and Eilan, both having the same problem with their targets.

Eilan looked to the bone that was being held up by the wights, smacking into it with her saber, but as soon as she made contact with the charged ivory, lightning chained off of it, zapping her, sending her flying several feet off the platform, tumbling down the hill unconscious.

The chain had triggered all other touchpoints, energy sparking thick through the air, forcing Kissa and Gale to run back away from the violent destruction taking place across the platform. The reaction vaporized the specters into nothingness as a rift, hundreds of feet high, spanning the whole platform across, began to phase into reality, opening wide the gates of a deep hell, slowly beginning to appear more solid as the lightning continued to thicken.

Sha'oul lifted his warhammer, seeing that the rite had been completed, ready now to put his full attention to the pathetic band that had hounded him for so long. He looked to Reza, grinning as he looked upon her familiar face.

Lightning arced, flaring dangerously close to Kissa as she ran, one rope of lightning connecting with Gale's back, cracking him forcefully forward, tumbling across the platform in front of Sha'oul.

Slamming his heel in the man's back, he lifted his iron maul, smacking it down on the electrified man's head, cracking his helm and skull open easily under the heavy force, spilling his brains out in all directions as Reza and the band watched in a moment of disbelief.

Metus' steadfast Praetorian Guard, Galeren of the Nightfall, had been slaughtered quickly and brutally before their eyes, and none took it keener than his Praetorian companion who had served by his side for years.

Jasper rushed in, silently, a tumult of rage within, slashing furiously at the cruel executioner.

The warhammer's shaft came up, blocking the saber's cuts, Sha'oul dodging back, stepping in with a swing from his warhammer that Jasper attempted to block with his shield.

The mallet head ripped the shield from the guard's arm, tossing him to the side, but as Sha'oul went to follow through with his fatal smash on the man, he staggered as a deep chanting voice pierced through the chaos of the moment, Henarus standing to the side of the platform, robes whipping about him as his prayer of confusion muddled Sha'oul, sending him backpedaling, attempting to regain his posture.

Kissa tossed a throwing knife into the protective web that formed along the side of his head, turning just as she slashed in at him with a short sword, stabbing again and again along the weave of protective aether, attempting to pry the magical substance open with her steel blade.

He backhanded the haltia, barely clipping her. It was enough to fend off the assault momentarily though, and as Sha'oul tried to stabilize, Reza came in, the point of the longsword she had received from Metus slicing through the hexweave that protected Sha'oul, ripping apart its sinews slightly as a few inches of blade dug into his shoulder.

He spun his hammer around him, forcing everyone back, knocking Jasper in the side just as he was getting up, slamming him to the platform's edge, badly broken.

Sha'oul took a knee, the insidious voice of confusion continuing to wreak havoc upon his balance and reaction time.

He groped for the dagger on the ground, scooping up Kissa's knife, and chucked it explosively at the voice.

It had been a lucky throw, even Sha'oul knew it, and the voice halted as the prophet fell back, clutching his side as the sharp pain of the deeply embedded dagger bit in.

Sha'oul snatched Kissa's short sword mid swing with his protected hands as she came in again at him, and as he turned to look down at the puny foe, a terrible sense of dread flooded her as he hefted his warhammer once more.

Cavok slapped the man's head so soundly, that loud pops

could be heard from Nomad's torqued spine over the lightning and sound of battle all around them.

His head snapped back into place as a demonic smile replaced the look of rage he had prior to, as if to show how futile the fight was that the large man engaged in.

His sword slashed past Cavok's arms, leaving a clean cut along his thigh, forcing him back as Nomad brandished his sword, grin wide on his face as he saw the flaw in the man's defense. Cavok's tattoos flared, and he braced for Nomad's strike, knowing he needed to disarm the skilled swordsman if he didn't want to deal with further wounds.

Nomad raised his sword high overhead, holding the aggressive stance menacingly as he waited for his foe to make the first move.

The two circled around each other, sparks of lightning carving destructive lines in the stone right between the two, springing both forward on the attack.

Cavok blocked the overhead chop with his hardened arm, snatching Nomad by the cowl. Nomad tore away from the rags, slashing back in to gouge Cavok along the side, the blade glancing along Cavok's ribs.

His blade snapped back towards Cavok's gut, and he barely slapped it away from his stomach before Nomad redirected his thrust, cutting into the large man's thigh.

Cavok lurched back at the wound, and Nomad followed up with demonstrable speed, slamming him in the nose with an elbow, delivering a kick to the stomach straight after, sending the unarmed man to the ground in a thud.

Just as he raised his sword to execute the man, a burst of energy, rolling towards the two, blasted Nomad in the chest. Light brighter than the sun at noonday scorched a hole through his clothes, revealing a now blackened burn along his torso as he stumbled back.

He looked up to see Terra holding aloft Bede's talisman, a white glow mounting once more from the medallion as Terra prayed, eyes closed as electricity bounced all around him from the rift.

Nomad's blood-red eyes locked with the glowing girl, and Terra did tremble, her faith wavering slightly in the sight of the wrath of Telenth's guise.

The possessed man rushed her, his movements unnatural, his speed unexplainable. He was upon her before she could take a step back, snatching her up in the air by the neck, holding her close to the wall of lightning as he grinned, crushing her throat as he recoiled his arm to toss her into the wall of red angry light behind her.

A blue-sigiled hand latched onto Nomad's, Cavok's grip so strong that Nomad was forced to let go, Terra dropping to the ground gasping for breath raggedly as Cavok's vice-like grip tightened, snapping high-strung muscles in Nomad's forearms.

Nomad reversed his blade grip, jabbing it through Cavok's thigh, continuing to stab him where he could as he latched onto Nomad's ankle, bringing the demonic man up in the air. Cavok brought him down, slamming Nomad's back to his knee, snapping the man's spine in a gruesome crunch.

Cavok heaved, completely exhausted. He tossed Nomad's limp body to the side before moving to Terra to help her up from the ground where she sat recovering from almost having her throat collapsed by the man that was now folded in half.

Just as Cavok reached out for her hand, a wick of lightning slammed across his chest, jolting the man violently for a moment before sending him flying across the platform, his tattoos flashing with the flow of electricity for a moment before going out, a few more bolts pocking off chunks of stone all around her as she huddled in terror.

Nomad's upper half began to move, turning around to untwist himself, snatching up his sword that had fallen to the side.

Terra looked on in horror as Nomad's red-blazing eyes met hers once more, smile gone, replaced with the rage of a murderer.

He grimaced as his spine snapped into place, sinew lashing it together, a boon from the devil, getting him up and running on borrowed time, helping him to find his footing, tentatively at first, but as he stepped forward, Terra knew she needed Elendium now more than ever.

She began to pray and held up her grandmother's heirloom, the pendant shining brightly, as if simply waiting for the call. It bloomed into a blinding ball of aura, blasting out a beam of light that gave the demon little time to react.

Nomad reflexively threw up his sword in front of him to block the beam and sneered at the expected impact...but the sword held the light at bay, the blade absorbing the holy light, brightening itself as the sword began to glow white hot in his hands—the same sword that had been blessed by Bede herself so long ago. It flared to life as if to fulfill an oath that had laid dormant for far too long in his corrupted hands.

Life, or unlife, drained from him rapidly, causing him to scream out in pain and horror as the white glow cast out the corruption within him.

He dropped the weapon, the handle sticking to him for as long as it could as though it were magnetized to him, but as it clanged to the ground, he dropped to his knees next to it, shriveled, staring ahead unresponsive as the glowing red left his eyes.

The voices left him. Telenth receded from his mind, seeing the inevitable decay of what was left of the husk, even the dark force no longer being able to hold the broken thing together.

Nomad smiled, withered beyond recognition, and though his emaciated husk of a body was quickly failing, for once in what seemed like an eternity, there were no thoughts, no voices, no strings pulling upon his mind except his own.

Black ooze gushed from his back, spewing all over the stone behind him as he collapsed, using his last motion to weakly place his hand upon his blade.

It faintly glowed a peaceful white for a moment, flashbacks of Bede weakly fleeting before his eyes, her kindness and love, her last gift to him through his family's sword—a reminder of the light that had shown the way to his freedom.

Then, his eyes closed. Free from the red. Free from the hellish dreams.

A silent blackness.

The blackness of death.

41

UPON THE STEPS OF HEAVEN AND HELL

Red strands of electricity whipped down along the ground, pulverizing bone and stone into dust as it cracked along the stairway to the rift, causing Lanereth and Malagar to back up against the alcove's wall next to Wyld who flickered weakly in and out of reality.

"What is happening?" Malagar shouted over the upheaval of the scene about them, the whole structure shaking under the maelstrom of energy that was expanding into existence before them.

Lanereth looked on to the light that streamed down through the chaos of the rift's edges, seeing glimpses of another world's sky beyond, it fading to night, then to day, then to night again, as if time were speeding up, adjusting to the gap between realms as the rift matured into a more solid portal.

"It's a realm rift!" Lanereth shouted, tears streaming down as she clutched her amulet.

It was what they had been hoping for—the only hope they had within the hellish realm—and though neither had voiced the hope the distant light had given them, it was the reason for their persistent journey. The gods had heard their prayers. They had given them a way out.

The lightning reached further, snapping out to the structure's limits, raking a line of angry destruction along the tranced denizens unfortunate enough to be among the first there, ripping through their bodies in explosive fury, blasting dozens in one arc as the thunder clapped repeatedly through the air.

"Back!" Malagar yelled, but neither Wyld nor Lanereth could hear him, both shoving close against the bone structure that protected them from the lightning shower as the rift widened, opening all the way now, touching the ground, encompassing the structure's frame as the bolts began to die down as the window into the other realm became fully formed.

"The rift is open!" Malagar yelled. Lanereth could barely hear, even as the man shouted in her ear, the din of hearing loss ringing in her ear from the bombardment they had just witnessed.

Malagar grabbed her, tugging for her to make a bolt for the rift just a hundred feet away, but Lanereth held back, causing Malagar to turn, confused.

"The rift is open," Malagar repeated, assuming the statement itself was enough to explain why they immediately needed to leave the place.

"Yes, the rift is open," she said, looking now to the hundreds of thousands of demons and abominations that continued to flow out of the large city in the distant plains across the realm.

"This rift was not opened for us, Malagar," she said, remorse heavy in her throat.

Malagar turned to behold the army of hell that lay before them, crestfallen by the crushing weight of the realization. Though they may have a path home, they would bring with them the full might of a realm of the Deep Hells. It was chance timing that they found a way out, and though they could take advantage of that opportunity, the portal was a death knell for wherever that rift led to.

He looked to the reddening light in the sky, the Blood Eye flaring across the horizon, the looming figures watching the portal with fixed intent.

Was the Lord of Ash himself among the titans that stared down upon them? Watching the scheme play out as the forces of hell marched onwards to initiate a war of the realms?

"What could we possibly do against that?" he asked, pointing to the sea of demons, swaying unnaturally in disjointed rhythm, a chilling chant beginning amongst the front line.

She stepped out from the alcove, looking from the sea of evil carpeting the lands before her to the rift that now shown the nights sky she once knew, the pale green light of Kale shining its moonlight down upon them from a distant dimension.

She raised her amulet, closing her eyes, and channeled herself into the relic, using it as a focus, calling out to her god—her mother. It was the cry of a child in danger.

Her call reached across the planes, transmitting from the twisted place she was in, into the heavens of Una and beyond. Her cry spanned out through the distant lofty realms of the heavenly host, the watchers high above, reaching the ears of Sareth—Eleemosynary—the beginning of her line and eternal mother of her kind.

In the night sky through the rift shone a light, soft at first, expanding gently, peace and stillness radiating from the heavenly beam shining down from the heavens of Tarigannie's desert skies.

It was a rare junction between three polar realms—three different places and times existing at once only yards away from each other's thresholds.

The celestial shaft of light descended upon her, filling her with warmth and repairing her scared and beaten body, restoring her to her former glory, the wave of healing extending to Malagar as well.

Her eyes lit up, Malagar watching as she entered a trance, communing with higher powers that did not choose to make their thoughts known to him.

He turned back to the hordes of ash, tormented souls, moaning, breaking from their communal trance and chants, slowly marching forward now, seeing the rift ritual complete, open to them, ready to deliver them to a ripe world filled with sweetbreads of flesh, and pleasures their world had not seen in many eons.

"Lanereth—we need to leave," he said, hesitant to touch her while she was consumed in the light.

The wretched line of hungry devils rushed forward towards them from down along the base of the steps to the rift.

"Telenth-Lanor has long been planning this rift gate's construction—" she said, coming out of her communion, looking to the massive structure's height, knowing full well now the amount of souls the boned frame would cost for the formation of such an impressive rift portal. It was a rift not built for an army, but an invasion of realms.

"Lanereth...," he said, his voice being drowned out as the horde continued their approach up the steps. He could see now that she did not intend to retreat through the rift.

"It has to be destroyed from within, or they'll open another rift somewhere else in Una using the same gate," she replied, dashing his hopes that she was going to simply take his warnings and rush through the rift gate with him right then and there.

"It is my duty to close the gate, not yours—"

He shook his head, cutting her off. "I stand with you. If there's a way to close the gate, close it now before it's too late. I won't leave you in this hell alone."

He felt the comforting grasp of the saren's delicate fingers intertwine with his, a tear of thankfulness easily welling up in her eyes.

Looking to the horizon, she could now see dark shapes drifting through the ashen skies towards them, and the dark statues tall above the battle began to move jerkily, their shrouded faces creaking to look down upon the intruders into the realm.

Black mouths opened wide, an endless void within, pitch black beams of energy, lined with white, shot out towards the two, dark rays carving into the dirt before them.

The Guardians of Hell began to stand up from their massive thrones, rocks creaking and groaning under the titans' weight.

Squeezing Malagar's hand in hers, she turned to see the undulating sea of torment rushing to the rift, hundreds of thousands of damned souls, desperate to escape their hellish prison, the titan guardians slowly marching forth, mouths beginning to gape open once more.

She needed to act swiftly. She spoke into the light a short prayer, pulling out the cylinder marbled staff, expanding it to its full size.

"Provide me with a portion of your light to break down this window between realms."

Holding her staff up, she drowned out the tumult all around her, blocking out the noise from both the battlefield in the Ruins of Solstice on the other side of the rift, and the charging horde of the ashen realm to her back.

She reached out to the flame within her staff, connecting with it instantly, Sareth pouring a portion of her celestial light into it all at once.

Power, pure and hot, pulsed forth from its crystal tip, sending out a beam that cut straight through the left side of the arch's support.

Ten more beams fired from the glowing rod, slicing through the structure in all segments, the portal to Una flickering out in the blink of an eye as the arch groaned, riddled with structural fractures that snapped and popped as bone crunched against bone, threatening to come crumbling down at any moment.

Malagar grabbed Lanereth, pulling her from her trance just as a piece of ivory as large as a boulder smacked down next to them.

More parts of the structure fell, and the two rushed back in with Wyld, seeing that there was no hope of them outrunning the massive structure's collapse, getting as far under the cavity in the bone as they could.

Wyld was barely recognizable now, her image blurred, faded, distorted.

The world around them began to collapse, and their only means of escape fell with it.

42
THE DEAD OF NIGHT

A green flame engulfed Sha'oul as Reza's flaming sword drove again through the warlord's hexweave armor, causing him to stumble back just before he could deliver a blow with his warhammer that would have smashed Kissa flat.

He looked to the saren in disbelief that she was so easily ripping through his magical defenses.

Her ring, the one blessed by Leaf, spread an angry fire across her blade, flaring bright as she brandished it, swinging it down on the tyrant, keeping him on his heels as he dodged and blocked the strikes with his warhammer.

She rapped him across the shoulder, making it past his defenses, the green flame licking up the purple tendrils, flaying them away from him, peeling back where the flame had touched him.

He bull-rushed her, slamming into her with a charge, jolting her in the face with the shaft of his hammer, bloodying the saren as he sent her reeling.

He thrust his hammer's head forward into Reza's stomach, knocking the wind from her, laying her flat on the ground with no sign of a quick recovery.

A baritone voice began up in prayer once again, instantly unbalancing him. He staggered as he looked in the direction the voice was coming from.

Henarus clutched at the dagger that was still embedded in his stomach, holding a teal glowing hand towards Sha'oul as he prayed to Hassome, speaking words of confusion at their adversary.

Sha'oul withdrew into his most inner wells of thought, attempting to block out the befuddling voice, finding the strands of hexweave that permeated the air about him.

Blood welled up from his wounds and he began to gather the liquid into a heavy orb, the ball of blood sloshing about as his consciousness struggled to hold form.

He yelled ferociously as he pressed his telekinetic hold on the liquid to send it floating across the platform at the holy man, stretching the orb into a thin rope of liquid that stretched from the lightning wall, slapping into Henarus.

The instant the connection was made, the unending outlet of pure energy arced, sending a jolt so explosive that the prophet's body could do little to hold together, instantly ripping him into an unrecognizable mess of blood, robes, and charred flesh that smattered the surrounding area on the platform.

Sha'oul shook his head from the lingering daze, looking around him to get his bearings of his enemies.

Kissa and Terra had helped Reza back to her feet, and the three had regrouped to face the large man, but all three held back, watching him, waiting.

His eyes narrowed, not sure if they were stalling for time, or simply waiting for him to initiate the attack. He stepped forward, seeing the white glow beginning to form around a broach the youngest one held close to her chest. He knew the aura of the holy light, and knew he needed to squelch it before her prayer could be answered in full. He wanted no more interference from any other gods that night.

Reza's longsword lit with ghostly green flames once more,

causing his march to hesitate slightly as he eyed the dangerous brand the saren held.

The broken web-weave of hex that partially still covered his body lit up as a throwing knife skipped harmlessly off the back of his head.

As he turned to see who dared strike him from behind, Fin leapt through the air, latching onto the large man's back, stabbing through the opening in the weave along his shoulder in the exact spot he had stabbed the man days earlier.

His retribution was swift, snatching the cape of the assailant, flinging him down in front of him, the knife hilt still in his shoulder, raising his hammer against Fin.

A curved blade sword cut deep into his armpit, causing him to immediately drop the heavy weight, his arm jerking protectively tight to his body as Yozo slashed again and again at the arm that had been exposed by Reza's flame, cutting deep gouges along his arm before Sha'oul roared, runes along his armor burning so hot that the iron withered and flaked off, like paper in a flame.

A rolling wave of black sharp flame rippled out from around him, sending Yozo and Fin scrambling, knocking Jasper, who was already struggling to draw breath, clear off the platform by a superheated wave of sizzling air, the shockwave blasting Cavok and Nomad's limp bodies off the edge as well.

Kissa dove to the ledge, sliding off just before the blast could touch her as it continued on towards Reza and Terra who had their backs to the dangerous lightning wall.

Both knew there was no time to escape to the sides.

The blast overtook them, enveloping the two in a torrent of nightfire, raging over the whole platform, eating into the back of the rift, the lightning angrily sparking in retaliation, mixing with the hellish firestorm to create an overly fatal storm of infinite explosions that crackled all across the shelf.

He dropped to his knees. The move, even with the stored hexweave within his armor's sigils, had exhausted him, and his wounds were mounting. For the first time in decades, he was very aware of his mortality.

He heaved, drawing breath even as black blood gushed from his shoulder and arm, looking around, making sure he had flicked the fleas from his sight.

The waves of fire rolled over a bright white bubble enveloping Terra and Reza, the shining light holding firm until the last of the flames licked past them, dissipating into the lightning screen behind them.

Terra's eyes were white orbs of light, the amulet at her heart radiating of energy and power. Reza paused for a moment to look to her savior in wonder as the young lady floated just above the ground, the lightning behind her attempting to slam into her, but being deflected, carving angrily into the ground all around them.

Sha'oul snarled, thrusting forth his good hand, one black ring burning a hot white before turning to coal, a burst of aether materializing in the shape of dark tendrils, lashing out at the two, reaching for them desperately, but being held at bay by the light Terra shed.

She floated closer to him, Reza advancing with her, and while he attempted to break through the maiden's holy aura, Reza rushed to the side, her brand lighting in vibrant green once more, flaring as she easily slashed through a dark tentacle that lashed out towards her, slicing into another as she closed the gap between her and her foe.

Shouting a battle cry, she swung hard into the giant man's broken arm, slicing it from his torso, redirecting her cut into a thrust, her sword point sinking past what hexweave aura he still had across his body and punched through his plate mail. She roared as she forced the meteorite blade further in, cracking the steel in twain before releasing the hilt and bounded back.

Sha'oul stumbled back a step, green flames eating away the rest of his hexweave shell just as the rift and red lightning abruptly ceased, the hell gate closed off now.

The battlefield quieted with the evaporation of the hell gate, the night still for just a moment, as if Una itself let out a sigh of reprieve amidst the chaos of the battle.

He ripped the sword from his chest, dropping it in a clatter, a gush of black blood spilling out onto the floor.

"Telenth—" he voiced, holding his good hand forward, as if reaching for a savior that was not there, his arm and body starting to shrivel, the years of taint that had sustained him, withdrawing now.

"Telenth saves no man," Terra said in a voice not her own.

The light that surrounded her, consolidated, shooting forth in a blink, enveloping the fallen Avatar in cascading rays of pure energy.

His frame held together for a moment longer, the edges of his silhouette flaking apart into dust, carried away by the eternal light of Elendium.

The blinding light narrowed, trailing off into the darkness of the night.

Sha'oul was gone, nothing left in the place he had stood save a scorch mark of ash along the platform where he once stood.

Faint cries of anguish lingered in the air, Reza could hear, stuck between their reality and another. One where Sha'oul was headed. A place deep, dark. A place where few went, and none in her realm could ever find.

His were the cries of the eternal sorrow. And for a moment, even after all the evil he had brought upon their realm, she pitied the soul for the unspeakable horrors he was bound for in the Deep Unseen.

43
RECOVERY OF THE VICTORS

Reza breathed deep, getting to her feet again, scooping up the discarded sword, slicking the black blood from the blade before sheathing it. She rushed to Terra who was lowering back to the stone beneath her, eyes returning to her usual bright blue hue.

Reza caught her as she touched down, seeing the youth drained and on the brink of unconsciousness.

"Elendium showed me this moment, months ago," Terra weakly said as Reza laid her down on the stone.

"I was never scared for you or I—what of the others? We need to help—" she grunted, trying to sit up, but the strength was completely gone from her.

"Rest," Reza whispered, placing her hands back on her chest, clutched around Bede's glowing necklace for comfort.

"Reza!" Kissa called, jumping back up on the platform, rushing to the two.

Reza looked around the platform, seeing that all her friends had been brushed from the grounds during the final stages of their fight.

"Kissa, where are the others?" she asked, scooping up Terra in her arms as she shakily started towards the edge of the platform to look for the rest of her beaten and battered allies.

A reassuring hand rested on Reza for a moment, Kissa gently taking Terra from her shaking arms, following her to the ledge to help look for those Sha'oul had thrown off the platform.

"Fin!" Reza shouted, seeing the burned man cradling Yozo who was unconscious.

"I'm...alright," he said, his clothes along his right side badly scorched, looking down to Yozo, adding in a subdued tone, "Don't know about Yozo though. That blast...he's touch and go."

Reza leapt down from the shelf, taking a moment to steady herself, getting her footing before kneeling beside the two.

She placed a hand on Yozo's brow, bowing her head and dipped into the wells of aether her ring provided. A rush of air gently ruffled Yozo's tattered burnt clothes and hair, his skin healed over within moments.

She released her gentle glowing hands from him, Yozo shaking awake, looking to see Fin and Reza looking down on him.

"Your face," Fin noted, smiling to see the man's deformities gone, his bone structure returned to how it was the first time he had met the man.

"You alright?" Fin asked, helping Yozo to his feet.

Yozo looked to Reza, assuming she had put an end to Sha'oul for good, seeing the rift now closed, then looked to Fin and replied, "I left Revna, Jez, and Alva to come with you to help Reza. They still need us."

The two looked down the hill, through the broken streets and building husks to the quickly dying battle to the south, seeing the ranks of Captain Durmont that likely the sarens still fought alongside.

"Reza," Fin said, turning back for a moment, smiling and saying, "Good to see you," before rushing off with Yozo down the hill, slashing through idle dead that seemed to have lost the motivation to fight back.

"Reza, over here!" Kissa called, the haltia placing a slumbering Terra down beside Cavok's heavy frame, Jasper also there who was propped up against the wall.

"They need help," she said, checking each for vitals.

Reza made her way over to the group, slowing as she saw Kissa bow her head when she got to Jasper, the trauma from the battle proving too much for him to withstand, his chest collapsed and badly burned.

Reza kneeled between Terra and Cavok along the cool night sand. The large man was unconscious, fried from the lightning jolt, bleeding freely from the cuts Nomad have given him.

She laid a hand upon them both, giving what she could from the ring's essence, rejuvenating their life force back to homeostasis.

Cavok breathed in deep, his wounds looking mostly healed up, though he remained slumbering.

Terra roused, sleepily opening her eyes for a moment, trying to sit up as Reza advised her to rest where she was, calling Kissa over to help tend to the two.

"Stay with them," she entreated as she looked out along the platform's base. There was one other she needed to find.

She looked to the Hyperium pressing the failing line of dead back to the walls as they connected with what was left of Saadir's riders, the tides of war now vastly favoring the living since the arrival of the Plainstate reinforcements and the fall of Sha'oul.

She stood, stumbling through the rubble along the edge of the platform, looking for Nomad that had been by Sha'oul's side until Cavok had intercepted him. She had not seen what became of him after that.

She scrambled around the base of the platform, searching for her old friend, the image of his burning red eyes flashing in her mind as she stumbled over rubble piles.

Her eyes fell upon a lone figure in the sand, dark shrouds covering the broken body, a backdrop of dead soldiers and arisen underpinning a stillness of death as she rushed over to identify the figure.

She turned the figure over and uncovered the shroud from his face.

It was Nomad...emaciated and withered, as though the corrupt black blood that had been within him all those months had, upon its departure from his body, left him a husk of his former self.

"Hiro!" she cried, cradling his withered frame, his head lolling sickly to the side, the surrounding area clear of friend or foe as Reza sobbed freely over her companion.

She brushed the man's crow-black hair, weeping over him, her tears falling upon his mummified skull-tight skin, his withered features a clear indication of his finite fate.

She placed a hand upon his chest, and her hand began to glow.

His frame...was empty. The beautifully unique weave of aether that once clearly marked his scent and trail as the one they had come to know as Nomad, was not there.

He was dead. She was too late to catch him.

She opened her eyes, looking down on him blankly in silence for a moment, then held a hand to his chest once more, reinitiating her connection with his body.

Her ring flared to life, green flames licking along her hand as they mixed with the white glow of her healing powers, engulfing Nomad's body.

She dove further in.

The more she transferred herself into him, the more she became aware of a trace of something. The faintest flow of hexweave, a path that led to some other place, to some other state of being.

The green flame engulfed the two figures, igniting in a pyre of flame. Both bodies glowed a strange flickering of white and green as the winds picked up, spiraling up into the night's sky.

Reza was no longer aware of the surroundings she once inhabited. She was on a journey, adrift amidst the astral realm, recalling the strange feeling that she had been there once before, also with Nomad, upon the steps of a great transition, the place of eternity, both the beginning of all things, and the end of all things.

"Nomad," she spoke through her thoughts, the waves of her consciousness rippling the same word out through the expanse.

There was silence amidst the void. She had lost his trail. She floated now, slowing—an empty, lonely depression lingering near.

"*Hiro*," she whispered, her hope dwindling as she floated along the endless stretch in silence, no ripples of company bouncing back her way.

"*I...*" the faint thought struck her, awakening her senses. "*...remember...you*," a familiar presence spoke, coming into focus, a stillness and peace resting over the both of them.

Her spirit shivered with elation at the long-awaited answer. She reached out to him, stretching for his essence.

As they touched, they merged, their souls sharing a connection that would have been impossible to relay through the rudimentary methods in their bodies back in the physical realm of Una.

They danced there for a duration without time, as simple aether in the expanse, basic structures of energy, similar to infinite others before and after them, but impossibly unique at the same time.

The white-green flames slowly died away, her ring, once glowing a verdant green, crumbling to ash, falling away from her finger.

Nomad's body, before a husk, now was revitalized, restored to his previous state.

He sat up, looking ahead, acquiring where he was, making no sense of it, then looked to Reza, still with a look of slight confusion in his eyes, not quite understanding the situation.

"Hiro," Reza whispered, taking his head gently in her hands.

He reflected upon the title for a moment, slowly nodding his head, agreeing with the name.

"It has...been a long time since I was that man, Reza Malay," he said, a distant look in his eyes which still seemed to be attempting to adjust from his wanderings along the fields of the eternities.

She jarred him from his reflections, enveloping him in a hug, both tipping over in the sands as she squeezed him tight almost in disbelief that he laid there whole before her after so many long months of fretting over the man's soul, so many times giving up hope in ever being able to see his melancholy smile or distant reflective eyes ever again.

Yet there he was. She had searched his body and soul for the taint of Telenth, and she had found no trace of his inky corruption. Nomad had been purged by the light.

The two looked out over the remaining pockets of combat along the battlefield. The arisen were all but put down at that point, none seeming to know what to do without the constant drone of hate and command from their dispatched puppeteer.

The sounds of battle slowly came to an end, replaced by cheers and victory cries from all around the ruins. The night had been won, and relief was in the air for those still living, having endured a night of hell none had lived through before.

The arisen had been put down. The long season of necromancy that had been such a blight upon the region, finally put to rest with the last arisen being slashed in half by the united peoples of the Southern Sands.

Part Five: A Time of Renewal

44

A RENEWED PEOPLES

"Fort Wellspring has not had this many visitors in quite some time," Captain Durmont said as he looked over the leaders in his command room, wearing a melancholy smile.

"We all lost many men last night. I have been briefed by various sources on the Plainstate's attempt to reach out and aid in unifying a defense against the threat. It seems the judges that sit upon their thrones in the capital refused their kind offers and even harassed them on the trail home.

"That they continued to chase the arisen threat is noteworthy, and as you return to report of the happenings in the Ruins of Solstice, Captain Saadir, Captain Sakar, I would hope you give our neighbors proper respect in telling of their true motives and bravery upon the battlefield. Without their support, our people would have been slaughtered, every one of us."

Both leaders of the Rochata-Ung infantry and cavalry divisions gave a curt nod, allowing Captain Durmont to continue his war debriefing with all leaders of every unit involved in the battle that had just taken place northeast of the fort the previous night.

Field medics and the resident surgeon of the fort were busy helping those they could as hundreds of wounded cycled in and out of the expanded medical bay in the courtyard, many of the healthy soldiers helping where they could to move the injured in and out of the operation room, helping to bed them in the barracks for rest and recovery.

"General Bannon, Primus Hathos, both of you have wounded in our medical bay. You are welcome to leave a detachment behind to oversee them and help them return home once they're ready for travel. We have many open bunks now, unfortunately. The room is available to house them for as long as necessary. They will be safe here."

Bannon bowed, accepting the generous offer, pleased to have finally found a Tarigannie leader he had respect for and that showed them even the least bit of willingness to work together.

"We have thirty soldiers critically wounded and unfit for the road back to Sheaf. Your offer is very generous. I'll leave an additional ten with them to help with preparations and care. If you can house forty of my people, then we will proceed as such," Bannon said, speaking for both his company and Hathos' Hyperium.

"That is fine," Durmont agreed, adding, "The same hospitality is extended to your men, Captain Saadir, Sakar."

"Indeed," the Captain of Horse promptly affirmed. "There are a few men that we will leave behind in hopes of a recovery. Most will come back with us to Rochata-Ung. It is not that difficult of a ride."

"Scars, see that the militia men from Gunnison are paid from the treasury for their service," Durmont noted to the auxiliary officer.

"A special commendation to Revna and her company. Without them, we would have been caught off guard to this threat. Yozo, Jezebel, Alva, and Revna—you are welcome at my fort as long as I remain captain. You risked much in coming to us and fought by our side in battle. You have my thanks," he said, Revna and the rest bowing in thanks to the recognition of their efforts.

"I also understand that it was by your company and efforts,

Reza Malay and Terra of Hagoth, that Sha'oul, the arisen's warlord, was put down. There is no one here that could thank you enough for your valiant contributions in this war. It is my understanding that it was you who helped stop his uprising in Brigganden a year ago as well. Your name and deeds shall be noted in Tarigannie's records. I will personally see to this," Durmont reverently said, bowing his head in honor of the two.

"Here, here," Hathos said, clapping for the two, smiling, a rare sight to be sure, causing Bannon, Revna, and the rest to join in the applause in respect to the two women who, without their help in the fight against Telenth's avatar, the outcome of the battle would have been drastically different for the worse.

Both looked uncomfortable accepting the cheers, seeming relieved when Durmont continued with his debrief.

"Kaylic will see to any supplies each of your companies require before your journeys home. Once again, we thank you for heeding our call to arms to defend our homelands.

"Tell the judges to expect my presence in the following days where I'll personally deliver my report of the recent events," he said to Saadir, his demeanor showing his displeasure of the judges' latest display of conduct.

Even though the man ranked beside him, he knew of his favor amongst the ruling class of the capital. He had no doubt if the judges could be chastised by anyone, it would be the captain of the fort, holding sway with not only the aristocrats in the capital, but with all the southern towns and countryside of the region. He was, in many ways, seen as the people's general, even though he ranked only as a captain.

"I will," Saadir said.

With that, Durmont thanked all for gathering, and wished everyone safe travels on the road, the room letting out as each leader dispersed to give orders to their officers in preparations for moving out.

"Reza," Revna said, catching up to her as she was one of the first to escape the crowded room.

Reza turned, looking to the three saren who came up to her, each wearing a comforting smile.

"In the past, not many talked kindly of you in the monastery,"

253

the priestess admitted, guilt showing through her timidness with the statement. "But we have seen your strength and connection with Sareth. I know she has her eye upon you; and—I know Lanereth would be proud of what you have accomplished.

"Please come visit us in Jeenyre sometime soon. There are so many empty seats now at the table. It will be a lonely rebuilding without you. I promise to keep the old guard's tongues in check. They don't mean ill, it's just, your strong-headed spirit rubbed them the wrong way when you were with us."

"I...," Reza paused, mixed emotions of the monastery causing her to hesitate with her response, "...will consider it. At the least, I need to pay my respects to Lanereth. She...was important to me."

Revna did not want to press the point further, and seeing Yozo talking with Fin in the courtyard, she called them over.

"You're both welcome at the Jeenyre Monastery any time as well. You fought by many saren's sides during this war, and Sareth will remember your deeds. I will make sure that both your names are added to the records of allies. If you should ever need the aid of the saren, we will do what we can on your behalf."

Fin and Yozo both bowed, Fin with a big smile on his face, looking gloatingly to Reza, while Yozo could not look more stoic, putting much weight on the honors.

"Fin..." Reza warned, causing the man to harmlessly bring his hands up in defense as if to ask what he did wrong.

"Yozo," she said, looking to the man. "You have had grudges and troubles with my allies in the past. I need to know that we can trust you in our company. Both Cavok and Nomad are with us in our camp outside the fort walls. I need your word that as long as you stay nearby that we will not have further issues with your grudges with them."

The man looked her directly in the eyes, answering without hesitation. "I have put my path of vengeance behind me. I can agree to your terms, on my word."

For a moment, his mannerisms and intensity reminded her of Nomad, and for the first time since meeting him, her intuition of the man was that he was indeed no longer a threat to her friends.

"Watch yourself around Cavok," she warned, knowing the large man had a bit of a grudge himself towards the foreigner.

"Speaking of our indomitable warrior, it's been too long. We're overdue for a drink together. I need to catch up on what became of him these past few months," Fin said, bowing out of the circle, heading out of the fort to the camp Reza's company stayed at.

"You are heading back to the monastery now?" Reza questioned Revna, curious to know their timeline.

"Yes. It is a long ride, and a report to the High Order is needed. The sooner, the better I should think. Please visit, Reza. Within the season would be nice. I should like further details on the part you had in all this, and it would be good to talk," the priestess replied, holding Reza's hand lightly before looking to Alva and Jezebel who had already rounded up their horses and supplies for the road.

"I will. I promise," Reza agreed, giving the surprised priestess a quick hug, seeing the three out of the open gate as they rode off along the road to Sansabar.

"What are your plans now?" Reza asked Yozo as he was walking away from the gathering.

He stopped, considering the question, answering, "I don't know," pausing as he thought through his options. "I might ask Fin what he suggests. I have grown to...appreciate his advice. The man is very wise—much like Matt was. He has guided me in a positive direction thus far."

Reza held back a chuckle at the thought of Fin being *wise*. He had always been an airy jokester in her eyes, not necessarily a fount of wisdom.

"Reza," Terra called in her gentle voice, shyly nodding to Yozo as she greeted the two, her amulet she wore about her neck lightly glowing the way she had remembered it had around Bede's neck during her last days.

"You know what that means?" Reza asked, nodding to the glowing amulet.

"I do," Terra softly said, coming to Reza's side, away from Yozo, which she still remained tentative around, remembering his foul demeanor back in Sheaf.

"It means you are a saint. Elendium has graced you with his power, as he had done with Bede in her final days upon Una,"

Reza said to the girl, a bit of pride in her voice for the young lady's position.

"To attain sainthood in this life is to assure a place in Elendium's favor for all eternity. Make sure you walk upright and remain worthy of that calling," Reza added, patting her on the back.

"I will," the girl confirmed, a bit of confidence entering her voice as the three slowly made their way out of the gates, the Tarigannie sun beginning to set upon the busy fort.

There was a sense of thankfulness blanketing the fort that housed the many peoples from various lands, all grateful for being alive after such horrors of war. There was also a bittersweetness in the air—all those that survived holding in reverence those that they had lost in the fight against the evil dead.

The Tarigannie people were free, and the desert air itself seemed cleaner as light winds swept through the land, clearing the stench of death from its sands.

45
JUDGMENT DAY

The dark streets of Brigganden were rife with the same level of unease and foreboding as when they had passed through it the first time, priests and soldiers following the small army of four hundred riders that made their way through the unwelcoming town led by Bannon, Hathos, and Reza with Terra at her side.

"We did not come through the city gates when responding to Fin's call. Brigganden seems no longer a safe place to pass through these days with its current rulership," Bannon whispered to Reza as they trotted through the quiet streets, being watched closely by the priests and soldiers.

"Forgive my sayings, lady Terra, but this sect of Elendium has brought a foulness over Brig these last months."

Terra looked upon the priests in white robes who were sneering at her, particularly entranced by the glowing amulet she wore openly, one sprinting off through the streets as if suddenly on an urgent mission.

"To think, we liberated this place not that long ago, and now their people hide indoors under constant watch," Reza spoke, not worrying to keep her voice down, sickened by the city-state's citizens kowtowing to the bishop's influence and harsh laws.

The soldiers looked down from their city towers dispersed along the main road, watching the army march their way through town, the priests following the group closely, not saying a word as they shadowed their steps.

"Few would dare walk the streets of Brigganden on the lord's day of rest," came a slithering voice Reza and the others heard, looking to see Bishop Tribolt fast approaching the band.

"But I am not surprised it was *you* who disobeyed our ways. You have violated our treaties, and as such, recompense is required," the bishop announced as a large detachment of soldiers began to make their way down from the judges courtyard, the soldiers in the watchtower being ordered to load their crossbows, the sounds of clicks of taut strings snapping into place all along the city towers.

Bannon stepped forward, addressing the man in robes. "We were not told of this custom at the gate. If you would punish visitors walking through the streets on your *lord's day*, why let them in through the gate in the first place?"

"We do warn those travelers that have not been given the doctrine of Elendium. Sultan Metus and his men have been informed of our laws. I see some among you that were there that day in court. Did you not read the treaties?" the scrutinizing man sharply asked, soldiers filling in behind him as he drilled Bannon.

"We just came from war, Bishop Tribolt. This is no time to harass your neighbors who just last year saved this very city from the hands of the arisen," Bannon said shortly, done with the ridiculous spite the religious man held for those he was supposedly serving.

The bishop ignored the comment, continuing with his sentence. "Punishment for breaking the Lord's Day is time in the oubliette. Seeing as we cannot send your whole company to the oubliette, penance by the flagellant thongs will suffice."

The streets were quiet as Bannon stared the bishop down, all awaiting his response.

"We will not be paying your god's ridiculous penance," he said at length, a very tense hush falling over all close enough to hear his response.

"Elendium demands it...," the bishop sneered, stepping closer to the general, Bannon seeming not in the least intimidated.

"You do not speak for Elendium," Terra said, breaking the tense silence. "False is your authority, and perverse is the sect you lead. This is not the way of the faith."

"How dare you challenge my authority, child. We may not have an oubliette for a whole army, but we have one perfect for one small as you," the bishop scolded, turning his wrath to the girl who stood her ground, rushing up to her.

Cavok, always at her side, took one step forward and snatched the frail bishop by the throat, squeezing just enough to stop him from speaking, watching emotionless as the man squirmed and struggled for breath.

"Let him go, Cavok. He needs to answer for his corruption of the faith," Terra said, Cavok releasing the bishop from his grip, still standing between the two in case the old man still wished to continue his hostilities.

The robed man coughed and sputtered, composing himself, going still after his eyes glanced upon the glowing necklace that Terra wore around her neck. Terra saw what he fixated upon.

"You see the sign.... You're trembling," she noted aloud, watching as the man looked back to the soldiers that had come with him, seeing that none moved up to protect him, seeing the other priests among his fold eyeing warily the pendant Terra displayed.

"You have nothing to say now—now that you see that you stand in the presence of a true follower of the faith—a *saint* of the holy one?"

"Blasphemy," the man said, but his speech was weak with fear, no conviction in his voice any longer.

"Blasphemy?" Terra shouted, and her pendant shined bright, causing the bishop and his priests to turn away, her voice taking on an otherworldly tone as she stepped forward.

"The church has been corrupted, these last generations stifling my chosen—my saints," she said, gently beginning to levitate above the crowd, her eyes glowing just as they had upon the platform in the ruins, her voice shifting to another's voice—one from the heavens.

"I speak to all here in the name of Elendium, the Eternal Light. All here bear witness to the fate of those that preach false doctrine and dole out unjust punishments in my holy name."

The bishop collapsed, weak with fear, hysterical on the ground. He was frozen in place, unable to move. His priests looked as if they were ready to bolt from the scene as Terra looked over the crowd from above.

She raised her hand, and as the fear of God became complete in all of the priests' countenances, light fell from the sky, parting the grey clouds, pillars of white falling upon each follower in white robes, enveloping them in a blinding light.

Through the noise of the dying screams sounded the click and whizz of a crossbow, the bolt flying from the steps above, sinking into Terra's chest.

Her eyes returned to blue in an instant, dropping her from the sky as the rain of light abruptly ceased, leaving scorched spots along the street where the priests and bishop once were.

Cavok had a hatchet in hand in an instant, hurling it at the dumbfounded guard, realizing his mistake just as the axe head thudded into his face, knocking his helmet from his head as the blade cracked open his skull, dropping him dead on the spot.

"Hold!" Bannon boomed, holding his hands up before both groups, repeating, "Hold," as he attempted to stop things in the street before they escalated into a bloodbath.

"Reza, see what you can do for her," Bannon ordered quickly, looking back to the girl, seeing that she had unfortunately been struck squarely in the chest, limp and unresponsive upon the ground.

He turned back around to the city guards, most seeming confused as to what to do, the priests apparently murdered en masse all at once, and one of their men down with an axe embedded in his skull.

"No more bloodshed—we want no more bloodshed," he started, hands still raised peaceably, attempting to quail the uneasy murmurings along both sides, swords and bows being drawn.

The crowd did quiet slightly as he held everyone's attention, and he continued to speak as Reza made it to Terra's side, propping her up as Cavok pulled the bolt from her chest quickly, plugging the hole in her as blood from her heart shot forth, reddening her white robes.

He knew the shot was fatal unless Reza could help.

"We have not come here to war with you. This false sect has hobbled your city instead of providing protection. The arisen threat is no more. We saw to their end.

"Open your eyes. You have not been oppressed by anyone but this corrupted religion. We have done nothing but try and aid your people from the beginning—do not make an enemy of one of your strongest allies. I can promise you, it would only end poorly for you and your future here in Brigganden."

Bannon's words calmed the low rumble of mounting tensions amongst the two groups, a few from both sides making moves to put away their weapons in shows of good faith.

"Cast off this false religion, protect your city by your own hand, and we will be at your side in troubling times," he ended as more weapons were lowered.

"How is she?" Bannon asked after seeing the crowd had been momentarily pacified, turning to Cavok who watched Reza working with Terra, attempting a healing as he spoke.

"They're both struggling," Cavok mumbled, looking frustrated and helpless with knowing there was nothing he, or anyone else, could do if Reza wasn't able to pull through with the healing.

Reza no longer had Isis' ring, the aether within it being completely spent on Sha'oul and Nomad in the ruins. She was working through the healing, but the bolt had pierced Terra's heart, the damage was massive, and it was draining her essence quickly as Reza did the best she could to patch the delicate structures along the girl's most precious organ.

"Reza!" Nomad called out, making his way through the troops to make it to her just as she collapsed, catching her as Cavok tended to Terra.

The hole where Terra had been shot had been mended, but both girls were barely breathing, and the two men could do nothing but hold them as everyone in the crowd turned now to someone making their way through the line of soldiers upon the steps.

"Report," a frail man in black robes barked out at one of the senior guards in the crowd, the guard quietly explaining all that had just transpired to the bent over old man.

"Metus' troop, eh?" he said after a brief pause, taking it all in, shouting in a shrill voice, "Weapons down, unstring those bloody crossbows you idiots! These are our allies."

There was a shuffling amongst the guards from both sides, all readily now sheathing their weapons and lowering their bows and crossbows as the order was given.

"General Bannon, correct?" the old man said, hobbling through the soldiers to appear in front of the scene where Terra and Reza lay upon the ground.

"Yes, and who are you?" Bannon answered, not having seen the judge the last time they had been through the city.

"Judge Hagus," he answered simply, eyeing the girls. "I remember those two, and you, big man," he said, poking Cavok's bicep with his cane, a strange wiry eye upon the lot of them.

"We've not had a good run of luck these past months...," he admitted, alluding to events he figured none he spoke to knew of.

"The captain of the guard tells me you blinked away the bishop?" he asked, a bit of pleasure in his voice.

"Yes, I suppose we did," Bannon answered, uncertain himself what had just happened with Terra's channeling.

"Good," the old judge spat, issuing no further explanation of the sentiment.

"Forgive us this exchange," he continued, looking down to Terra and Reza. "I'll have our best medics tend to them if you would allow us this recompense."

Bannon looked to Hathos, wondering how wise it would be to allow their injured to be taken care of by those that had attacked them in the first place. One look to how shallow Reza and Terra drew breath, however, forced his compliance.

"We will send a detachment with her," Bannon announced, no flex in his position.

"Of course," the old man agreed, whispering a command to the lead guard, which went to work dispersing the crowd of soldiers that encircled the area.

As the streets cleared, light patters of rain began to fall, plinking off the armor of Bannon's soldiers as they stood in formation, watching as Cavok and Nomad carried in their arms Reza and Terra up the scorched and bloodied stairs, following behind the old man in black robes with the city guard captain by his side.

46
THE UNCERTAIN PATH

"She...doesn't even look like Wyld anymore," Lanereth said, disturbed by the unnatural jerking afterimage of the kaith they once had traveled beside.

Malagar sat across from what was once his former friend, cross-legged, studying the mixture between Seam tear and what once was a person he had known so well.

Lanereth saw that her companion was deep in his thoughts, showing no sign of replying to her comments anytime soon. She stood, moving to the large bone segment that had fallen in front of the cavity they were in. After the dust had settled from the arches collapse, they had found their escape blocked.

She pressed against the large beam of bone. It was as solid as the other walls around them—they were not going to budge it with any amount of force they could generate.

She looked to the gaps along the cavity's lip. They didn't look promising either. Perhaps they could attempt a squeeze along one of the corners, but there was little room available, and rubble filled what gaps there were.

She sat back, looking upon the marbled cylinder that was her staff, tucking it away once more into her vest pocket. With the rift now closed, she knew no further channeling of Sareth's might would be possible, and even if she could once again channel her gifted power, within such close confines, she doubted that another blast like the one she had delivered earlier wouldn't rip them apart within the small, ivory coffin.

It seemed destined to remain there with them, along with her amulet, hidden away in rubble, holy artifacts underneath a pile of bones in a distant, forgotten hell.

What a sad fate....

A flicker and a flash of brilliant color snapped Lanereth's attention from the bone obstruction to where Wyld had been. Malagar was meditating, eyes closed as he chanted, sitting in front of the iridescent warp of space that rippled out towards him from where Wyld had been.

Malagar held forth his arm, and from it flowed the same aura of color as within the rift, creating a polar field of energy exchange. To her, it seemed he was communicating with the thing.

"Malagar," she hesitantly whispered, the strange flux melting onto his arm. She eyed the creeping material worriedly.

"Malagar, what is that?" she fearfully asked, as it quickly engulfed his arm.

He did not verbally answer her, but instead, opened his eyes, looking into the brilliant void within the rift that had opened where Wyld had been, the Seam stretching out before them endlessly.

He looked to the saren, holding his other hand out for hers. The Seam continued to engulf his body.

She looked to the rift, seeing eternities within. She knew very little of the Seam, it being banned from study at even the highest levels of records across all major institutions. It was a place she had heard was full of uncontrollable and endless pathways— pathways that by their very nature, flouted in the face of all standard practices and schools of organized thought and theory.

But even with the apprehension, the absolute vastness of

265

what lay within, she could not deny there was an unreal beauty to what she saw, what she could feel coming from within.

The Seam continued to envelop Malagar, freezing him in place, his otherworldly eyes now staring into hers as if from another time, an afterimage of where and what he once was.

She grabbed onto his hand just as the flow enveloped it, growing onto her arm now, a numb, icy feeling tingling along as it reached up to her, jittering along as it engulfed the rest of her body.

Her mind was assaulted with fractioned views of the place within, and as she shifted to move into the rift, her thoughts continued to muddle and multiply, thoughts flowing into her consciousness—thoughts she had previously had—thoughts that she would have sometime in the future—thoughts that were not her own all together.

As they walked forward, time both slowed down painfully while simultaneously slinging forward incredibly fast, leaving her not knowing if seconds had passed since they walked into the rift portal that once marked Wyld's death place, or eons.

Malagar looked steadily onward, and she still held his hand.

His hand was the only constant that tethered her mind to a set reality. His hand, and the image of him leading her forward.

To where...she did not know.

Through the endless rift of everchanging realities, the two trudged along, making their way along the narrow path where existence and physics could still somewhat hold together, just enough to allow for their travel.

Years would pass away, decades, lifetimes beyond measure of them holding onto each other, onto their very existences, before a light would shine before them.

A light that they both could sense they once knew very well. A light that smelled of the foreign concepts of soil and air, of trees and rivers. The sounds of life. The place they had once known an existence upon.

They had found their way through the endless Seam web back to the world of Una.

47
AN UNDYING FRIENDSHIP

The darkness of unconsciousness gave way to the shade of night as Reza opened her eyes slowly, looking around in the dim room, the only illumination being that of the open window letting in the fresh, night air.

Nomad stood, back to her, looking out of the window, the view of the quiet city below too mesmerizing for him to break free of the view until he heard Reza stir in bed.

Turning around, the two met eyes, smiling, Nomad coming to her to embrace her in bed.

"You rise again. After so many days...I had begun to worry," he said into her shoulder. She could tell by his voice that he was struggling to keep his composure.

"Nomad...," she dazedly said back, returning his strong hug, giggling lightly at the desperate embrace, as if he were worried if he didn't hold her tight enough, she would wisp away.

"Nomad, I'm fine. Lighten up or you'll crush me," she said playfully, gently pushing the man off of her so that she could have some room to breathe.

"What a relief you're with us again," he reiterated, his smile and wet eyes proving his sincerity.

She tried to sit up, struggling slightly as weakness still remained in her limbs, asking, "You say it's been days? How long have I been sleeping?"

Nomad helped her sit upright, explaining, "Three days. You had begun to worry the physicians—as well as your friends. Even with knowing how resilient your spirit is, three days is a long time to slumber."

Her eyebrows raised, remembering why she had gone unconscious in the first place. "What of Terra? Is she alright? I did the best I could with the healing, but without Isis' ring..."

"She's...had a rough recovery, but she is alive. Without your quick response, the wound would have killed her within seconds. The bolt had torn her heart open. She's weak, but in better condition now than the first or second day. Today was the first day she was allowed visitors. I checked up on her with Hathos just a few hours ago."

She thought over the news, whispering, "I wasn't able to complete her healing. Perhaps in a day or two—"

"—you focus on yourself for now. The physicians are doing a good job of taking care of her," he said, easing her conscience.

She looked to Nomad. That he was fretting over her, it was clear.

"How long have you stayed with me?"

"I've taken a few breaks here and there, but mostly the whole time. Everyone's come to see you a few times. Everyone that stayed behind that is," he replied.

"Stayed behind?" she asked, not sure who Nomad was referring to.

"General Bannon led most in the army back home to Sheaf. He left a very small attachment, mostly Hyperium leaders, to watch out for you and Terra. Cavok, Arie, Fin, and...Yozo...stayed behind as well. Though, Cavok and Fin just left to hike some mountains nearby—Arie went with them as a guide as she knows the mountains better than they do, and to keep them out of trouble. Fin said it was to visit the grave of a friend of theirs."

"Wait, we're still in Brigganden?" she incredulously asked, confused as to why they were still in the hostile city.

"The Judges threw out all the decrees and laws the priests had made once they learned of the arisen's downfall. There were few priests of any standing left after Terra's display of judgment. Thankfully, the judges and people took Terra's power with Elendium as a sign and cast out all remaining false priests from their walls.

"They offered to see to you and Terra's treatment in recompense of what transpired in the streets. Bannon left our small detachment just in case further issues arose. So far they've been nothing but hospitable."

She let the past few day's events sink in, thinking upon those that had stayed behind, just for her and Terra to ensure their safety, thinking upon Nomad who had stayed at her bedside through the worst of it.

"Help me to the window," she ordered, Nomad quickly moving to help, seeing that she was going to attempt the journey with or without his aid.

She was weak, her strength not fully there, as was usual after exerting her power of healing, but the cool stone floor felt good on her warm, tired feet, the slight breeze of the desert sky drafting in, ruffling her sleeping garments as they made it to the windowsill.

Looking out brought the sweet smell of desert bloom, the dim torchlight of the sleepy city setting a low glow along the scene before them, but not bright enough to subtract from the beautiful vista of the Imhotez mountains in the background and the stars and sky beyond.

There were a few people out in the streets still. Nomad had heard and seen many celebrations the nights earlier now that the restrictive laws had been torn up.

Tonight was quieter, but the distant songs of merry gatherings along the celebration street could gently be heard from the high window of the magistrate's court where the doctor's medical wing was located.

"I was past this life's gates, Reza. How did you bring me back? I feel...as though I was not meant to return this time. But when I felt your presence, reaching for me—" Nomad left off, still not sure how he felt about the event.

"I...know. I did not know what I was doing. Isis' ring, the life sap, I drew upon all aether at my disposal, and then some. I am not sure if I should have been where we were. That place—I get the feeling that one should not return from that threshold. I wonder if anyone else *has*. What might the consequences be for those who see beyond the veil?" She paused, considering her open-ended question.

"You were gone, and I brought life back into you, somehow finding your soul from the other side and coaxing you back to me, here, in Una. Perhaps it was selfish of me."

Nomad looked to Reza, and she looked to him, as if awaiting an answer to her question.

He looked away into town, whispering, "Perhaps...but that doesn't make it an unwanted gift. The other side was peaceful, expansive, different. It's not a place to fear, I see now. But," he said, looking to her with a smile, "you went to a great deal of trouble to return me here, so here I will stay a few years longer—with you."

She leaned into him, not out of weakness, but to be closer to the man she had come to love—to need—and with the way he had embraced her earlier, it was clear that he felt the same way for her.

They had, through time, realized that without one another, neither of their lives would be complete.

Embracing her, they kissed, their soft lips feeling each other passionately, sweetly, tears of both joy and sorrow over the past year's tragedies, trials, and victories coming out, their romance playing out in a dark room high above the city that was still healing from the same evil that had ironically brought the two together in the first place.

48

BURYING OLD GRUDGES AND REGRETS

"Green tea and whatever the special is today," Nomad said to the waiter at the little outdoor restaurant close to the judicial district, having seen to both Reza and Terra's needs that morning.

It was midday and having skipped breakfast, he was happy to have found a promising eatery that lured him there with tempting smells lingering from a street away.

"No green tea here. We have red tea, wild dagga and chai rooibos. We have a rack of lamb on the spit, fresh with cherry tomatoes, asparagus, chives with a basil baste, buttered naan with kefir—" the man announced, Nomad cutting him short with a wave of his hand.

"Sounds lovely. I'll have that," he said, agreeing to the suggestion.

"That'll be four silver strips," the waiter replied, Nomad handing over four small silver metal strips from his change purse.

Cinching the pouch back up, he kicked his feet up on the other chair at the small table as the waiter went to get his order ready.

The day was a quiet one uptown where he was visiting, most of the busyness happening down in the market district where the crowds were. He had the sitting area out under the vine-covered lattice all to himself, the shade from the naturally covered patio awning keeping him cool in the gentle breeze that flowed through the cozy shop's dining area.

He sat there, eyes closed, head back, enjoying the quiet moment, wonderful aromas wafting out of the kitchen inside when he felt a presence by his side.

Squinting an eye open to see who it was, he sat up, seeing Yozo looking down at him out in the heat of the sun.

Nomad hesitated for a moment, surprised to see the man there, gently kicking the chair he had propped his feet up onto, offering him a seat.

Yozo looked to the kitchen for a moment as if second guessing on coming to Nomad in the first place.

After some hesitation, he took the chair and ducked under the hanging vines, sitting in the shade across from the man he once knew as Hiro.

The two shared glances at each other for a few moments in silence before the waiter came back out and asked, "Anything I can get you?" to Yozo.

Keeping his eyes on Nomad, he replied, "Green tea."

"We don't serve green tea. We have red tea," the waiter answered, irritation slightly in his tone.

Yozo looked at the man, giving him a face, asking blatantly, "What the hell is red tea?"

"It's a blend of wild dagga and chai rooibos, sweetened with honey—"

"Fine, whatever. Red tea will do," he replied, sitting back in the chair, waiting for the man to leave them.

"One silver," the waiter said, holding a hand out for the payment.

"Let me," Nomad said, adding once he saw Yozo about to protest. "You treated me to tea on the road in Jeenyre, after all."

Handing the man another silver, the waiter left the two men

to gather the tea, the both of them settling back down to continue their staring match.

"Something...has changed with you, Yozo. I'm not sure where we stand, though I have much I wish to say to you. I just...don't know if you'd be in the mood to listen."

The waiter came to their table with a cast iron red teapot with two clay cups. Pouring both of them some vibrant red tea, he left the pot and cloth with the two, returning to the kitchen.

Looking at the steaming earthenware, Yozo thought on his words a while before reaching for the tea, smelling its vapors, sipping a few drops to test the taste before idly replying, "Maybe someday. That doesn't concern me like it once did."

He snapped a honeysuckle flower from the vines overhead, mumbling that the drink was bland, using it to stir the tea to cool it off faster, giving the flavorless tea more of a floral note.

"I once very much cared about *why* you did what you did. These last few months have, as you said, *changed* me. Your friend Fin—his teacher, Matt—and many others, showed me a different way—a better way.

"Once, you were the focus of everything to me. Your punishment for what destruction you had upon my life was my reason for carrying on through all the torment and pain...."

Yozo sipped his tea now, letting his words sink in as Nomad sat there, contemplating the words spoken.

"Now...things are different. It is ironic, those who you befriended reached out a hand to me, even after I rejected them so many times, they persisted. As I hounded you, I couldn't escape those who thought the world of you—that would lay down their lives to protect and fight for you.

"Fin once told me that the past is dead, history cannot be rewritten, and as I was chasing down memories of past phantoms, I only further enslaved myself to it, giving up all the beauty the present holds. We ourselves are the only ones that can relinquish the shackles of the past that holds us down.

"I'm done focusing on you," he casually said as he sipped from his tea, and where Nomad might have expected a tone of malice in the statement, he was surprised to hear peace in its place.

"There are those here and now that I've come to appreciate,

and those that appreciate me. Now is *my* season. I believe... I will focus on living my life for now. Perhaps there is some peace I can find here in the presence of those that saw something good in me, even when I had nothing but spite within my heart."

Nomad was left speechless, looking at his untouched tea, the waiter shuffling in the kitchen, coming with his platter of food.

"That's...all I had, Hiro," Yozo ended, drinking the rest of the tea, leaving the flower in the earthen cup, walking off just as the waiter arrived with his meal.

Nomad stared blankly at the flower in the cup before the waiter asked a second time, "Can I get you anything else?"

"No...that's fine," he distantly replied as the waiter left, annoyed at once again having to repeat himself.

Nomad picked up his cup, taking a sip of the red tea, considering Yozo's words deeply.

Yozo had been right. The tea was bland.

49

THE ROAD HOME

The caravan moved slowly along, Hathos snapping the reins from time to time at the head of the carriage that held Terra comfortably inside. Kissa followed close behind riding their wagon full of their supplies, everyone else walking along beside the leisurely coach.

Terra was up chatting to Reza far past her usual bedtime the physician had prescribed to her, the crew deciding to walk a bit into the night as the air was nice and cool, the weather being unusually pleasant to them the last few days.

The coach's curtains were rolled up, Terra looking out at her companions walking quietly along as Reza continued to attempt to coax her back to the large couch in the back she had been using as her personal bed, having fluffed it up with blankets and pillows to make it more comfy.

"You think we'll be making it to Viccarwood before we stop for the night?" Terra asked lazily, interrupting Reza's argument for why she should be getting to sleep.

Reza considered the likelihood of the question, replying in a tired tone, "More than likely, though you shouldn't be up to see its lights. Go to bed, Terra. The doctor said you shouldn't tax your heart more than is needed. Do me a favor and lie down. There's nothing to see out there anyways."

Terra gave one last look out of the coach at the caravan of friends, looking at Nomad walking beside Yozo, neither talking to each other, but seeming to enjoy the stroll together. Cavok, as stoic as ever, walked alone ahead of Fin and Arie, who both seemed quite engaged in conversation with each other, snickering in the night at some private joke they kept between themselves.

"You think Arie has a thing for that man with all the daggers? They've been talking a lot together this trip," Terra asked, prodding into topics she knew she shouldn't be.

Reza wondered that herself.

"Go to bed," she answered, instead of indulging the frivolous gossip. Terra finally fluffed her bedding, looking as though she actually was ready to turn in this time as Reza opened the door, stepping out of the slow-moving carriage, closing the door behind her, hoping the girl actually listened to her this time.

She approached Cavok. He had been through tough times, as they all had over the past months; but out of all of them, he seemed to be the most alone in his depressions. He often had shut others out, even during the highs. She knew with the lows he had gone through of late, he would be one of the slowest ones to mend, especially with Fin, his best friend, being torn between Yozo and Arie of late. Reza wondered how much longer he would stay with the group, seeming how the man could not stand Yozo and still having raw feelings towards Nomad. Without Terra there, whom he had grown rather close to, she wondered if he would soon drift on down the trail without them.

"You want to ride in the carriage with Terra for a bit, Cavok? I'm sure she'd love your company," Reza prodded the stern looking man as she matched his pace beside him, knowing he might very well need company more at that time than Terra needed extra rest, even after all her arguing with the girl to bed down for the night.

"No. She needs her sleep," he spoke in a matter-of-fact tone, continuing along.

The night was quiet again save for the creak of wagon wheels and clop of hooves along the trail leading to the next town with the occasional chuckle from the two in the back falling slightly behind.

"Cavok, have you...spoken to Nomad since the war? It wasn't *him* that did those things to you in the dunes months back, it was Telenth."

The two looked at the swordsman far up ahead now out of earshot and Cavok answered readily without much thought, "I have not."

"You should," she replied, knowing a rift had formed between the two since the many days he had to fend off the wild man in the desert months back—how large and serious the rift was, she was not certain of as the man had become more solitary than usual of late.

"Perhaps we will have a talk," he huffed in a tone that did little to put her at ease.

She wanted to place a comforting hand on his arm, but his stiff posture seemed to announce his wanting to be left alone.

She walked beside him instead, hoping her presence the rest of the walk ahead of them that night, would be enough to comfort his wounded soul in some way.

50
A TABLE OF REMEMBRANCE AND AMBITION

"Friends," Sultan Metus' soft voice sounded, quieting the dining room, many there already displaying their bad table manners by starting to dish themselves food from the buffet along the center of the long mahogany table.

"We break bread here together, one more time, and it warms my heart to look upon each of your faces, for things could have turned out much differently without the effort of all here around this table."

Cavok and Fin stopped serving themselves, seeing that Metus was wanting to have a serious speech, all else in the room already quiet as Metus paused for Fin and Cavok to follow suit.

"We've lost many through recent years. Those who were close and dear to our hearts. Those whose spots will not be filled—who left an indelible impact on our lives.

"We are grateful for their service and sacrifice. Let us honor them this night by enjoying each other's company in their memory."

Metus held up his silver chalice, announcing, "To heroes!"

"To heroes!" all others agreed, sharing in the cheers to those they loved—to those they lost.

With that, the table of ten began the feast which had been prepared specially for them.

There had been a celebration in the palace court days earlier that the group had just missed when Bannon had arrived home to Sheaf with the good news of the successful campaign waged against the arisen. It had been deemed a national holiday, and the whole city had enjoyed banquets hosted throughout many of the upper-class establishments.

Food and drink had been borrowed from the city's stores and merriment had been shared freely in the streets in celebration of the victory over such a dangerous foe that had plagued not only their lands, but other neighboring regions, a swell of national pride rightly bubbling those within the Plainstate.

Having missed the festivities, Metus had made sure upon Reza's arrival that a catered feast was prepared for her crew, knowing full well their pivotal role in fighting the agents of Telenth those past years.

Reza, Nomad, Arie, Fin, Cavok, Terra, Yozo, all passed food, eager to eat, free with jovial remarks and comradery, well lubricated with an endless supply of the finest wines and spirits, enjoying the Sultan's company, and that of Bannon and Hathos who had also been invited.

Though the military men had accepted the invitation, they showed much more restraint with the wine than the others, save for Metus, who never took more than a glass of wine for any occasion.

"So what now for your company of champions, Reza?" Metus asked, enjoying the company more than the meal itself, not having had time to properly visit with the crew after their arrival early that morning.

She deliberated on the question, not really sure herself what everyone's plans were after things were settled.

"I...cannot say for everyone else, but for myself and Terra, I aim to visit my people in the Jeenyre mountains once more. Her heart is still not fully mended, and after my last attempt...I fear she needs a saren with better hands for healing than I," she answered, attempting to stay fluent through the glass of strong wine she had already downed.

"Besides that, I made a promise to pay my respects to a friend there, and visit others that miss my presence. I believe I will spend a season at the monastery and Terra has said she would very much like to study there with the record keepers in our great library. It should be a restful winter there for us—one much needed."

"You have not told me of this," Nomad piped in, slowing down with the drumstick he had been working on.

"Me neither!" Fin agreed, piling on.

"Surely you're not going just the two of you? It's a long and hazardous road. Remember those Sephentho guards that gave us chase?" Arie added.

Before Reza could answer, Yozo spoke for the first time that night at the table. "I would lend my sword to your caravan if you would have it. I would like to visit Revna and her shieldmaidens. I owe much to your people."

"Sorry," Metus said as Reza looked all around the table, trying to figure out how to answer everyone.

"Reza wasn't hiding it from you all, she just wanted to speak to everyone individually to let you know of our plans," Terra attempted to defend for her.

"Has everyone had their say yet?" Reza asked, somewhat put out by everyone's interjections prying into the matter.

"I didn't get to say my piece," Cavok said, raising his hand in protest, Fin and Terra snickering at the man, a bit uncertain if he was attempting at some well-timed dry humor, or if he actually wanted to speak.

Reza let out an exasperated sigh. "Yes, Cavok. What?" she snipped.

"If Terra's going, I'll be coming too. She's too reckless to be watched over by *you* motley crew," he announced, folding his arms, dead serious about his installment in Reza's plans.

"Is Terra's mother alright with her running off with this rowdy bunch of hooligans?" Bannon chimed in, asking Metus facetiously.

"Have you indeed talked to Ja-net about all of this?" Metus asked smiling, though in honesty.

"Yes, my Sultan," she answered a bit tipsy from the half glass of wine she had had, overworking her manners in the presence of royalty. "I spoke with her on the matter as soon as I made it into town."

Metus and Bannon both nodded their approval, murmuring "good, good," as all attention turned back to Reza who looked very put out over the takeover of her newly announced plans.

"You have something to say, Reza?" Bannon asked, seeing that the woman was clearly pouting about something.

"No further interruptions," she ordered, looking around the table, ending with a glare at Nomad.

"Nomad, I had planned to ask you later this evening to join us on the road to Jeenyre." Nomad received a look that seemed to indicate that this was not a subject up for debate.

"As for the rest of you. If you all have nothing better to do with your time, I suppose Terra and I wouldn't mind company on the trail—as long as everyone can get along together. If I am allowed to be frank for a moment amidst the mirth. Our group of friends has grown over the last year or so. There are rifts between some of us. Deep rifts. You will be required to work through your differences if you are to travel in my caravan. Even *I* have worked countless hours besides that prattling praven, Jadu, and somehow managed to not silence him permanently," she paused, Nomad and Fin suppressing smiles as Reza took a deep breath to attempt to lower her blood pressure after the mention of the little enchanter.

"What I'm saying is, I expect you to behave yourself in the group if you voluntarily join my company. I'll not be a babysitter on this trip. The last thing Terra needs with her heart condition is to fret over strife and brooding among us," Reza ended, looking to Cavok and Yozo specifically.

The room was quiet for a moment, all reflecting upon Reza's words. Hathos, in his quiet, measured voice broke the silence.

"In war, it becomes easy to set aside differences. In times of peace, it becomes much harder to do. When it is hard for me to appreciate particular soldiers I command, I try to remember their past accomplishments and contributions. All in the Hyperium have commendations, or they would not have been accepted into our ranks. I have witnessed firsthand that the same is with your crew. All here have accomplished many great things and have shown great loyalty and valor in selflessly serving those around this table, and the people of the Southern Sands region as a whole. Think not of the worst a person has done, but them at their best, and you may find appreciating them as a companion will become easier."

The room was not quiet for long after, Fin asking, "So when do we leave?"

Reza nodded her head, glad to be back on subject. "A week. We've all been on the road for some time, we've all earned a good rest; but the sooner we get Terra to the monastery, the better."

"Sounds reasonable," Metus agreed after sipping the last of his wine. "Though I'll be on the road myself at that time, unfortunately in the opposite direction. A matter I actually needed to discuss with you, Hathos, sometime about. It'll be a simple deployment, but I was hoping the Hyperium would accompany me to Barre.

"Darious has had time to get his people settled there and I plan to bring a supplies caravan and a ward of physicians to help them get started as official Plainstate citizens on the proper foot."

Hathos readily pledged his support to Metus' wishes, Bannon offering his updates on the refugees' time thus far in Barre, as he had just received a report that day from returning service men from the town, allowing all others time to continue with their meals and individual conversations.

Reza calmed herself, pouring water in her chalice instead of more wine, clearing her head slightly as the night wore on, and she smiled, appreciating how easily all present seemed to fall back into high spirits, even after all they had gone through, all they had lost over the war of the arisen that was still so fresh upon their memories.

That night gave her hope, that no matter what horrors they

had gone through, or might go through later in life, that they'd get through the worst of it, together.

51

FAREWELL TO THE ENDLESS DUNES OF THE SOUTHERN SANDS

Reza gave Nomad one last kiss before they headed out of their room in the housing district. It was going to be the last time they'd have any degree of privacy once they started on the open road with their friends in the coming months, and she had begun to thoroughly enjoy sharing herself with the man she loved. It was, after all, the first time she had been with anyone, and the newly discovered realm of pleasures and comforts were all too tempting not to take full advantage of.

"Ready?" Nomad whispered as he tucked her platinum hair back behind her ear to show her face, admiration clear in his features of the beauty before him.

She tugged tight her doeskin travel gloves and nodded, both

carrying packs full of gear they'd need for the road ahead.

Opening the door, Nomad let Reza out first to see Terra, Cavok at her side staring off into the desert dunes that rose just above the city walls far beyond, the autumn air gently blowing a brisk breeze through the housing district as they waited for the two lovebirds to finish up whatever it was they were doing alone in their room.

"Hi you two," Terra facetiously greeted, a suspecting grin on her face as she patted Cavok's strong arm to prod him to acknowledge how adorable the couple was.

Cavok did answer, but not in the way Terra wanted him to, grunting, "Love...it'll weaken your knees. Can't have weak knees on the road."

"Maybe...you should work on getting stronger knees then, 'cause mine are fine," Reza jabbed back with a wicked smirk, getting an approving smile from the large man as they headed off to pick up the other three down by the stables.

The walk to the stables had been quiet, each enjoying the song of birds often accompanying the morning early light. They had decided to forgo stopping to eat at a café, against Terra's pleadings, but they did not want to keep the others waiting, and so they had picked up a few breakfast items along the way in the market to share with everyone on the road.

They settled all costs with the stable's master, Cavok and Nomad busying themselves in tending to their rides as Reza and Terra watched for the arrival of the other half of their company.

"Well, well, well. Ain't this a sight," Fin boisterously announced, Yozo and Arie at his side as the three walked into the stables where Cavok had been hard at work hitching their carriage up with Nomad gathering the other four horses for those not riding in the carriage.

"Seems like yesterday we were headed up to Jeenyre to break your sorry ass out of jail, Nomad. We'll need to watch the roads by Sephentho. We're all wanted criminals around those parts now," Fin warned, a bit too loudly for Arie's liking, smacking him on the back. Yozo shook his head at the inappropriate behavior of the two as the two groups met up.

"Your carriage, my sir," Cavok said, bowing to Fin, designating him as first rider to start their journey off.

Fin gave Arie a hug goodbye, kissing her openly as everyone awkwardly watched the passionately long smooch. Everyone in the group allowed their public display of affection without protest, knowing the couple would not be seeing each other for a good few months as Arie stayed behind to attend to her duties at Sheaf while Fin was on the road.

"Me lady," Cavok said to Terra, playfully offering her a royal welcome into the bed-like bench she had grown to like on the road from Brigganden to Sheaf the previous week. If she had to travel, this was her preferred mode of transport.

Fin tipped his wide-brimmed hat to Arie from the rider's bench and without further ado, smartly snapped the reins along the horses' sides, starting the carriage off in a brisk trot down the street to the city gates leading northward.

Nomad and the others mounted their horses, following Fin's lead, exiting through gates they had come to know well through the years, departing the city that held great significance to each of them.

They made it a short ways out from the gates along the road before Fin drew to a halt as he looked back at the city amid the dusk of the evening, lights already burning in windows and the bustle of evening shoppers clear and lively in the business district they had just left, seeming as though life in the region, as it once was during wartimes, had been some distant memory, a past that didn't even seem real to those busily going about their lives in peace.

"It's a strange thing, life," Fin softly spoke, everyone reverently observing the same melancholy scene of a place they wondered, as with every time they set out on the open road for distant lands, if they'd ever see it again.

"Strange indeed," Yozo answered, a depth in his voice that shook them all at the remark, the two of them speaking the thoughts they all were feeling so simply, so eloquently.

They turned back to the path ahead and were off along the red-orange dunes of the arid lands they had devoted so much effort to protect over the last few years, ready for a season of rest and uneventful travel along paths they knew well to places they expected little trouble from.

As it is many times in life, fate had other plans in store.

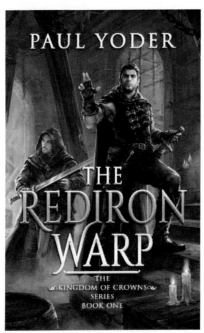

Continue the adventure with Reza, Nomad, Fin, and the others in book 4, The Rediron Warp available on Amazon!

A mysterious mania-inducing sickness is ravaging the kingdom of Rediron. Nervous itching, grey skin, glowing blue veins—all symptoms of this cursed disease that warps and torments minds beyond repair. No cure is known. Death is their only reprieve.

The Rogue assassin Fin and his renegade swordsman companion Yozo enter the land's borders in search of their long-lost friend. However, they can't help but suspect his disappearance and the disease are connected.

The two sleuths find themselves in hot pursuit of the

dangerous organization pulling the strings of the devastating illness. But dark gods watch over their every move, ensnaring them in their wicked plans. With the whole kingdom and its moral values at stake, can Yozo and Fin find their friend and rid the kingdom of this unholy blight draining the life of the populace?

**The Rediron Warp** is the first book in the Kingdom of the Crowns trilogy and the thrilling continuation of the _**Lands of Wanderlust**_ saga, which puts captivating heroes against the Lovecraftian horrors in a hellish world plagued by threats from the undead. Pick it up on Amazon and start reading today!

FROM THE AUTHOR

Through the course of this book, I've left my job to start writing full-time. It's been an exciting transition, and I'm looking forward to all the extra time available now to focus on writing.

I hope you've enjoyed the Lords of the Deep Hells Trilogy! Writing it has been the start of something that has changed my life, and it means a lot to me to know that you were there for the journey. If you've enjoyed the books, make sure to leave a review on Amazon and on Goodreads. It's greatly appreciated.

You can start in on the next book in the series with The Rediron Warp where you can read more of Reza, Nomad, Fin, and the others in their next big adventure, discovering the many wonders of the world of Una!

Visit me online for launch dates and other news at:

authorpaulyoder.com
(sign up for the newsletter)
instagram.com/author_paul_yoder
tiktok.com/@authorpaulyoder
Paul Yoder on Goodreads
Paul Yoder on Amazon

Made in United States
North Haven, CT
31 October 2024